AWAKE IN THE WORLD
Volume III

Riverfeet Press Anthology

Riverfeet Press
www.riverfeetpress.com

AWAKE IN THE WORLD, Volume 3
A Riverfeet Press Anthology
Various Authors
Natural World || Fiction, Non-Fiction and Poetry
Copyright 2023 © by the authors
Edited by Mara Panich, Tyler Dunning and Daniel J. Rice
All rights reserved.
ISBN-13: 979-8985398847
LCCN: 2017937546

No part of this book may be reproduced, scanned, or distributed in any printed or electronic form without permission from the publisher. Please do not participate in or encourage piracy of copyrighted materials in violation of the author's rights. Purchase only authorized editions.

This title is available at a special discount to booksellers and libraries. Send inquiries to: riverfeetpress@gmail.com

Cover design by: Creative Pear Graphic Design LLC
www.creativepeargd.com

This is a work of fiction. Names, characters, businesses, events and incidents are the products of the author's imagination. Any resemblance to actual persons, living or dead, or actual events is purely coincidental.

CONTENTS

FROM THE EDITORS
Poetry: Mara Panich—Mud . . . 3
Fiction: Daniel J. Rice—How Wild Wolves and Classic Literature Saved My Life . . . 5
Non-Fiction: Tyler Dunning—One Thousand Silent Apologies . . . 19

POETRY
Selected as Best in Poetry: Irene Cooper—drift . . . 35
Mark Gibbons—Cool Blue Dawn . . . 41
Michael Garrigan—Slate Run . . . 45
Todd Davis—Lost Blue . . . 47
Dazar Frihet—A Place much Farther Back . . . 51
Ana Maria Spagna—where sky blue beckons . . . 55
AJ Donley—April in Covid . . . 57
Brad Garber—What Animal I Would Be . . . 61
Benjamin Green—My Place . . . 63
Chelsea Jackson—Honeysuckle: A Ghazal . . . 71
Gary W. Hawk—River Town . . . 75
Donna Mendelson—A Family of Clark's Nutcrackers . . . 79
Gillian Kessler—Suspended Somewhere Animal . . . 81
Mark Christopherson—The Small Hours . . . 85
Heidi Sander—Carmanah . . . 87
Steve Wilson—A Transfixion . . . 93
Lynn Fast—Filling My Eyes . . . 95
Mark Oswood—The Obligations of Being a Flicker . . . 97
T-M Baird—A question, little lady: Do you know where you come from? . . . 99
Yetta Rose Stein—In My Dreams, I Die in an Avalanche in the Bridgers . . . 103

FICTION

Selected as Best in Fiction: Logan James Campbell—I'll Just Wait Until It's Quiet ... 107

Billie Hinton—We Are the Charm ... 127

JoeAnn Hart—Flying Home ... 131

William Burtch—Animal Crossings ... 141

Theresa Rice—The Summer I Loved Three Fish ... 147

NON-FICTION

Selected as Best in Non-Fiction: Daniel P. Hoffman—In Search of Flowing Waters: The Seasons of Alaska ... 163

Valerie Innella Maiers—Wyoming Four Ways ... 189

Amie Adams—In Which Spring Makes An Appearance Once Again ... 199

Chris Waltz—A Geologist, a Bear and a Priest Walk into a Bar ... 205

John Jacobson—Sprouting Leaves ... 225

Kelli Short Borges—The Void ... 229

Monica Devine—Many Things Were Visible When the Earth Was Thin ... 239

Scott McMillion—Hunting Among Wolves ... 249

FROM THE EDITORS

POETRY EDITOR

Mara Panich is a writer, artist, and owner of Fact & Fiction Books in Missoula, Montana. She holds a BA in Creative Writing and English from Purdue University and completed post-graduate studies at the University of Montana. Her debut book of poetry, *Blood is Not the Water*, was published by Foothills Publishing and named a Montana Book Award Honor Book in 2021.

Mud

dirty wet hubris growing warm with thaw and reaching   crowded letters form words of expression eaten by awakened worms   when you told me that birth is magical and ugly I imagined the expelling of all the undergrowth in spring   where slop proceeds beauty smelling of the rot that feeds life   your giving comes from the damp places between legs   where existence begins in pleasure and pain what breed is this emotive birthing one born of sunlight wakening   or a mushroom's surprise at the richness obtained when our egos thrive in the decay of darkness   fight guilt with confusion   tell each rhythm that it is unworthy of appreciation because seriousness is equal to sadness   but this happy well-wishing inspiration feels

                so energetic

on my   tongue

FICTION EDITOR

Daniel J. Rice was born in Weisbaden, Germany, and moved frequently during his youth. As an adult, he has engaged in such occupations as: Drywall Carpenter in Minnesota, Hydrologist in Wyoming, Restaurateur in Montana, Fly Fishing Guide in the Blue Ridge Mountains, and Book Publisher. He enjoys the silence of serene landscapes, and in 2011 he fully immersed himself alone in a northern MN wilderness where he lived in a wall tent deep in the forest for five months and wrote two books (*The Unpeopled Season*, and *This Side of a Wilderness*). This led to the inception of Riverfeet Press, through which he has published the nature-centric work of more than one-hundred other writers. If he's not waist deep in a river holding a fly rod, or at his desk editing a manuscript, he's most likely in the backcountry hiking trails with his wife, daughter, and two rescue dogs. He's been known to howl—both in darkness and daylight.

How Wild Wolves and Classic Literature Saved My Life

I woke up this morning and opened my computer to check the news. In my feed was an advertisement for a new TV series similar to Cops. *The screenshot had three Sheriffs in the background with guns drawn and a man up front on his knees wearing handcuffs. I paused for a moment because I knew the man on his knees as a friend from my youth. I was with him the day he got the panther tattoo displayed on his forearm. Memories started building up inside. I stepped outside and watched the winter sunrise over the hills to the east. It was time to wake my daughter and prepare her for school. While she was brushing her teeth and selecting her clothes, I used my pocket knife to stir instant coffee and raw cocoa into a hot cup of water. Whenever I am in a quiet moment of reflection, I can still hear them howl. Both the wolves and the monsters I knew before them.*

We parked at school and I walked her to the gates. She said I love you three times and gave me a hug around the waist. I sat in the Jeep and watched her play with her friends until they went inside. As I pulled away there were the mountains of Paradise Valley broadcasted before me, so I took a drive. It is January and this time of year where I live the landscape is dominated by heavy winds pushing up the valley from Yellowstone National Park, which is fifty-one miles south. The valley is interspersed with cattle ranches where long grass is dry and brown from the wind. To my left are the Beartooth Mountains with sharp angled peaks full of snow and touching low clouds. On my right is the Gallatin range which is more rounded and lower but still covered in white. I pulled off the road and stepped out to the edge of a river.

Around here they call the Yellowstone the Last Free River. *I stand on a slick boulder and listen to the cold water making chimes along the icy shore. My father grew up on a farm and then worked hard his entire career to make a good life for us. My mother stayed home to raise her children and she put her whole heart into this every day. Yet when I think about my past, it is not the things they did for me nor the privileges they provided. It is the monsters that I knew and the monster I was.*

...

I remember the day it started and the person who introduced me to a dangerous way of life. I always had a wondering mind and adventurous spirit, so it was easy for me to jump into something new and different. His name was Nick and halfway through my junior year of high school at a suburb of Minneapolis he arrived in the halls wearing a blue newsboy cap cocked to the right and baggy pants with a blue bandana hanging out of the back pocket. The other students in our small rural town didn't like him, but I wasn't too popular anyway. On his third day I asked if he wanted to skip economics class to go for a ride and smoke a joint. He agreed, but when we got into my Mercury Tracer he insisted on rolling a blunt. Neither of us had a cigar but this wasn't a problem. We pulled into Casey's convenience store at the edge of town and I distracted the attendant by asking for directions while Nick stole a pack of Black & Mild's from the shelf. It was easy and I wondered why I hadn't thought of this before.

We continued skipping class most afternoons and quickly grew an entourage of other misfits who preferred the education of being free to roam over the isolated monotony of schoolrooms. There were the twin brothers Ken and Carl who didn't look too much alike on account of the large scar on Carl's face and the fact that Ken wore his hair in a crew cut while Carl let his grow wild. They were raised by their single father who always had a stash of cheap beer we could snag because he was typically passed out by mid-afternoon. Ken had a reputation for being kicked out of class because he would yell *Fuck You* anytime a teacher called on him. Carl had recently been removed from the hockey team because he broke some sort of record for starting the most fights in a season.

Matt had a devious face with squinty eyes. He walked with a slouch and talked with his hands. He was our leader, not due to any wit or logic, but because of his cunningness. He had dropped out of school several months ago and his single mom worked days so we hung at their house when we tired of roaming the streets. We'd hang on his front porch rolling blunts and shot-gunning beers while talking trash and singing along to gangsta rap cassettes playing on the boombox. We were high as hell and this dilapidated porch was our throne.

When Yusef landed in our little town he brought a whole new level of mystique and credential to our crew. He came from the big city of Detroit and said that if we joined his gang we would have the support of other members from cities around the country. We were each initiated in a paved parking lot outside of a hockey rink after dark which required standing in a circle of six friends who we fought with fists for two minutes. The next day the blood had dried and the bruises formed, and we were put on the set with new literature to memorize, hand signs to perform, and specific methods for wearing our hats.

It didn't take long for the local cops to know us each by first name, and they made a habit of creeping past the front of Matt's house. Sometimes they would flick on their siren lights to try and scare us. Then one day they parked at the curb. Two cops got out of the cruiser and approached the porch. Yusef quickly disappeared because he had warrants out in several states, and he was the only one of us over the age of eighteen. Matt walked to the curb to greet the cops with a blunt dangling from his lips. "What the fuck do you want?" he said when they got closer. The cops made a comment about extinguishing his blunt and putting his hands up. Matt pulled in a puff of smoke and blew it into the officers' face, then said, "This is my land. Show me a warrant or get the fuck out." The cops grabbed Matt by the arms but he gave a good tussle. When they wrestled him to the ground the blunt was still in his lips. They cuffed him and put him in the cruiser then took him to a holding cell where he stayed until his mother picked him up later that night.

...

The wind is crisp on my face as it blows cold air off the Yellowstone River. I have spent many days in wild places trying to make sense of the people and events from my past. It often seems like that life must have been lived by somebody else. I couldn't have done it. Not the person I am today. Wild landscapes can ease the mind, but change must be intentional because this doesn't happen by accidentally stumbling upon a beautiful piece of scenery. I pop back into the Jeep and drive upstream.

...

The first night I was arrested they should have kept me locked up. I had recently brought in a new member to the gang. His name was Emanuel and he had moved here from L.A. On this night his cousin José was visiting so we rolled the streets in my Mercury Tracer. There were a pair of subwoofers in my trunk that pounded out bass as we cruised the small town streets with our windows down so the weed smoke billowed out. We had the blue rags on our heads and flashed gang signs to passing cars and people on the sidewalks. People passing by looked at us as though we were aliens or some other foreign species they had never seen.

At a stoplight in front of Casey's convenience store a pickup truck pulled behind us. The truck bed was loaded with members of the football team all wearing their letterman jackets. Emanuel flashed a gang sign out the window and yelled "Fuck you honky jocks!" Four of the boys jumped from the truck and rushed at the Tracer. The light was still red but I hit the pedal and a chase was on. I turned north and pretty soon we were on a gravel road with the pickup on our tail. I maneuvered the dark streets around dairy farms and corn fields. We hit a cul-de-sac and I spun around to head the other direction. The truck was coming straight at us so I swerved into the ditch. The pickup turned around and was creeping toward us with its brights on.

José hung out the backseat window and fired two shots from a pistol. The sound shocked me so much I hit the pedal hard enough to cut ruts in the ditch. I looked in the rearview and through the gravel dust saw their headlights hadn't moved. We burned out of there and it was several minutes before any of us spoke. It was Emanuel who said, "Did you get those fuckers?" "Hell yeah," replied José who still had the pistol on his lap. "We need to get the fuck out of here," I said.

Emanuel had a girlfriend the next town over so we drove that direction. She lived in a brown trailer with three large dogs and her older sister. Their parents had died a few months back and her sister was old enough to make the adoption legit. Her name was Tracey and she was extremely beautiful even though she used the word *Fuck* three times per sentence. We hung in her room and smoked enough weed to cut logic from our minds and the nerves from our veins. It was decided that since José fired the shots, he was the one the police would be looking for. We left him at Tracey's for the night while Emanuel and I headed back to town.

It wasn't the police who were looking for us, at least not yet. We didn't make it two blocks into town before getting surrounded by pickup trucks full of young dudes with letterman jackets and trucker caps. Small town boys were a militia of force. The chase was on again but this time we weaved through the neighborhood streets. Three trucks trailed directly behind us honking horns and flashing lights. I cut into a narrow alley hoping to lose them. The alley dead-ended at a red brick fence with no room to turn around.

We popped out of the Tracer and the first thought in my head was *Tonight I will die*. There were thirteen of them standing in the dim alley and several held baseball bats. One boy stayed in the Dodge pickup truck and watched us in the headlights. I figured he was the one who held a gun and was told to only get out if things got heavy. I remember thinking how brave they were because for all they knew one of us still had a pistol. The biggest of them started his approach and Emanuel yelled "Fuck you white boy!" The two squared off and Emanuel caught a solid punch to the face but didn't go down. He was a tough dude big enough to carry his own. After a few swings it quickly turned into a wrestling match as most street fights did. When the bigger guy had Emanuel on the ground, one of his friends rushed up and kicked him in the back. This clicked a trigger inside me, and even though I had never been in a street fight in a dim alley, all fear was forgotten by adrenaline so I rushed in. This got the rest of the boys involved and all I can tell you for certain is there were a lot of swinging fists and taking punches. Some bats were used.

The fight didn't last long before a woman came out from one of the houses along the alley. She said the police were on their way. This sent the boys into a scurry and pretty quick it was just me and Emanuel left limp on the ground. He had blood coming out of his mouth and nose and I'm pretty sure I got hit by a bat several times because my back was tingling. I must've connected a few punches because the next day my knuckles were swollen and my wrists were sore. You don't think too much about your knuckles and wrists when you're outnumbered in a fight. I recall looking up from the pavement to see a single street light in the alley and it burned dim yellow.

Three squad cars rushed in before we could make it to the Tracer. They emerged with guns drawn while yelling words I was too oblivious to comprehend. By this time I had made it to my feet but Emanuel was still on the ground. I was ordered to put my hands on the roof of my car so that's what I did. One of the officers picked up a bat the boys had abandoned and slammed it into my back then put cuffs around my wrists.

At the station they rolled my fingers in black ink and then placed me in a concrete cell where I waited alone for several hours. The first man to enter was in street clothes so I figured he must be some kind of detective. He said I was going for a ride and they placed me in the back of an unmarked car. Thirty minutes later we were parked outside of Tracey's house. The street was dark and they kept me in the backseat while they knocked on the front door and then told José to come outside. They shined a flashlight in his face while he was looking my direction, and then asked him some questions before sending him back inside.

When the two detectives returned and opened the backdoor to

the seat where I waited, they asked if I recognized him, José, and I said no. They said I'd better be sure, because if they could prove I was lying it would be my ass in juvie. I told them I had some good friends in juvie, but that wouldn't change my answer. During the ride back I came to the conclusion that Emanuel must've given them José's location, so I never talked to him again.

...

I turn left in the Jeep and drive up a canyon road along a small trout stream that comes out of the mountains. Last time I was here I caught seven cutthroat trout on dry flies and then a brown bear walked past me along the near shore. I don't have a logical fear of bears and I think this is because of my assimilation to creatures more dangerous. I drive thirteen miles into the mountain and get out of the Jeep where a small tributary dumps into the main stream. There is a trailhead here and if I walk two miles there will be a waterfall that pours off the side of a rocky cliff. Once I am there it will be a good place to think, and the walking will help.

...

I was placed on probation after that fight in the alley and so my parents wanted me to take a job in another town to put some distance between the bad influences. I started working at a fast food taco joint wearing a black embroidered hat and apron. My first night of work I was at the three-compartment sink in the back spraying grease off of dishes when Lamont approached and asked if I could score some weed. I said I could but it would be tomorrow. He had a roach in his pocket and so after work I drove him home and we smoked it in a copper pipe. He lived in a housing project near the Mall of America—it was the closest thing the suburbs knew of a ghetto. When we pulled up there was a crowd of young dudes in the parking lot passing joints and freestyling gansta rap. Lamont asked me to join them, so I got out of the Tracer and walked into the crowd. A bunch of dudes I had never met shook my hand, but not in the normal way. They angled their pointer finger up and latched it to mine, then curved it toward the sky with the thumb and middle finger forming a pitchfork. There was a sense of something indomitable in our union of smoking weed beneath yellow streetlights, swaying to music and sharing secret handshakes.

The next day I wanted to make a good impression with the weed so I drove out to Nick's brothers' place. They moved here from Chicago and his brother still had connections for the best sticky greens you could find in our little town. He lived in a shack on a dead-end street where he kept automatic rifles beside his windows. There were always a handful of dudes getting high on coke, shrooms, acid and opium. Nick's brother would sit by the front window holding a machine gun with an anxious look on his face saying they were coming for him. I never thought to ask who.

After work that evening I offered Lamont a ride home. This time Josh joined us and we drove to a trailer park where I met Jason and Teddy. Quality weed shouldn't be smoked from a pipe because you didn't get the good resins. None of us had papers or cigars so Jason went into his trailer and came out a couple minutes later with his mom's bible from which he tore out the back page and we used this to roll the fattest joint I ever smoked.

I quit that job after a few weeks but continued to tell my parents I was going to work so that I had free time to run the streets in a different town with my new crew. I continued school in my hometown but didn't go to class much because after the fight my entire school was against me. Pretty soon I got in another fight and this time it was in a classroom so they suspended me. I convinced my parents to transfer me to an alternative school in the town with my new crew. My argument was strengthened by a letter from the principle who said he didn't think I had a good future at his school.

On a Friday night we went to a party at Vicki's house while her parents were out of town. Vicki was Jason's girlfriend, but I don't think you could call her that because when I asked him about her, he said, "I just like fucking her doggystyle." I had made a routine of buying weed from Nick's brother and selling it to people at my new school and their friends. I needed to have money since my parents thought I had a job. The money was mostly for show because we stole all of our Newport cigarettes, baggy clothes, 40 ounces of High Life beer and gas station food.

Vicki invited a guy she worked with and his friends to the party so there were a total of fifteen of us getting fucked up and fucking around. Jason started messing with the new kids saying they were gay and dressed like preps. They got up to leave even though Vicki said they should stay. After they went outside Jason waved for Teddy, Lamont and myself to follow him. He said we were gonna fuck 'em up.

Outside Vicki was talking to her friend trying to convince him to stay. Jason walked up all casual while the rest of us followed slowly behind. He got up close to the guy's face and said he wanted to apologize, that he was joking around and didn't mean anything by it. Then he said he wanted to make it up to them and quickly popped the boy square in the nose. The boy stepped away and put his hands up saying he didn't want any trouble even though he was easily fifteen inches taller than Jason. Blood poured from his nose, around his mouth, and dripped off his chin. Once Jason had an idea in his head he saw it through. He rushed the dude with several more punches until the kid went down and then proceeded to stomp on his head.

Teddy was a big guy and he knocked one of the other kids out with a single punch. If you've never heard what a solid punch sounds like in the front yard of a suburban house after dark let me say that the old Batman comics explained it accurately. *THWAP!* Vicki tried to rush in and save her friend until Lamont grabbed her by the arms and held her back. Jason sat on top of Vicki's friend punching him in the ribs and the kid Teddy knocked out was lying on the ground with his right foot twitching. I remember being mostly astonished and thinking this was something that happened in real life. This was what real people did.

...

I arrive at the waterfall after post-holing through deep snow for the final half mile. The water is mostly frozen but I can hear it flowing behind the ice. I light a match to my camp stove and fill a tin cup with water as it tumbles down. When the water is boiling I use my pocket knife to stir instant coffee and raw cacao. I keep one hand warm with the cup and the other holds a copy of Nausea *by Jean-Paul Sartre. The first time I read this book was while living alone at a small cabin in the Northwoods of Minnesota. A good book will make you feel at home in its pages and I felt related to the alienation of this protagonist.*

...

I started my senior year at a new school, this was the fourth one I had been placed at during the past two years. I didn't attend class too often because I was still more interested in what was happening on the streets. I had earned a reputation as one of the largest dealers of good weed in our area so I spent most of my days bouncing around from town to town making the rounds and getting stoned while always having at least two of my boys along for the ride. I sold weed for the popularity and meeting people more than the money.

My family went on a vacation later in the semester and wanted me to go but I said I had to work. It was nice of them to provide me several weeks' notice because this gave me enough time to plan a party. No one knew where I lived because it was out in the country so I drew a map on a scrap piece of paper and took it to Kinko's where they printed three-hundred copies. I passed these out to everyone I saw for the next few weeks and knew they would come because nobody ever said no to their dealer. Most of the people who I invited never met each other because I traveled in a large circle encompassing multiple cities and towns. I thought it would be pretty cool to tie them all together.

Teddy and Lamont were the first to arrive and they had broken into a liquor store the night before to help prepare so the trunk of Teddy's old purple Mustang was filled with cases of beer and bottles of booze. We had a long driveway that bent around a pond and before dark it was lined with cars from the garage to the road. It was a warm night so most people stayed outside. Behind our house was a large yard of grass that went down to the lake. Ken and Carl had a friend who worked at Radio Shack and they *borrowed* some equipment to play music that was loud enough to be heard throughout the property.

When Usaw arrived it was the type of announcement that traveled through the crowd fast. Usaw was from the Mdewakanton tribe and his family ran the casino so they had a lot of money and he used his share to do cool things like collect fast-shooting guns and antique Corvettes. One day while I was delivering him a pound of the stickiest green he gave me a tour of the vault where he kept his guns and said these would be needed when retribution came. He was known for being a crazy fucker who once stabbed a guy in the mall and then returned to the reservation where he claimed sovereignty. It helped that his uncle was a famous lawyer who had recently been on the cover of Time Magazine. He showed up to the party with a gang of his cousins and they brought a large bag of shrooms which he laid out on the hood of his Hummer and invited everyone to help themselves. The only drugs I ever did were weed and alcohol but a lot of the others partook.

Jason pulled in driving a brand-new silver Honda Accord and I had never seen this car before. He was calm and cool as he explained how he was waiting for a taxi outside of a tattoo shop in downtown Minneapolis when some asshole left the car running to go inside. He jacked the fucker and drove straight here. This, combined with his fresh panther tattoo, made him the popular focus for a while as the party roared on.

There was a point in the night when I paused and looked around as a tourist at a museum or carnival. A lot of shit was happening all at once. A crowd of people had moved into the dark forest and I could hear them yelling and tripping and running into trees. Another crowd was at the lake where Lamont had managed to ignite the boat dock on fire and a bunch of kids had jumped into the lake to try and extinguish it by splashing water. In front of the house a car full of girls had driven off the side of our driveway and slid into the pond. One of Usaw's cousins was lighting fireworks in the front yard and Nick was shooting people with my pellet gun. He claimed it was only one pump so wouldn't break the skin and then he fired at my ankle and I still have the pellet there to prove it.

Lyndsey was wiping blood off my foot inside the house and we were just beginning to feel each other up. I was dizzy and elated from the combination of booze plus the sensation that comes from feeling popular. A loud collision came from the driveway followed by the instant commotion of young men yelling. I didn't want to leave what was happening because she had just wrapped her legs around me, but Lyndsey seemed worried by the noise so I went outside.

Matt had been driving Ken's car to go into town and pick up some girls, but he backed right into the Accord which made Jason furious. Just as I stepped outside, I saw Jason pick up my dad's shovel and hit Ken's twin brother Carl square in the face. This sobered me up quick and I heard 150 voices all exclaim "Holy Shit!" at the same time. Action escalated fast and before Matt had even made it out of the driveway with Ken holding his brother in the backseat the entire yard had erupted into a fight.

I rushed around and tried to break it up but this was no use. Usaw was waving an Uzi threatening to shoot anyone who came close. I stood in his face and said if you don't get the fuck out of here I'm going inside to get my shotgun and then blowing your head off. I think it was the bravest thing I ever did but it was fueled by arrogance and drunken adrenaline. I didn't feel the punch or see who it came from but they must've been strong because when I regained consciousness the crowd was mostly gone except for Sandy who was holding a wet clothe over my right eye.

...

I finish my coffee and turn away from the falls back through the deep snow. Even when I am alone in the mountains I feel the presence of someone coming up from behind who has been looking for me all these years. I return to the Jeep and in the trunk there is always a bag full of books. I pick up The Stranger *by Albert Camus and flip through a few pages. I remember the man who committed a crime of killing a stranger, but the real stranger in the story was the man to himself who seemed distant from his actions as if watching an actor on a screen. I'm not ready to return home so I drive south again through the valley and along the last free river.*

...

I never saw Ken or Carl after that night but I heard Matt died from an overdose several months later. I hadn't even thought about Jason in a number of years until I saw him wearing handcuffs on the computer screen this morning. Teddy and Josh stayed in touch for a while because they wanted me to score them good weed even though they knew I quit dealing. Nick's brother was murdered in his house and they never caught the killer so Nick went into a mental hospital and last I heard he was selling clothes at Gap in the Mall of America.

Lamont continued thugging around the suburbs and I heard rumors of his reputation for jacking people by selling them fake weed he ordered from a magazine. I saw him one day outside of a movie theater wearing fancy clothes with a shiny long necklace and he showed me the chrome 45 under his shirt. We talked for a moment about the old days and then he said that I was an interpreter of the madness. I felt goosebumps on my legs and realized I had misjudged his character. The person I had seen on the surface of his behavior and action did not do justice to the ideas circulating in his mind. He mentioned seeing Usaw recently and when he did Usaw was still hung up on the threat I made that night of the party. Usaw wasn't one to forget an offense too easily and the only reason I didn't die that night was because I got knocked unconscious. He said that if Usaw ever saw me again there would be a bullet in my brain and I still believe this was true.

...

I pull into the town of Gardiner which is at the north entrance of Yellowstone National Park. There aren't many people around this time of year and most of the shops are closed even though this is the only entrance to the park that stays open in the winter. There is elk scat on the sidewalk and the sun is beginning to set as I wander around alone. I see a poster on a window that is advertising wolf viewing tours.

...

The day I turned eighteen I dropped out of school and moved out of my parents' house into an apartment around south Minneapolis.

I worked a construction job and tried to keep to myself but anywhere I went people knew me and seemed drawn to the chaos they thought I represented. I changed the way I dressed and the music I listened to but this was not enough to change their perception of me. The first book I ever bought as an adult was *The Metamorphosis* by Franz Kafka and I read it on a Friday night while alone in my apartment. It was about a character who turned into a hideous insect, but what I remember most was how during this transformation the people in his life changed their perception of him. This happened slowly, starting with neighbors, then teachers, friends, siblings and eventually his parents no longer recognized him.

Several years later I moved out of the city into the Northwoods and rented a cabin on a lake near the town of Ely. Everything I owned fit in the backseat of my sedan so it didn't take long to unpack. It was mostly books and some old camping gear passed down from my father. I sat at the lake and looked out at the water. There were several islands with rocky shores and large pine trees, and across the lake where a river flowed out was a portage into the Boundary Waters Canoe Area Wilderness.

The next morning I woke early and rented a canoe in town then paddled the lake alone. Paddling a seventeen-foot canoe alone was tricky for a novice like me so I stopped at the second island and got out to explore. The island wasn't too big but the foliage grew thick and gnarly. I sat on the shore and listened to loons echoing their song across the water. I began reading *Rosshalde* by Hermann Hesse and was hooked once I saw this line: "A new atmosphere, pure and free from guilt and suffering, will envelop him."

I read that book until I fell asleep on the island and then was woken in the dark by a sound I never heard before. It was a deep, solitary and mournful song and it felt like it was bellowing from my own chest. The single wolf howled alone from the near shore and then it went silent. A few moments passed and then several others returned chorus from across the lake. I was alone on an island between wolves communicating in the dark. There was a temptation to howl back but it wasn't my place so I stayed silent and listened to them. I didn't understand their language but could tell it had nothing to do with the worries inside my head. I fell back asleep knowing that tomorrow the sun would rise and the air would smell clean over the lake and everything in my view would be in its original condition.

NON-FICTION EDITOR

Tyler Dunning grew up in southwestern Montana, having developed a feral curiosity and reflective personality at a young age. This mindset has led him around the world, to nearly all of the U.S. national parks, and to the darker recesses of his own creativity. He's dabbled in such occupations as professional wrestling, archaeology, social justice advocacy, and academia. At his core he is a writer.

One Thousand Silent Apologies

According to Lee Whittlesey, former park historian of Yellowstone, water hemlock "is considered by many authorities to be the most virulently poisonous plant in the earth's North Temperate Zone ... one mouthful of the root is enough to kill an adult male." The human body on this wicked weed then includes nervousness, muscle twitching, dilation of pupils, tachycardia, rapid breathing, frothing at the mouth, apnea, tremors, pissing and shitting yourself, vomiting, grand mal seizures, comas, and necrosis. In short, a roller coaster you wouldn't wait in line to ride twice. One park ranger, witnessing such a fatality, and let's just assume for the sake of this sentence that he's seen more than one, claimed it the most violent death he'd ever seen. This alone is fair enough warning: don't go "Into the Wild," and eat unknown members of the vegetable kingdom. Ever.

That's why I set out, morbid information in mind, plant identification book in hand, to locate the killer. Because looking is fine. Because, like snagging a candid selfie with a celebrity, we enjoy novelty and equate the shutterbug moments to power, and power astonishes, whether positive or negative, and astonishment, according to physiological responses, is as an effective drug as any. I felt this celebrity high when a haggard mountain man, face shrouded in beautiful beard, lumbered into my café writing grounds with eyes that begged "please don't recognize me" but his mumbly Boston voice, making the city-slicker mistake of requesting vegan options in rural Montana, could only belong to one man: Casey Affleck.

Again, later in life, when strolling the streets of Harlem, I saw the same eyes on a woman sharing the sidewalk and knew, despite her apparent being-out-in-public fears, to take a second look:

Tina Fey. I got an instant high. Lung blood right to the brain. Like pot or cocaine or psilocybin or ayahuasca. Novelty is dope, and the hope, being a flower nerd, was that water hemlock might offer the same—

But listen, I'm not equating Tina Fey to a poisonous plant. Or Casey Affleck (well, maybe). What I'm saying is that we like to find shiny things, agates amongst the river-rock mundane, that are predicated upon conceited belief systems, like a collective culture that tells us celebrities have more value than school teachers and municipal workers and military members combined, or upon individual interests that offer intellectual erections to more nuanced things, like birds or rocks or plants. (For Christ's sake, people have paid hundreds of thousands of dollars to own a single orchid.) My point: opposed to, say, pot or cocaine or psilocybin or ayahuasca, there are other fun ways to get kicks from crops. Looking can be just fine. And I wanted my selfie with Yellowstone's most herbaceous assassin.

The challenge with water hemlock, however, is that it resembles so many other plants from the parsley/carrot family. It doesn't have that telltale Affleck voice or wry Fey smile. People confuse it for wild carrot, parsnip, and camas (hence, why they eat it . . . and die). It has the same compound umbels—with small white clustered flowers—like many other parsley plants, but what makes it somewhat identifiable are the leaf veins, running to the notches and *not* out to the points. Also, it grows only in wet seepage areas. Being a novice to all vegetable kingdom matters, this was just enough guidance to embark on the fool's errand.

Whittlesey, our aforementioned historian, is to blame. He wrote this book called *Death in Yellowstone*. The cover design is an old headstone image superimposed over a hot, steaming field of geysers. Looks more like hot, steaming—well, it doesn't look great—but the thing sells. You can analyze the cover for yourself when perusing Yellowstone gift stores and visitor centers; it's one of the most purchased books in the park. Because people adore death stories. Because people relish catastrophe. I bought a copy too, but for other reasons than adoration, something closer to academic obligation.

My college career was straight-laced and sloppy. I got above-average grades. Didn't party. Worked hard. But I also fragmented my graduation timeline by dropping out for several years to pursue a professional wrestling pipedream. I completed three undergrad semesters prior to leaving for wrestling school in Missouri, and, when crawling back to Montana State University years later, I found myself with little to show but cognitive dissonance and a transcript advertising mismatched credits with no sensible direction. To make sense of it all, then years behind most other students my age, I assessed my options and selected the fastest route toward graduation—I had history credits, so history is what I'd study (text me if you need life coaching).

The strategy worked fair enough, though I was quick to realize I didn't enjoy history much at all. The discipline seemed too naval gazey in the ways we rehashed other people's written accounts to convey the same outcomes: that humans are predictable in their greed, self-preservation, violence—

History repeats itself. So do history students. Ad nauseum.

Besides, what did I care for the evolution of the market economy in the Southern colonies (beyond this reference from my favorite movie, *Good Will Hunting*, featuring—guess who—Casey Affleck) or the pre-revolutionary utopia and the capital forming effects of military mobilization (ibid)? I lost interest somewhere between "Origins of Western Civilization" and "Civil War and Reconstruction," with old white men informing us young white students of dead white men who'd built the patriarchy upon us, but the stagnant path did lead me to more important conclusions than complaints. That's how we get to Whittlesey.

You see, to the best of my recollection, formulated from interdepartmental gossip, the university fucked up. Montana State had miscalculated, or just overlooked, the number of graduating seniors within the history department the spring of 2007. Roughly sixty students were then vying for thirty spots in a necessary capstone class—to miss the class meant missing graduation. I became one of the thirty who didn't make the cut. One of the thirty left to MSU's problem-solving ingenuity, which, as with most bureaucratic processes, wasn't a reassuring place to be.

As a hail Mary, the school hired the historical archivist at Yellowstone National Park, Lee Whittlesey, to make the commute from Gardiner, MT, once a week, to teach us academic outcasts the history of the park. What I'd stumbled into was every national park aficionado's holy grail, an academic accident that tipped in my favor. What's more, capstone classes are supposed to comprise the culmination of your studies over the last four years (assuming you're graduating on time and didn't take time off to wrestle other men in spandex), but this course, in terms of difficulty, was horseplay. Wasn't surprising though, considering its last-minute formulation, and considering our acting professor wasn't a professor at all. With the ease of the workload, appreciating Yellowstone became the sole focus.

Whittlesey's wisdom swept through my mind like wildfire, my preconceptions of the park an accumulated kindling that burned into deeper curiosity. The information was surprising and astonishing, yet shame-inducing. I was one of those take-it-for-granted boneheads who grew up ninety miles from the park but rarely went, while others traveled from around the globe for the once-in-a-lifetime experience. Had you asked, I could have named maybe five national parks at the time: Yellowstone, Tetons, Glacier, Yosemite, the Grand Canyon. Any memory with these places was mute, a family vacation to Glacier the strongest: elevated boardwalks through damp forest; us kids sharpening sticks to hunt squirrel; an alcoholic grandmother losing her footing on a decline, drink in hand, tumbling the hillside in cartoon fashion, and, as the legend lives, not spilling a single drop of bourbon (inconspicuously concealed in a Diet Rite can).

By the time I took Whittlesey's class, age twenty-two, I'd been to Yellowstone only a handful of times, and when places like "the Grand Canyon" were mentioned, I wasn't sure if we were talking about *the* Grand Canyon, or some different earth trench closer to home (turns out there is a "Grand Canyon of the Yellowstone"). Likewise, other landmarks were explicated that I'd never given much heed: Grand Prismatic, Yellowstone Lake, Norris Geyser Basin. Whittlesey waxed eloquent about it all; there was no better person to learn from.

According to an interview with *Yellowstone Insider*, he'd started in the park as a garbage man—well, adolescent—an eighteen-year-old Oklahoman riding the backs of refuse trucks and collecting Yellowstone's human-generate waste. He'd fibbed his way into the position, simply showing up at the Yellowstone personnel office, at the behest of his father, and requested a job. He was told the park only hired those who'd submitted applications by their deadline, but times were different then, sans the Internet and with less rigid administration (this was the same year, 1968, when Edward Abbey's *Desert Solitaire* had been published, truly giving us a look into the easygoing nature of NPS culture), so he lied, saying he'd done as much, and was offered the position.

The opportunity created predictable habits—hiking, backpacking, reading park literature. The pay was decent, the work easy, and summer after summer he'd return. He eventually made his way from West Thumb to Old Faithful, where he became a non-driving commentator for a concession company, and where he was told by other employees that there would be more excitement—and girls.

But summer jobs being just that, college drew the Oklahoman home where he received a degree in radio and TV communications, which he applied for a while, but, after a few years, couldn't ignore the distant call of Yellowstone. He returned, now with his wife, and became a bus and snowcoach driver. He became a "lifer."

He moved through the ranks, attending ranger school in North Carolina where he earned his law enforcement commission. Then he went to law school, back at his alma mater of the University of Oklahoma. This training prepped him for his future with research and writing. He came back to the park in 1988 as a law enforcement ranger, based in West Yellowstone, and was on duty that season when the historic wildfire hit. Nearly forty percent of the park was affected.

That fall his first book came out, *Yellowstone Place Names*, including backstories of nearly every place name found in the park. Whittlesey then became an interpretive ranger at Mammoth Hot Springs in 1992, allowing him to embark on a controversial project—wolf reintroduction. Working with Paul Schulllery, they began producing a wildlife inventory of all historic wolf sightings—an important document for the 1995 reintroduction. This same year he put out another book, the best-selling *Death in Yellowstone*.

His technical writing ultimately got him hired as an assistant park historian. When his predecessor left, he applied for the position, his law degree lending important credentials, making him the park's fourth official historian.

As his students we read various books on the park, many authored by Whittlesey himself, including his flagship *Death in Yellowstone*. It's exactly what you'd expect: 276 pages recounting Yellowstone's recorded deaths, from drowning to falling trees to falling off cliffs to noxious fumes to maulings to lightning strikes to murder. All the good stuff that makes us wonder, "What were these people thinking?" There's lots to get worked up about: children slipping off boardwalks into boiling hot springs; a man gored twenty-nine times when trying to feed a bison. But of the accounts, a decade removed from my first reading of the book, the fatalities that lingered most, perhaps inspired by their unassuming yet hyperviolent nature, where those of chapter four: "Don't Eat Wild Parsnips!"

I didn't care about flowers when taking Whittlesey's class in 2007, wouldn't until 2016, but that chapter from *Death in Yellowstone* was a precursor. Water hemlock, beyond every other account, affected me. Could have been that, growing up near Yellowstone, you hear of the recurring glamorous deaths and become desensitized. I was no stranger: my neighbor, Sarah, was mauled by a grizzly while exploring the park with friends. She survived, but not without cost: a punctured lung, a broken and nearly severed arm, seven fractured ribs, a thigh ripped open, canine teeth through an eye socket and sinus, lesions everywhere. I'd see her gardening through cracks in our shared fence, like stealing a glance at the scene of an accident, a human body dissected by nature and rebuilt by modern medicine. But her heart remained strong: one of the first things she said upon returned consciousness, knowing park policy with problem grizzlies, was "Please don't kill the bear."

So it went. Stories recirculated, every passing summer, with new players plugged into the same scenarios—animal attacks, drownings, cliff falls—but never once did I hear about water hemlock. Because, to the untrained eye, Yellowstone's 2.2 million acres are a place of magnitude: herds of bison lounging under prominent peaks; moose, wolves, bears in the Lamar Valley; pools of boiling geothermal goo. Scanning for megafauna, the eye easily overlooks the minutiae: glacier lily amongst the lodgepole pine; lupine on Mount Washburn; fairy slipper near Hellroaring. Entire worlds go unnoticed. The park is just too monumental for such inconspicuous deaths. The expectation was that if you were going to die in the park it better be epic, not a drawn-out battle with neurotoxins causing you to piss, shit, and puke yourself into a coma.

My brother Troy, fifteen years my junior, knew the stories too. I'd been dragging him to Yellowstone for most of his life. He was there the first time I saw the Grand Canyon of the Yellowstone, the first time I walked the boardwalks of Norris Geyser Basin, the first time I took a snow coach tour in winter, the first time I cycled the park in spring. My Yellowstone story became his.

He was seven the first time we went, too young to comprehend the significance of the visit. I was too. But I regurgitated Whittlesey stats to both him and our parents, sponsored by my college-education elitism, pointing to rimrock cliff faces and speaking of ancient calderas; pointing to fields of bison and confessing them the last wild herds; pointing to place names on the map, like Absaroka and Hayden and Shoshone, and explaining the significance. A national-park-loving seed had been planted in me, unbeknownst at the time, and like all truth hardwired into an embryo, I was tasked with one mission: to propagate. Troy would be my convert.

No surprise then that I coerced him on this current journey, plants the agenda, making a daytrip to Red Lodge, through the Beartooth Mountains, and down to the park's northeast entrance. He and I somehow always coordinate these summer trips amidst Sturgis motorcycle rallies, which lure all hogs and choppers to its Midwest epicenter, making for a less peaceful enterprise one expects amongst our wilderness. And loud, unnecessary noises bring me closer to second-degree murder than any other stimulant I've tested. Troy has other irritants: he wants to murder *me* for stopping at all roadside flashes of paintbrush pink and columbine yellow, or the faint purple of arctic gentian and the pale baby blue of mountain forget-me-not. Fireweed, replete when the season's ripe, is also a favorite. These stops, collectively, delay us by hours.

The bikers stop, too, mistaking my massive Sigma DG 150–500mm camera lens to mean I'm a professional (I point, I shoot, I let autofocus do the work) and any stationed car to mean discovered megafauna, appreciated to this ranking and proportionally dictated by the amount of traffic gathered: 7) pronghorn 6) elk, 5) bison, 4) moose, 3) black bear, 2) grizzly, 1) wolf. They look where I look, perplexed, slick leather chaps chaffing as they mill about, until I point and say, "yellow toadflax."

"Toad?"

"No, that flower."

They don't even pretend to care, no quick deference, then rocket off with a sonic fucking boom—

Jesus Christ, to think they expect to see *anything* out here. May the bears subscribe to my sentiments on manslaughter. Luckily the snapdragon-like structure of toadflax soothes me, a meditation in flower form. Troy, being a rural teenager, calls my interest "gay," as if to mean stupid or lame or uncool. As if to be the perfect insult. It's not. I tell him "pansy" would be wittier.

This kid, Troy, becoming a man, is the closest I may come to progeny. You see, my mother, at thirty-six, became pregnant with an accidental embryo that subdivided and subdivided into a body of cells that soon become my little brother. The annunciation was first shared at a hotel furniture convention, my older brother, Treaver (correct spelling, no joke), and I sitting across from my parents at the GranTree Inn, us on one bed and them on the other, my mother sobbing to the dread of their unplanned reform. She'd gotten off birth control for the first time in fifteen years, due to an advancing side effect, something to do with blotchy skin, and sibling germination was the result, though at the time I was certain her tears meant divorce, a longstanding fear throughout my childhood. But, yet, instead of separation, there was addition, a fifth pea to our pod, Troy.

I'm now currently the same age as my mother when she conceived with this final child—I thought her so old at the time, maybe influenced by her too-old-to-be-having-a-child woes, yet middle-age is upon me, mid-thirties not a gentle transition but a cruel highjack, the body leaving the mind behind to assume it still chic and spritely. Fleeting hairlines and potbellies are the dissonance, a mental trial only time can bestow and taunt with the irreversible. By this age I thought I'd've matured into wanting kids but never did, perhaps too selfish with my alone time and too quickly annoyed with anyone wanting my attention. It's why I don't like dogs. Or people. A new brother then, fifteen years my junior, became perfect for parental practice while maintaining a fraternal distance. He would be my test dummy.

After the annunciation, my mother's belly began to grow, Troy inside like a tumor, yet I never opted to test his "kicking" with a hand to my mom's taunt stomach, an act too akin to the 1979 *Alien* chest bursting scene. No thanks. But even when an alien on the outside, especially in those initial infant years, Troy still frightened me; I thought my clumsy teenage body would bring harm to his fragile perfection—the same fear as driving a new car or wearing out-of-the-box shoes (A ship in harbor is safe, right?). Still, I remember the first time he fell asleep on my chest. It was an invitation to something tender, like unconditional love, that I hadn't applied for, curse his branches, which led to an honorary membership in worry. I didn't want him to have depression like me. Or to self-loath. And from that softness grew flowers, as if *actual* unconditional love, a nursery to our budding brotherhood, producing the glorious garden that had me appreciating the act of raising kids and the glorious garden that, mind you, this asshole was now calling "gay."

Once inside Yellowstone's boundaries, we park and hike alongside Soda Butte Creek—one of us is hoping to glance a carrot-like white blossom. One of us is also trying to gift the other a love of wild places.

"Here, smell this." I roll a sage leaf between my fingers, releasing its aroma, and hold it nose level. "And this," I say, doing the same with yarrow. We barely make it through the first meadow before he's done with me. Since undertaking this flower hobby, I've become less fun to hike with, the hypnotic flow of trail movement interrupted over and again by the stopping, squatting, identifying. But there are deeper sins to commit in a national park. Troy will be fine.

We skirt Soda Butte Creek's edge, somewhat of a seepage area, as the vegetation thickens. Visibility is lost to the knee. Plant after plant fails, according to the veins, to be water hemlock. No surprise though, I've done zero research on anything. Not even a quick Google on dispersion, habitat, or growing season. But that's how you best spot celebrities, nonchalant, little effort. And if there is any crossover between plants and TV personalities, I trust my luck, because my blasé sighting shortlist is impressive (excluding the aforementioned Affleck and Fey) and to be appreciated, like megafauna, in this ranking: 7) Pauly Shore, 6) Flavor Flav, 5) Kathy Griffin, 4) Paul Giamatti, 3) Michael Keaton, 2) Anne Hathaway, 1) Prince. (Forget that the list suggests "You need to spend less time in Vegas casinos, Tyler.")

My face inches deeper into the undergrowth, the swamp oozing up over my boots and soiling my socks, until a creature, not but four to five feet out, somewhere hidden in the marsh, chatters like a house cat chirping at yard birds. A river otter maybe. It's cute. A playful noise.

"What is that?" Troy asks, interest piqued.

"Don't know . . . I've never heard anything like it."

We linger, looking for a culprit, when out waddles an oversized creature, stout as a tiny bear. "What *is* that?" Troy says again, only glimpsing hindquarters before the animal disappears into its den.

"A badger," I whisper, putting a cautionary arm across Troy's chest, directing him behind me. "These things can be mean as hell." And it's back up, emerging from a different sagebrush-shrouded hole, fifteen feet away, grunting like a little pig. The fur pattern is beautiful, like Affleck's beard, black stripes accenting a white face, oversized paws looking dopey. The creature keeps circling, dipping in and out of burrows, occasionally emerging to stare head-on. Yep, clown feet. But I'm still cautious, bear spray readied. Our dad taught me to be.

Before I could legally drive, before Troy was born, Bruce let me practice on prairie service roads and throughout favored hunting grounds, his durable pickup my chariot. One session, we jostled along as per usual, my style cautious and controlled, when Bruce said "Stop." Without saying more and putting a finger to his lips, he opened his door, took his .22 rifle off the window rack, steadied the forestock on the frame of the truck, waited, eye to scope—

Then gunfire.

We Dunning boys are obsessive, perhaps a genetic legacy of Bruce, which led to the collection of a lot of kitsch—snow globes, commemorative coins, action figures, McDonald's toys, comic books, trading cards—but Bruce's interest at that time, for a few months' stint, was roadkill. More specifically, he wanted skulls. Any trip then, whether to the grocery store or to a different state, threatened the possibility of the biohazardous, him pulling over to inspect a carcass. It was a short stint, thank god, but boy were those productive months.

If the head was salvageable, he'd wrap the dead animal in a blanket, maybe put it in a cardboard box, rot and decay and maggots a nonissue, and bring it home. From here, and after decapitation of course, he'd ready two big vats on the kitchen stove: one to boil the flesh from bone and the other for bleaching. I hope you can't imagine the smell because, if you can, it means you, too, have endured something equally as putrid as decomposition expedited. Our space of shared meals would reek for weeks as new skulls started lining the curio cabinet: squirrel, mouse, raccoon, skunk, porcupine, fox, coyote, etcetera, etcetera. Everything roadkill . . . until now.

He and I got back in the truck and drove the direction of his bullet. Again he said "Stop." We got out. Before us was his prey, two squat legs, black fur tapering into a beige tail, the animal ass up and half submerged at the lip of its den. It blended imperceptibly with the landscape, a visual defense, but my father, even in older age, has hawk eyes. He poked the haunches with the rifle barrel. "A badger," he said. "These things can be mean as hell."

The animal showed no sign of life, no reaction to the prodding, so Bruce slipped work gloves on and began tugging at the hindlegs. We expected a smooth removal, but my old man pulled with the force of his body weight, 170 pounds, yet the fifteen-pound carcass didn't budge. "Dug its claws in before it died," my dad said, walking back to the vehicle with intent.

Next, we tethered a tow strap to the badger's waist, the other end to the truck's hitch. At the wheel again, I inched the truck forward, per Bruce's hand instructions, till the strap was taut. "Okay," he then said, "gun it." With fear and trepidation and one thousand silent apologies, I floored the accelerator and, for a brief golden moment of rebellion, the animal's steadfast claws—two-inch blades for digging, defense, and maiming—held before the force of butchery until finally succumbing to the combustion engine's horsepower. The truck jolted forward. Through the rearview mirror I saw the body launch twenty feet skyward, still attached like an umbilical cord to the hitch, a reverse birth violently bringing this poor animal to an opposite outcome. Its decapitated, rendered, and bleached skull still sits on my bookshelf, all thirty-four boding teeth intact, and a reminder of how far an obsession for collection can take us.

Troy and I now stand petrified to this living badger, it nonplussed to our presence. Just in case, my trigger finger remains on the bear spray. It would be fair retribution for past transgressions if this animal wanted to harm me, but Troy is innocent to that crime. I resolve to at least protect him. I will not let my little brother become a stat in any updated version of Whittlesey's book.

His second edition came out nearly twenty years after the first, in 2014, now revised with new maulings and fatal hot spring fiascos with almost 200 pages added (and with a much better cover). But the book remains forever anthropocentric; these cautionary tales tell only of human death in the park. My dear badger friend has no historical archive, just like his cohort of wolves and bears and bison, to the injustice done on this land through poaching, poison, and malice. For example, there are nineteenth-century images of bison skulls stacked on the prairie like pyramids in Mexico; images of hundreds of wolf pelts filling hunters' cellars. *Death in Yellowstone* is only a small portion of this land's grief story. One thousand silent apologies could never be enough.

I whisper a new requiem each time I trek Yellowstone. Barely a month goes by now that I don't visit the park; much has changed since I took that capstone class and finished my undergraduate degree. Yet, people keep dying in the park. Much has stayed the same. Whittlesey has since retired, looking to work on personal projects and further explore Montana, but he also left because of the outright denial of climate change by federal officials who are supposed to be in charge of protecting the environment. Since the creation of the planet's first national park in 1872, Yellowstone, politics have always peppered our bucolic places.

Still, Yellowstone remains wild, from the obvious to the unsuspecting. I rarely tread in a state of ease; many things can kill you out here. Even the plants are dangerous. *Even* searching for the dangerous plants is dangerous. But I continue on, badgers or not, brother in tow, water hemlock my current target of intrigue—curiosity and ignorance and bad timing the unifying factors amongst all the fatal departures in this park. These neurotoxins unto ourselves.

Troy and I decide to circumvent our transgressor and head home. We set a wide berth and begin moving around the little clown and back toward the car. The badger scratches in the dirt. Grunts. We make it back to the car with no altercation, my water hemlock goal abandoned. "That was awesome," Troy says. "I love coming out here."

"Pretty amazing, isn't it?"

". . . Sorry you didn't find your plant."

"That's okay," I say, knowing it was never really the goal. "You want to try again sometime?"

"Fuck yeah," he says.

"Fuck yeah," I say.

And in accordance with the innumerous circumstances that got us here—unplanned pregnancy, pyramids of skulls, poisonous plants—my plan has worked. Troy cares. And from the softness, I pray, flowers will grow.

POETRY

SELECTED AS BEST IN POETRY

Irene Cooper is the author of *Committal,* poet-friendly spy-fy about family (V.A. Press, 2020) & the poetry collection, *spare change* (FLP, 2021), a finalist for the Stafford/Hall Prize (Oregon Book Awards). In 2020, she co-edited *Placed: An Encyclopedia of Central Oregon*, an anthology of Central Oregon writing. Poems, stories & reviews appear in *Denver Quarterly, The Feminist Wire, The Manifest-Station, phoebe, The Rumpus, Witness,* & elsewhere. Irene teaches in community & supports AIC-directed creative writing opportunities at a regional prison. She lives with her people & Maggie, the corgi, in Oregon, where she pretends to garden, but mostly just watches the birds.

drift

1. [confluence/divergence]

hydrologic sponge of volcanic bedrock
feeds the river of falls
which joins the Crooked and
                        Metolius at Billy Chinook
reservoir is French for *keep,* Old English for *hold*
but nothing holds. under our slow eye
rock yawns and stretches at our feet
                              in geologic terms
it's only a minute or so since lava flowed
and cooled to form the porous basin that seizes
and draws the rain from run off
                        watery keep sinks, circulates
emerging months and years ahead as spring
          unless it doesn't. Whychus Creek, old
steelhead paradise saw none nor no Chinook
for fifty years and more
                                   peculiar
web of waterways and *stable*
diverted to dry and dire straits
               what if there was yoga for rivers,
an asana to raise the winter flow from its score
of cubic feet per second,
                      gentle the summer floods
raise all boats and restore
the nimble reaches to their hardy oddities

2. [bas(in) nature]

jay bathes in a sprinkler-puddled swing

lawn mower stirs a doe to lift her gaze

coyote cruises Deschutes River Woods at noon
at twilight, bucks leap like sk8rboyz on Colorado

black bear paws Tumalo Creek,
moony racoon wakes the chickens, riles the dogs

vixen skitters her red kits across highway 97
sudden owl swoops before the headlights

bobcat skims the dusty rimrock
sights us, surprises us on our careful trails

    3. [greater sage grouse]

they numbered 16 million 50 years or so ago
and today the rough count's 500K, plenty
to grouse about for the living three percent, plus uncrushed
         species that swim the sagebrush sea:
pygmy rabbits, pronghorn, golden eagles, coyote;
yellow bells, milkvetch, tarweed fiddleneck,
—350 entities native to the brush
         a lek is the place male grouse display their moves,
spike the air with punk fans of tailfeathers, puff their masculine air sacs,
gloop gloop. sage chickens mating on the sage steppe
losing ground and cover fast to fire, juniper creep,
people. in Oregon, at least, the ranchers are onboard:
         save the bird, save the herd
across state lines, nothing rhymes with gas, with oil
but back to sex: the choreography commences at golden dawn,
competitive and feathered as any rodeo
    many are called to the ancient do-si-do, few get to do the deed
lonely males await their season in a patch of scrub
females get busy with the babies
        the grouse is not endangered, *per se,* but we watch,

we watch, this bellwether, this indicator, we watch,
tick tock, the canary as it dances in the coal mine

    4. [river critters]

macroinvertebrates lack a spine
& are nimble environmental indicators of:
        nutrient availability
            temperature
                oxygen levels:
the ethereal dragonfly, the lowly flatworm
eco-mates to the macrolepidopteran:
              swallowtail butterfly at the Metolius
gothic window paned splendor, red ombres to gold to coolish black

hatch chart in January:
        mayfly in slack slow water and back eddies
        caddis in deep slow runs
        the stonefly, the midge—
in April they're in the riffles, the soft runs, the tail-outs
in May the salmonfly risk the fast and heavy boulder runs
fish only want what anybody in their position would:
        a gravel bottom
            calm backwaters
                side channels
—& for hiding,
deep pools
sunk debris

declared a threatened species in 2014, the spotted frog
has it rough—
no wetland in winter, eggs flushed downstream in summer
makes it hard to get a jump on the whole survival thing

a spot can be a blemish—or
a spot can be a fixed point on the horizon
a way to focus

5. [straight]

           straight as the crow flies
           isn't so straight after all
         Charles Dickens made it up
     and who doesn't like a good story.
   straight shot, straight away, straight
    as an arrow, give it to me straight
       straighten up and fly right
        they're a straight shooter
         can't think straight
      the straight and narrow
       path is not for rivers
who've no need of moral
compass, they've got gravity.
    narrow path squeezes out
  the complexity. circuitous
    eco-logic, unassailable:
     witness the soaring red-
   tailed hawk in a high wind
   the golden eagle following
      the curve of the earth
sighting and capturing its supper.
   the river's neither line nor
parabola, and balance is seldom
symmetry. drive and cycle, water
      is opportunivore bent
         for the sea,
  and there's the curve again
    stable in its peculiarity
    imperiled if bereft
of meander and bend

Mark Gibbons was named Montana Poet Laureate from 2021 to 2023. He is the editor of FootHills Publishing's *Montana Poets* Series. *In the Weeds*, his eleventh collection of poems, was published in 2021 by Drumlummon Institute. A lifelong resident of Montana, Gibbons has been scribbling poems and working a variety of blue collar jobs from laborer to teacher to truck driver with his high school sweetheart and partner of fifty years, Pamela Leigh.

Cool Blue Dawn
—for Miles Davis & John Prine

Bring me the top of the mountain
at the top of the world
this dawn top of the morning
to stand in the eagle's lair, the air,
wind cool, steady, whipping
my hair, blue sky far as eye
can see, just me on this rock,
feathers ruffled, turning blue
till you arrive and that makes two,
three birds to share this view.

Bring me the backyard bluebird,
let it sing harmony with the finch
in the hedge, dance with the chickadee
hopping the spruce trunk, open for
the meadowlark's heartbreaking solo
of hope hidden in weeds—let
Miles scream a bitchy hawk whistle,
make Bird squawk camp-robber riffs,
have Monk crow and whippoorwill
(the only way to go home)
and beg Coltrane to blow coda
of mourning doves supreme.

Bring me the music of birds today,
those are the best words
of comfort for the feeling of soul,
help us learn the language
we don't know, this world, this life
we love, this light and noise
we agree exists, what we see
and don't understand, help us forget

the threat we constantly fear—
knowing we are going to disappear—
for some reason it terrifies us to be
as fragile and beautiful as birds.

Bring me the dream of wings,
of freedom aloft, that promise of
flight when fate closes and opens
the door into birdsong and joy,
fearless in the new dawn
breaking over the unknown—hearts
reborn into a new kind of blue.

Michael Garrigan writes and teaches along the Susquehanna River in Lancaster, Pennsylvania and believes every watershed should have a Poet Laureate. He is the author of two poetry collections — *Robbing the Pillars* and *River, Amen*. His writing has appeared in Orion Magazine, North American Review, and The Hopper Magazine. He was the Artist in Residence for The Bob Marshall Wilderness Area in 2021 and you can find more of his writing at www.mgarrigan.com.

Slate Run

Deadwood stacks across rock,
patterns stitched by quick wind
      slicing down drafts,
         waiting for high water.

Miles of bushwhacking to plunge pools, searching
thin red streaks across shins, exploration tattoos.

Spirits gather where creeks carve
granite leaving steps to some mystic
      hiding under the layered
        slate shelf waiting for dark
              to tail out.

Prayers palm and peel where water
runs deepest, runs darkest, runs to stillness.
      Earth holds tight to our elders,
        the Appalachian Mountains.

So much life is written watching rock gather.

Todd Davis is the author of seven full-length collections of poetry, most recently *Coffin Honey* and *Native Species*, both published by Michigan State University Press. He has won the Midwest Book Award, the Foreword INDIES Book of the Year Bronze and Silver Awards, the Gwendolyn Brooks Poetry Prize, the Chautauqua Editors Prize, and the Bloomsburg University Book Prize. His poems appear in such noted journals and magazines as *Alaska Quarterly Review*, *American Poetry Review*, *Gettysburg Review*, *Iowa Review*, *Missouri Review*, *North American Review*, *Orion*, and *Poetry Northwest*. He teaches environmental studies at Pennsylvania State University's Altoona College.

Lost Blue

For more than
a decade I stole
snowmelt
from spring,
lifted pink
and red bodies
twisting
from current,
the only fish
born rightfully
to this place.
But after
the fire ran up
the mountain—
(root balls
incinerated,
a scorched
absence large
enough to crawl
inside of)—
the stream holds
only ash,

water warmed

without banked

dogwood and willow,

the leaky canoes

of fir and spruce

sunk to the bottom.

I count every fish

as it swims away

to the main river:

orphans of the lost

blue I'd hoped

to show my son

before the debt

of loving a place

broke him.

First published in *Coffin Honey* (Michigan State University Press, 2022)

Dazar Frihet is a Norwegian-American who splits his time between a big city job and recreating (as in re-creating himself) in the wild places. He believes that people are always better than the assumptions we make of them, and that we are all at our very best when alone in the wilderness.

His first novel will be published by Riverfeet Press in 2024.

A Place much Farther Back . . .

In a place much farther back
Beyond the reach of recollection
I can hear the music of my childhood
Singing to me surrendering serenades
In a rhythm I still recall
Like not a day has passed
All these moments of my life
Have been tied into one event
A chain of circumstances
More elegant and irreplicable
Than a strand of double helix
My memories are only music in my mind
The images acquainted with my life
Are the only translation which could properly describe
The things I've learned
And the questions I still pursue
I am dancing an unscripted choreography
Getting lost inside this map of my time
Step by step spinning in circles down a straight line
I can still feel the cold wind on my nose
I can still taste the water from the river on my hands
I still smell the grass on my knees
I am still that old boy
Buried deep inside of this young man
My ambitions are much swifter than my feet
But someplace farther down this current of time
I am certain the two of them will meet
I am floating somewhere in between

The past and the future
At the apex of the pendulum
I balance in defense of all opposition
I take advantage of every spare moment
By giving myself the chance to dream
It always takes me to places
Where life seems to be so easy
Keeps me smiling inside
In pursuit of the greatest possibilities
I want to grasp the wilderness in my heart
Life is the exploration of constantly evolving opportunity
Only the sound of the winds
And a blue sky
Beneath the shade of evergreens
Will make me feel free
I need the water on my feet
I need clean air in my lungs
I must hear the screams of the wild
If I will ever understand
The sequence of my life
And all this worlds' existence
Only there
Where my thoughts can find isolation
Am I at peace
With the intoxicating rush
The rotation of this world
The only language I comprehend
Is the subliminal inclination
Implied by this orchestra of silence
I can hear it so loudly
Singing to me

In soothing sweet melodies
I listen to the timeline
For the chorus of my life
I hear the frogs and crickets singing
Near the pond outside my window as a child
I can see the sound of the loons' echo
So distinctly it fills me with goose bumps
So completely I feel the sounds of my wilderness
That no matter where I am
Whatever notes the future of my timeline may progress
I can close my eyes and hear the song of nature's finest
Singing to me full of emotion and bliss.

Ana Maria Spagna is the author of several books including *Uplake: Restless Essays of Coming and Going*, *Reclaimers*, *Test Ride on the Sunnyland Bus*, and two previous essay collections, *Potluck* and *Now Go Home*. Her poems have appeared in *Bellingham Review*, *Pilgrimage*, *North Dakota Quarterly*, *Split Rock Review*, and *What Rough Beast*, and are collected in *Mile Marker Six*, which appeared from Finishing Line Press in 2021. She lives in the North Cascades and teaches in the MFA programs at Antioch and Western Colorado Universities.

where sky blue beckons

ankle deep in ash where sky blue beckons
this worn descent where an ice sheet weighted
uplift we snap sticks through brush what you call
chaparral what you know how this outcrop
teeters how bear shit dries to berry hulls
bees hunt flesh all buzz and crackle this summer
reckoning ten years late how this bare ridge
drops past mercy down a deer path fire-scarred
where Basque sheep bedded an eagle flaps
as if in spite or fervor where kinnickinnick
clings to round rock if you could see
where blue sky skims my shoulders
closer now in shin-high grass where black snags bare
to bone you've seen me from afar now stand exposed
to touch this sky-glazed rim with curious grace

AJ Donley has her bachelor's in psychology and English and her master's in forensic psychology. Currently working as an advocate in the sexual violence field, she seeks to explore the human psyche and illustrates what she sees with poetry. AJ plays with form, language, and imagery in an attempt to interpret what she experiences. Poetry is a practice and is never complete; just as the mind is subjective and dynamic, so, too, is her writing. She is on a journey without destination in the hopes of glimpsing something decadent.

April in Covid

I have come to the yard to escape
the stagnant news reels, the same updates
the United States has surpassed Italy, China
fear has become monotony
and the winter has been long.
My friends are dying
of boredom, trapped in their homes, trapped
by a man who runs my country without science
but hides behind lies
I dive into books, resurfacing just long enough to work
from home then submerge myself again
into drink, into books, into Netflix shows
filmed in ancient times before mask mandates
and pandemic panic.
So when reality plunges in through my belly button
grabs hold of my sacrum and rips me
from the pages and drops me hard
back into the chair beneath the maple tree just in time
to watch the cool sap from some branch eclipsed by sunlight dissolve
into my sock, I am shocked
to see the colors that greet me here:
the grassy backdrop to my sap-soaked sock has shifted

from brown to green in less parched patches;
a blue jay sits between slumbering sumacs;
the purple ball the dog doesn't play with as dormant
as it was before the snow came;
and everything is still and silent and static until suddenly
a sense of movement lassos my vision and pulls
my focus to the left where a brown butterfly
waves to me from the leaves that autumn raking forgot
glowing iridescent under the almost-dinnertime light
and beneath her is sprouting a tentative cluster
of tulips, peaking from under musty mulch, as though
knocking at the door wondering if they are too early for the party,
almost apologetic, unsure, but imminent
and I realize that the reality that snatched me from the book
is named spring, is named transition, is named dynamic, says
"don't forget to look because if you only see
winter and then summer you will be ignorant
to the constant movement that creates and destroys"
and I know that
the grass will green
the jay will fly away
the ball will be there tomorrow
the tulips will blossom
the butterfly will be back next spring
to remind me to pay attention,
a prelude to an awakening summer.

Brad Garber has degrees in biology, chemistry and law. He writes, paints, draws, photographs, hunts for mushrooms and snakes in the Great Northwest. He is an avid birder and rock hound, a student of geomorphology and geology. His experience as runner, rock/mountain climber, son, father, husband, cook, bartender, carpenter, hunter, art model, fisherman, cancer survivor, musician and all-around aimless human being, informs his writing and bends his mind. Since 1991, he has published poetry, magazine articles, essays, photographs and weird stuff in such publications as *Edge Literary Journal, Pure Slush, On the Rusk Literary Journal, Sugar Mule, Third Wednesday, Barrow Street, Black Fox Literary Magazine, Barzakh Magazine, Five:2:One, Ginosko Journal, Vine Leaves Press, Riverfeet Press, Smoky Blue Literary Magazine, Aji Magazine* and other quality publications. 2011, 2013 & 2018 Pushcart Prize nominee.

What Animal I Would Be

It was about snow the hot coldness of it against the scales as I scrambled through brush as thick as otter fur ten thousand branches ripping the hide no hoof as agile as another no eyeball larger than a cuttlefish eye no claw sharper than a bush baby claw and I drifted in crashing tides against polyps and anemones all barbed up like Gulliver and tossed at the end of strings my monarch wings rigid in Mexican wind while I warmed my green turtle belly on Black Sand Beach a wandering tattler picking at morsels in seaweed and the anaconda of my soul twisted in antlers of wapiti next to heaving nostrils of wood bison all iced and wool-bound but the paws of panther shadows in Amazon mud and the reticent tapir led me into the mind of leaping lemurs all smiling like a party bursting out of a bowling alley into the streets of the jungle crashing into the brick side of a water buffalo all covered with egret shit and surrounded by leaf-cutter ants the black mambas slithering into tall grass where a mule deer might be waiting out the passage of an Oregon sun a pack of coyotes slinking by in search of kangaroo rats to gulp whole like jello shots and wildebeests dodged the snapping jaws of Nile crocodiles while lionesses carried their young into dark recesses for protection and bull elk bellowed like whistles on the broken side of a volcano and I thought about the deliberate peace of a sloth and the indifferent attitude of a 600-year-old Galapagos tortoise the swiftness and agility of the peregrine the imagined frivolity of otters and spinner porpoises twisty and splashy and decided as my spots blended into icy stone.

Benjamin Green is the author of eleven books including *The Sound of Fish Dreaming*. At the age of 65 he hopes his new work articulates a mature vision of the world and does so with some integrity. He resides in New Mexico.

My Place

I am in my place,
at the heart of things,
centered within my life
and the world:
I am standing in a small creek,
calf-deep over gravel and rock,
under steep cliffs of layered stone;
with trees and birds and butterflies,
the names for which I am still learning;
there are grasshoppers in the weeds.
The details are important, articulated evidence
that I am here, wholly present, aware, and observing;
I am not thinking, at least not thinking of other things,
or other times, even though I have been here before;
there are no questions of trespassing
or the arrogance of ownership,
even if I have purchased
a house a short walk up the road:
it is just me, and the sound
of moving water,
a fly drifting,
rod and reel in hand,
the chance of a fish.

Just me,
being here.

When I was twenty-one,
I dug up iris bulbs, and moved
them with me too late in the spring;
I re-planted them in the hardpan the locals
called "pygmy soil," but, they grew, somehow;
they found something to grow out of, and flowered
in colors that mimicked summer sunlight.
In the middle of a three-year drought
their petals looked like blurry waves
of heat-riddled yellow, like
the squint-eyed brass of direct light,
like a gathering, a proclamation;
they were a presentation.
Then, one day, they let go;
they wilted into the long dry
dying of an autumn day filled with
renewed hopelessness for wind, for rain, for storm.
Forty years ago, the blanched petals floated
like a leaf, kited on spirals of heat like a feather,
like a small bird soaring.
I remember
being there.

From that single moment
of presence to another:I stand
in front of a classroom full of

thirteen-year-olds; I am wondering
of the moments, wondering at the passage
of forty years,(of a lifetime),worrying at what was lost:
> deer ferns growing out of rock piles,
> the modest blossoms of labrador tea,
> morning dew on blackberries--
> (the fruit turned to mold by noon...)
> (I found them in the darkness under the spiny leaves)--

Again, the details are important: more fragments
of an observant mind, the results of having
paid attention, remembered while they
float away for one last time,
preserved in words in an
answer to a teenager's
question-- more evidence
of being there.

And, I think, it is good;
it *was* good to have a home
where I could see things and touch them,
where I could know things and love them,
where I could hurt things and try to make them right;
to have words that gained shape; to have aged,
matured into integrity, and to have found
more words, even in the shade
my body casts. It *is* good
to have held life
in my hands,
to have sung

in my voice
about
being
there.

And to have trusted in memory:
    how I cried the miracles of god,
    used words to genuflect, brought things close:
        storm wind on the ocean,
        points of land shouldering the waves like a prayer,
        fish struggling through flood currents
        to reach the green hills,
        the sky alive with
        sharp-clawed osprey
        intent on killing.
Beware! I cried.
And, *Joy!*
Be there!

Now, beneath
sheltering cottonwood trees,
rod and reel in hand, casting,
I contemplate the pain,
and lust, and love,
and, *yes!*,
the redemption
in being
there.

But, now, I
remember how the fog drifted,
how the world became gray, and more gray,
quiet, and more silent. On some days it seemed
it was no longer possible to perceive distinction--
(*Look!*, I implored, and again, *look!*).
I thought, No sun, no sky,
no earth. And all my desires,
the grace, the blessings,
the salvation,
the false curses
I once forgave
myself for—

>	A gentle breeze
>	of air loosens a cottonwood leaf;
>	it drifts stream-ward
>	past my face.

Just be here.
Now.

Look.
Wait long enough,
and beauty will happen:
tarantulas will walk from mesa top
to river bottom in autumn;
flowers will fold
their petals close

in the same way
that birds fold
their wings;
the sky,
voiced by the wind,
will hiss in the cottonwood leaves.
The sun slits the canyon's throat every morning
and washes in the creek,
and every evening
the canyon swallows
the light back
so the rocks
can bathe
in stardust.

In my place,
now, I am full of gratitude,
ready to testify in the middle of this blasting light
how shadows above all else
the sun makes....

And that yellow iris
with its staunched petals
floating close in early autumn
while blackened spiders hung in silvery webs
and dust oozed through window screens
and flies drank moisture from piles
of dog shit in the dried grass
and lichen turned gray

in the dark woods:

mortal transience for a moment made still.

I cast toward
a shadow under the
overhanging cliff of flesh-colored stone.
I have learned this: the world is the choice
to let it be, so a good place to start
is to let myself be faithful.

Look! Listen
to the unspoken language of silence
that answers prayers.
(Sometimes).
Look!

Look at how happy I am,
having been,
being here.

Chelsea Jackson is a writer, editor, and consultant. They use their poetry to ask hard questions, interrogate inherited social narratives, and explore what it means to be human. Their work is published in Passengers Journal, Fatal Flaw Literary Magazine, Touchstone Literary Magazine, and the Platform Review, among other publications. They were also a finalist in the 2020 Driftwood Press In-House Poetry Contest and the 2022 Animal Heart Poetry Collection Contest. Chelsea has an MFA in Poetry from Drew University and is the Managing Editor of The Maine Review. They love teaching workshops and helping others tap into the power of literature as a vehicle for social change. Originally from Southeastern, Virginia, they now live in Philadelphia with their partner and cuddly pit bull. You can find them on Twitter and Instagram @sea_c_j or at their website at chelsea-jackson.com

Honeysuckle: A Ghazal

A swamp child of the Chesapeake, of the honeysuckle
with sloshing nectar-belly, I waded in a bed of creek and honey-suckle.

Each sticky summer night I colluded with the Elephant-Hawk Moth's
protracting proboscis, filling our cheeks with honeysuckle.

Even now, amid the melancholy maturity brings, I catch their scent
before they catch my eye. Oh sweet reek of the honeysuckle.

My corpse revived by the sickly smell. Drooling
the child behind my ribcage shrieks, suckles honey.

One flower's candy fluid a pitiful harvest. I pull fistfuls.
Every flower mourns its twin, weeps *goodbye sister honeysuckle*.

Possessed I march, to melody of wind through tubular blossom
rain on petal, the beat of the invasive honeysuckle.

The gentle tug of calyx, slide of style, surge of stigma
dripping her carnal whisper over this body, weak: *honey, suckle*.

Unceasingly I thank the bush, kneel at her feet.
Draped in white, my priestess the honeysuckle.

Who am I to shower her with praise? Her flesh
turned mutilated feast, the honeysuckle.

It has taken me years to write of this haven
this tiny joy, to speak of the honeysuckle.

For many years **Gary W. Hawk** has perched on a three-legged stool: he listens to individuals and couples talk about their lives, taught for nineteen years in The Davidson Honors College at the University of Montana, and practices the craft of fine woodworking. All the while, poetry gets him up in the morning. His poems have appeared in *Camas, Gray's Sporting Journal, The Christian Century, Sojourners, Cedilla, Poets of the American West,* and The Island Institute's *Connotations*. He paddles a sea-kayak named *Bluebird* and writes at www.ospreypaddler.com.

River Town
Idaho Falls

Half dazed after July's Interstate heat
and the oven of red light intersections,
we leave the motel and go for a walk.

Near sunset the river flows like a thick green gel
over a bed of black lava, and downstream,
it rolls over the weir's rounded crown,
shattering in a chaos of white violence and noise,
the weight of it breaking on angular basalt.

With a crowd on a platform jutting above the river,
we defy our fear and lean over the rail,
astonished by the way the river's power
becomes visible in its breaking.
Who does not think what it would be like
to drift blithely on the slick above the falls
and then go suddenly over the edge?

On the same platform adolescent boys in white shirts and ties
try not to fantasize about the girls behind them.
All of them look like they've just been washed
in the white temple ablaze across the river,

remote as blessedness. It stands in the light of itself,
tempts us with promises too good to trust.

On the bike path children run toward mobs
of geese and ducks that giggle with hope
when they smell bread in the children's hands.
In deepening dark parents aim cameras at the scene,
light flashing off the young faces, as their young
throw bread to birds with long, sinuous necks.

At outside tables in the now solid dark
tourists from other countries, stranded between parks,
sip and whisper while the noise of locals
pours out of the bar.

Tall girls drift in a slipstream of perfume and speed,
the soft wheels of their longboards
carrying them along the asphalt next to the river.
We barely avoid collision with shirtless young men.
Heavy with sweat, they pedal as fast as they can,
spend desire like gamblers, hope only
to attract a gaze worth braking for.

Freshly washed after a day's labor in the fields,
other parents murmur to their children
like rams and ewes nudging their lambs
in a country with wolves.

Donna Mendelson and her husband drove 9,000 miles one summer looking for home. They found it in Missoula, Montana, where she taught linguistics and American literature at the University of Montana for some years. Though she no longer teaches, she is a faculty affiliate in UM's Davidson Honors College.

She loves the "broad margin" to life that Thoreau wrote about in *Walden* and tries hard to maintain hers. She listens for meadowlarks, looks for summer's clarkia and lewisia, and watches elk snout-nudge across the snow on North Peak. She is grateful for her home among ponderosas at the edge of town near the mountain called Nmqʷe in Séliš.

Donna's poems have appeared in *Rendezvous*, *Windfall: A Journal of Poetry and Place*, and *The Fourth River* and are forthcoming in *ISLE: Interdisciplinary Studies in Literature and Environment*. Her essays have been published in *Interdisciplinary Literary Studies* and *ESQ: A Journal of the American Renaissance*.

A Family of Clark's Nutcrackers

                works the ponderosas, one tree,
then another, circling, foraging branch to branch.
Each gray bird stops, stabs stabs stabs long corvid beak
into cone, drops scales and bracts, loses some nuts, then tugs,
holds a nut, whole-body wiggles, swallows, circles on,
hungry, persistent.

                The pines persist
in their own ways, survive beetles, budworms,
parasites, fungus, rust, decay, blight, flying embers
on west wind, the trees alive inside thick bark,
surviving while nutcrackers eat, stash, drop their seeds,

piney persistence like the ginnala maple's winged seeds
that cling, clicking in winter's east wind until spring,
like magpies who wait for what the nutcrackers drop,
as we do who hunger, hang on, guard our heartwood.

Gillian Kessler can be found dancing to loud music, teaching exuberant teens to appreciate language, writing in the early morning when everyone is asleep and exploring the wilds of Montana with her beautiful family. Gillian studied poetry at Santa Clara University with Edward Kleinschmidt, UCLA Extension with Suzanne Lummis and, more recently, in Missoula under the exceptional guidance of Chris Dombrowski, Mark Gibbons and Phillip Schaffer. Her poems and essays have been published in Mamalode Magazine and she writes frequently for Flapper Press. Her poetry was featured in the anthology, Poems Across the Big Sky Volume II. She has written two collections of poems, *Lemons and Cement* and the forthcoming, *Ash in the Tree.*

Suspended Somewhere Animal

The river rising, an orange
dog runs through the makeshift
marsh after a young mallard --

I enter my body of wild
chives and white lilacs, taste
buds, purified, drums blown blue

with flax, sweet grass, forgiveness
that's not accusatory, her
echo heavy in an upturned palm.

The creek could be road, daughter
heron in a gold velvet hat,
son sage grouse, fast and close to earth.

Husband not bird at all but something
like the trees, the surety of seasons.
Do you have your compass? Do you wear

it locked around your neck?
The monsters have settled, the
screen is shut, we're in real life.

There is nothing and everything
under the bed. I can't keep up
with wildflowers. We buried

Solomon's placenta beneath
the cherry tree,
defrosted poppy

in a metal bowl,
guarded muscle in
my hands.

There was no thought of
transmission then, the masked
vibrations of fear.

We held
one another beneath
this branch of starlight,

bloom girls in heavy
thicket, curls meld,
heads still,

held in aspen's

silent shudder –
they grow into families.

They breathe in the
expanse of open space,
thawing earth

and out of mist they rise,
the way woodsmoke rises
then disappears.

Mark Christopherson is an attorney, writer, and avid fly fisherman living in Minneapolis, MN. His work has been published most recently in Passengers Journal, The Dewdrop, and Wild Roof Journal. He can be reached at christopherson28@gmail.com.

The Small Hours

Maybe someday I will see the river as the river,
but tonight the moon drops its faces gently
on the water. They gaze below rather
than back to their source, at the watercress
and stone, into the depths where sculpin muddle
for straying nymphs. This strange world without air
is not unlike the realm of their father, yet it's brushed
by an ether, this flow and motion. When dusk
is forgotten the faces are everywhere, in the riffles,
the eddies and slow churning pools, circles of light
beneath the sweeping arms of willows. They gather
their terrestrial intelligence, hold fast images
of swaying fins over the crayfish sand. Here
is the thorny leg of a night heron in the shallows,
there is a glimpse of dark fur in retreat. It's a study
of flux and utterly novel to these minds etched
in silver, etched in rock. If they could speak
they might bid us to cease wailing over such riches,
over the change that is life and here so abundant.
We may even listen as morning returns and they
are forced from the water, receding back to spheres
timeless and pinned in the unresolvable distance.
Some say blue is a coolness, a color without passion,
but by day above the clouds you can see the face
of that worried father who has called his children home.

Award-winning poet, Pushcart Prize nominee and best-selling author, **Heidi Sander**'s poems have appeared in literary journals, anthologies, and multiple artistic collaborations. She is the founder of "Pathways To Poetry", a multimedia online program that helps emerging and established poets develop their writing, publish their poetry, and promote their work.

Her award-winning poem, "How We Live On", is being developed into a short film that will be touring film festivals in 2022 & 2023. The poem is also included in her poetry collection, The Forest Of My Mind, which was named a Hot New Release for Canadian poetry books. Her latest poetry books, Plant Your Words and the Plant Your Words Journal are focused on environmental awareness.

As a writer, storytelling is at the heart of everything Heidi does. To her, the art of writing is cathartic and opens doors of discovery. Her greatest joy is to foster the love of writing and to encourage others to share their stories and poetry. Her online program, "Pathways To Poetry" along with other writing workshops is part of her larger vision for the poetry and literary community.

www.heidisander.com

Carmanah

    1.

In Carmanah,
    dappled light muffles
        afternoon shadows.

Weathered trees
    shoulder the canopy,
        tender saplings sprout from

nurse logs and thick
    sword fern clusters,
        stretching to be

like their brothers
    and sisters, trunks so wide
        a dozen people can't circle them.

If these sitka
    could sing it would
        be hymns and chants

lifting their moist arms
    toward the coastal sun,
        roots lapping from

the stream bed,
    tidal pulses, deep
        rivers of starlight.

    2.

Isn't life itself an anthem?

    3.

In an area
      shorn by clearcuts,
          the devout followed

a holy decree:
      protect the old-growth,
          twice the biomass

of tropical rainforests.
      They left warm benches,
          narrow office spires,

subway halls,
      flocked to the
          mountains

scuttled over
      logging roads,
          dodged heavy

machinery,
      the bones of potholes,
          washboard rippled roads.

They congregated
      with the trees, took
          photos and videos

wrote music,
      poetry, canvassed
          door-to-door

through
      the veins of the
          country till a

multitude of 30,000
      signed, adopted and
          paid for each tree.

    4.

Isn't every life worth saving?

5.

The world's tallest
    sitka continue to sweep
        the sky with their halos

of green, higher
    than the towers
        of Notre Dame.

They climb with such
    lengthy determination,
        no one can verify

whether it's
    blind ambition,
        survival, or prayer.

Yet still,
    they turn their
        mossy wings upward.

What do we worship beyond ourselves
and our own creations?

Let us go to our churches,
    our synagogues, our mosques,
        our shrines, our temples.

The trees go to theirs
    rooting their mortal bodies
        in the hallowed ground,

the faithful sitka
    lift their cooper green
        steeples to the broad

infinite sky
    breathing in
        harp strings,

pure salt air,
    in this sanctuary
        they call home.

6.

Let us grumble,
    repeat our creed
        "Nothing lasts."

The Earth does.

Steve Wilson's poetry has appeared in journals and anthologies nationwide, as well as in his five collections, the most recent entitled *The Reaches*. His next book, *Complicity*, will appear in early 2023. He lives in San Marcos, Texas.

A Transfixion

                        Spun among
                dark
        isolations, dreams all

    roil and shadows: like reeds
        bent beside the river, or clouds

blown landward
    before a hurricane. Silence

                troubled within
                fracturing light.

Lynn Fast grew up skinning her knees in the small town of Winsted, MN. She went on to study opera and creative writing at the College of St. Benedict and the University of MN, though it was in romping with her two boys in the wilds of MN where she truly found her voice. She's been a Bluegrass singer, a tap dancer, and a homeschooler, she's dabbled with microgreens and praying mantis hatchery, and has been known to guerilla plant natives in wild places. It is these wild places which inspire the body of her work. Playful and intimate, her poems dissolve the barrier between us and the natural world.

Lynn currently works at the MN Landscape Arboretum.

Filling My Eyes

I am filling my eyes like grain stores for winter.
Filling my eyes, my nose, my skin—
gathering in birdsong, and tree
commingling,
collecting and cataloging the smell
and feel and vision
of green—
the green of the pond, the green of the hill,
the green of the moss, and grasshoppers
and leaves. I reap the copious bounty before me,
making hay while the sun shines,
burying my nose in palms of dirt
and memorizing the mourning dove's call.
I'm taking in all that is lush and lilting and alive—
filling my stores for winter.
I have more than enough to put by.

Mark Oswood is a retired biology professor (First Adult Life). He necessarily did the usual academic writing: articles in scientific journals, book chapters, wrote and edited books. Since retiring, residual academia, volunteering (mostly outdoor education for children), and life transitions (people and dogs) have been his Second Adult Life. Now starting his Third Adult Life, Mark is trying to read lots, notice more, and write at length (mostly poetry).

The Obligations of Being a Flicker

Last week I went on a field trip
to our yard, made glorious summer
in this winter of our discontent
by a flicker - a woodpecker -
warming a tall juniper, eating its berries.
(cones really, softly blue)
with the delicacy of chopsticks
plucking peas from prickly salad.

Then a single note - *kyeer!*
this flicker's call proclaiming
the *noblesse oblige* of frugivory -
to whom fruits are given, much is required:
ingestion, digestion, egestion -
accordingly, small hard seeds
will soon be bestowed
on places needing junipers.

T-M Baird has been writing poems since childhood, which took place in the midwest and upstate New York. They have a BA in Classics from Whitman College, an MA in Religious Studies from Lancaster University, and an MFA in poetry from the University of San Francisco. Their poems have appeared in several journals, including *Wild Roof, Deep Wild,* and *Sheila-na-gig*. T-M has followed a number of different paths, including many a hiking trail, swim lane, and garden furrow. Staying in motion and contemplating Mystery—especially where it concerns the Divine—are where they feel at home. They currently live in Vermont with their husband and dog.

A question, little lady:
Do you know where you come from?

Oh, yes sir, I think I do.
And you know what? It's not from your little rib.
I came straight from the spine of a cracking continent;
my bones hatched raw as malachite.

I slithered up from the silty belly of the sea,
only to bury myself again, by choice,
in the sweet-scented dust of wheat grass.

I have been carved from the bark of that tree;
I have dwelt lifetimes in its branches,
and again in the rooms of its every cell.

I am from fire. I speak volcanic ash.
I have spun wild in the universe,
and sat still in the wake of sudden stars.

I have spent weeks
in the sludge of salted streets, melting
steadily into rain.

I know you would never believe

                        how

                                I was born from my

mother's skull

               where it split

    to let lightning in,

though you dare—

you dare to claim me as your own creation,

sculpted dry from a disembodied rib

whose only marrow's in the river that fills your tap.

You're as breathless without the wind as I am, and

your God, and his

dusty

spine.

Yetta Rose Stein writes porch poems. Her work has appeared or is forthcoming in Grits Quarterly, the Montana Woman Magazine, Rejected Lit, and Orotone Journal. She is a graduate of Hellgate High School. She lives in Livingston, Montana with her partner and their dog named Cabbage.

In My Dreams, I Die in an Avalanche in the Bridgers

Alive in January like some unexpected miracle

Walking through the trees and past the trees

I am called to a ridge tucked back behind through

This promise of knowing more today than yesterday

Finding some certainty above the treeline

Living things fall apart at a certain altitude

Does this mean I am not a living thing when I find myself in thin air

The trees are a choking hazard I ignore

In January and alive like someone who knows enough but not everything

Considering each tree as a grave marker

I am alive and isn't that enough

The ridge shows itself like a fact

There is this shadow of a doubt

Reality stutters towards reality

Trees talking to one another like Christmas morning

I am left alone to my living

If I died without a sound would the trees hear me

There is this promise of being alive again tomorrow

I take it at face value like an eclipse

Snow melting where I can't see it

Wandering off an edge armed with vows I made to myself

Trees anxious to be included

I am called to a tomorrow that doesn't exist yet

I am left alone to my dying

These trees will live through everything that kills me.

FICTION

SELECTED AS BEST IN FICTION

Logan James Campbell writes fiction and teaches public secondary school literacy and multilingual development in East Oakland, California. Transplanted from Salt Lake City, he is a past winner of the Utah Arts Festival's "Ultra Iron Pen" multi-genre writing contest. A wallaby-looking dog named Zora accompanies him in the quest to write a prehistoric YA novel.

I'll Just Wait Until It's Quiet

I only invited this clown because if I trekked this far beyond cell range alone, Mom would protest on account of my Safety Plan. I told her Hugo would scare the grizzlies away. "You know it's not bears I'm worried about." I pictured her skeptical hands on hips. "Find someone to go with you. A *human*."

The only human I knew who also had (1) summer off, (2) no better invitations, and (3) the idiocy required for this obscure and arduous route I planned was Brian Sullivan. Moron showed up in sandals—no boots—so he's been limping along stiffly since day three. Never showed much brains at work either. Guy can barely find the power button on an iPad. At least he knows to leave trek decisions to me.

If Hugo were in charge, we would've taken some rest days well before Tungsten Pass. Hugo pup knows not the harrows of overdraft fees and the scholastic calendar. He just knows like I do that nothing beats the Uintas. They always provide a reset—like a defibrillator, restoring life's cadence into orderly peaks and valleys. Hugo loves the nonstop exercise and the cooler temps on his thick black coat.

But he and I are both over this whole fifteen-miles-a-day thing. This morning, he allowed a potgut to mosey across our path undisturbed. He'd spent the first few days bounding off-trail, harassing wildlife through the thick woods along the Duchesne. Since then it's been switchbacks up and over 12,000-foot pass after 12,000-foot pass. All the while Sullivan pointing out every falcon and accipiter. Dude can identify raptors by their flapping patterns. "No, that's not a sharpie. It's a Cooper's, with that flap flap gliiiiide. See?" I would point out how useless this knowledge was if I weren't so envious of it.

I uncrumple my map and doodle a hawk silhouette here on Tungsten, scribble in the margin: *Cooper's, Aug. 11*. One week till our anniversary.

#

For a while, Avril liked backpacking—just not long distances. She liked me, too, and she showed me the ropes of closeness. I counted her freckles: thirteen. We married. Here in the Uintas, of course, at Soapstone. And the August rains held off for an entire day of sunshine. We had thimbleberry cobbler instead of cake. A dozen species of wildflowers bloomed in lieu of frosting. Hugo wore a turquoise bowtie to match my thrift store shirt, and he observed reverently among our relatives as the brilliant Avril and I professed our endless love. "Conor. Avril. Do you promise?" I did, and she did.

#

My breathing exercises haven't been too helpful up in the steeps, not since yesterday on Red Knob when Hugo got cliffed out chasing a goat into the scree. I wasn't going to let Sullivan go fetch him over the cliff for me in those Tevas, though he swore he'd be happy to. One step off trail and a sandstone block beneath me teetered and threatened to dislodge, and I could not help but look down the rocky precipice toward gravity's welcome mat. The reality that *it can end now* returned to enchant me for the first time in eleven weeks. I tested the stone's reliability.

A deep bark resounded through the breeze and I looked up to see Hugo facing me, those eyes so human with doubt. Then he rediscovered his wolflike poise and vaulted his way back to me through the rocks, never stirring a single pebble. I suppose I was breathing the whole time.

Once the goat was out of sight I let Hugo off leash again, though he's stayed at my heel ever since, an invisible tether between us.

Our tent provides such an unsettling, defective form of privacy. Makes me think of the canary Mom used to keep, how sometimes she'd put a towel over its cage and it would stop chirping, go right to sleep. I wish my brain could shut off when I lay down in a tent, but beyond the nylon "walls," the world goes on. Sources of commotion are invisible. As with monsters under the bed, my imagination fills the space with convincing impossibilities. Hugo does the same, and we spiral together this way. He wakes me growling: a saber-toothed tiger approaches, departs. Now it's three A.M., and I hear Sullivan out there putzing around, probably trying to whittle a pine cone into a chess knight. Weirdo.

#

This summer I've been blasting music through the house, because I can. Whatever I want, whenever I want. I've steered clear of my usual sad bastard folk. I need an upbeat groove, and I've been feeling Javier Garcia's devilish "Tranquila":

observa todo el terreno,

súbete a una montaña,

quédate un ratito y después te bajas

Stick around a little while and then go back down.

#

We're atop Tungsten and finally have eyes on King's Peak. The valley before us is treeless, 10,000 feet above sea level. We'll camp there by a stream and be in range the next morning to ascend with daypacks, then return for our gear and start the day-and-a-half egress down Yellowstone Creek to the dirt lot to find Uncle Oscar and his getaway Buick. No cell service; no changing plans.

Sullivan's knees slow him down. The Tevas. I offer a trekking pole. "No thanks." He refuses help with a smile, a genuine smile. How does he do it?

#

Sullivan and I are both expected at the annual professional development "retreat" next Tuesday. That's when my soul must retreat from my body, when Mr. Tafel, Middle School Director, extracts it for safekeeping between Labor and Memorial Days. The exorcism involves Tafel chanting his latest mantras: "backward planning... differentiation... with fidelity... iterative process..." to a congregation of bagel-stuffed teachers in someone's living room, and they murmur the words back, nodding. "Remember your why," is Tafel's echoed *amen.*

Throughout the seance, I slouch deep into a cat-hair-encrusted futon and watch my suntan sublimate into a phantom, a Conor-shaped carapace floating before me. It waves goodbye, then sam-bas away to Tafel's chant. "Backward planning… fidelity…" Now I am Señor Dunn: a pallid, stress-acne'd zombie—not the virile sprite I had been in summer.

#

Snapshot of this zombie teacher's diet: Breakfast = Ho-Ho's and coffee. Lunch = Hot Cheetos and Coke. Dinner = Domino's and martinis. Fit as a flea.

#

I wish Hugo *was* in charge. We could just stay up here forever. I could swipe Sullivan's water filter and tell him to take a hike. To trudge his stupid Tevas the rest of the way out of my mountains, tell the world to leave me and my dog the hell alone. Or that I fell down a gorge and was washed away by the Duchesne. After all, we Irish-American Spanish teachers are a dime a dozen, it seems.

#

We were coworkers at the Hogle Zoo, Avril and I. My last year of college I cashiered in the gift shop, and her gig was painting kids' faces. That peculiar job gave me something to talk to her about, like why she always painted herself as a badger.

"I'm a Hufflepuff," she said. "Don't judge my Potter fandom."

"That's cool, but where do badgers come in?"

"Oh, Conor." I loved that she always said my name. "I've got to teach you some things." I laughed, and she held eye contact, giggling, scrunching her freckly cheeks; hexing me.

From then on I checked the staff schedule every Thursday so I could ask other cashiers to trade me for shifts that overlapped with hers. I'd talk to her about the animal kingdom enveloping us, and she'd tell me about her fictional one, each full of enchantment.

#

I'm convinced Tafel bottles teachers' souls against our wishes, like a reverse genie lantern, probably in that grimy coffee tumbler that has sat on his office window sill for seven years. I remember seeing it when I first came to interview, after I realized that in the real world with real empty bank accounts, a bilingual Ravenclaw is only employable as a teacher. The tumbler has a teacher skeleton by a chalkboard saying, "I'll just wait until it's quiet." Though Tafel doesn't use that line with middle schoolers. He uses *positive narration*, and he does so *with fidelity*. "Samantha has her eyes on me. Tanya's voice is off. Enzo is calm and ready for Town Hall." Señor Dunn is ready for Saturday.

Sometimes I worry that the transition back to school each year is even harder on Hugo than it is on me. Last September, he attempted the slow amputation of a dining chair leg. Separation anxiety; poor guy. I bought some chew-deterrent spray and went around embittering all our furniture.

#

The zoo had few guests that day and Avril was alone at her painting station, looking somehow more glamorous than usual in her ankle boots and sleek maxi coat; the world's most inviting badger. I left my register to finally go ask my burning question.

"Will you paint my face?"

"Sure, Conor," she said. "What kind of animal do you want?"

I blushed with the obvious reply that came to mind: *you're what kind of animal I want*. But I was not so bold. "What's your favorite animal to paint?"

"I can do anything with whiskers. Tigers, kittens. But you've already got the cute whiskers."

"Thanks," I said. "Maybe I could be a badger with you?"

My allusion to the definition of a species—organisms together capable of reproduction—did not cause her any blushing. "You're not a Hufflepuff. You're probably Ravenclaw," she said.

"What makes me a Ravenclaw?"

"You have a brain like a sponge."

"What do you know about my brain?"

"That you know enough to be a zookeeper instead of a zoo cashier." She pursed her lips a moment, then spilled the rest. "And you know like five languages, wilderness first aid, and how to rebuild a Dodge Dakota. Plus you play like fifteen instruments, even didjeridu." Google had told her more about me than I had.

"I'm terrible at didjeridu. I can't really circular breathe."

"Growth mindset, Conor. You can't circular breathe, *yet*."

I had also googled her, but there was little to find. Just her dazzling, quirky smile on a thumbnail photo from the zoo staff profile. *About me: more info coming soon!*

"Do you play any instruments?" I asked, determined for that promised info.

"Not yet," she said. "Maybe you can teach me one?"

"We sell panpipes in the gift shop," I said.

"Not at work, you dork," she said. "Speaking of work, you've got customers. Go sell panpipes, Conor. I'll paint you like one of my French girls some other time."

#

Five horse trekkers approach as we descend off the pass, and I'm too slow to grab Hugo's collar. I hate horses. Well, Hugo hates horses. He's going berserk and I worry a horse will spook, buck the rider. He's relentless, darting closer in and retreating, barking.

#

Avril surprised me, not asking to share Hugo. There was love in his huge, honey-brown eyes winning her with a gaze, a nuzzle; so straightforward. He'd lay on his back so she could scratch his "itchy itchy lightning bolt," the zigzag shock of white on his chest—a superhero emblem for his velvety, jet-black costume.

Had Avril wanted him full-time, I was prepared to fight. I would take a bullet for that dog. I'd wrestle a grizzly. I would Mortal Kombat a team of cougars and rip their aortas out before they could touch my dog. But with Avril, I'd be reasonable. If she wanted to split time fifty-fifty, I would, for Hugo's sake.

#

The gift shop cleared out again. Outside, Avril had cleaned off her badger mask and put on the thick-rimmed glasses I recognized from her zoo profile photo. Her shift was about to end.

I strode out to her, pretending not to hurry. "So, I'm a Ravenclaw. Will you paint me as a raven?"

"Ravenclaw's symbol is the eagle."

"That makes no sense."

"Just go with it." She dipped her brush in the paint, lifted onto her tiptoes, and studied my face up close. "Conor, I have no idea how to make you into any kind of bird. You're so *beardy*."

I chuckled, but her face remained serious. "Growth mindset, Avril. You have no idea how to make me into a bird, *yet*."

"I'll do a lion," she said.

"That's random."

"No, it isn't. Sit down, you're too tall."

A few strokes in with the brush, it seemed she couldn't get close enough for the intricate details. That's when I first counted her thirteen freckles, a constellation to orient my compass rose. She leaned even closer, I almost tipped out of the stool. The only way to keep balance now was to lean toward her, to reach up to her, and for the first time, to kiss.

#

Hugo's still barking at the horses. I attempt a commanding voice. "Hugo! Come!" No use. The leading cowboy, apparently a hired guide for the four yuppies following him, is unperturbed. The yuppies clutch the reins as he does, but with them it's different. I think of my grip on the oh-shit strap of the packed TRAX train. I have no control of the train, and they have no control of these horses.

Sullivan calls out, "Hugo!" Hugo tucks tail and bolts straight to him, lets him grab his collar. The idiot Sullivan looks gleeful.

Sheepish, I holler, "Sorry!"

Cowboy says, "Don't mind us. If anyone's getting hurt it's that dog."

My dog. I grab his collar from Sullivan and attach the leash.

#

Packing my gear, I recall when Avril tried to get us into Marie Kondo's method for tidying up. It has rules for how to put things away and what to discard. I remember Avril reciting Rule Six: "Hold each item and ask yourself: does it spark joy?" We drove six bags of joyless stuff to a donation center and I folded my socks for a few weeks.

Maybe Hugo and I could just stay. I figure we make it a fortnight rationing Hugo's lamb kibble and my freeze-dried Chili

Mac. Plenty time to take stock of our chances at more self-sustaining means. But I'll need to "borrow" more supplies from Sullivan than just his water filter. I should write the KonMari guide for backpacking. My Rule Six would be: "Weigh each item on a scale, then ask: can it sustain human life under duress?"

#

If we're going to do this thing, I need a better plan. There's no story I could give Sullivan that won't lead to Search and Rescue coming for me. I need to take his gear while he's sleeping, cache it, pack my stuff and head north up the ridge where Hugo and I can keep an eye on him. He'll eventually give up finding us. Then I'll get the cache. Hugo and I could log a marathon before anyone comes looking.

We reach the campsite. Tomorrow we're supposed to celebrate the summit with the gin flask, then start down out of the woods. I don't really care about summits, and I don't know why I planned this trip. It's not much of a getaway.

I ask Sullivan to pass me the gin flask.

I still can't believe Hugo ran to him instead of me. The horse must have scared him out of his senses. He bolted to the nearest familiar voice. That's all.

"Pass me that flask, Brian."

#

If I let Sullivan go on without me, I don't know that I'd make it far with all his gear and mine, plus Hugo's food, before SAR get up here. He'd make good time downhill, but I'd be overloaded. I can't just let him leave. But I really, really want him gone.

After this trip, Señor Sullivan and I will be stuck right back together next week. One part of Professional Development I do look forward to: First Aid. Being an EMT, I get to skip it altogether and enjoy two hours' silence in my classroom. I relish any size windfall of quietude in the chaos of teaching: a postponed meeting, a closure for swine flu, that shithead Enzo's unfathomably rare absence.

#

Less and less of me emerged from that school at the end of a day, a week, a trimester. We thought it was funny at first, how much a day of teaching could drain me.

"How was school today, darling?" she'd say.

"Fine," I'd say, and she'd laugh. But soon it was clear how not funny this was, and she stopped asking. My body maintained rote exercises: grilling pork chops, shaking martinis, renting indie movies; even suggesting road trips, a dog walk, a round of Taboo?

We never discussed household chores and who was in charge of what. In an unspoken duel of endurance, we'd just let scummy dishes fill the kitchen for days. The winner could tolerate the mess until the other caved and took care of it without comment, resentment soaking into the sponge.

#

I still don't have the gin. I'm going to kill this guy. "Hand me that goddamn gin, Brian."

"We gotta save some for the summit, man."

I laugh, but then I realize he's serious; he's not handing it over. I will break him.

"There's not much left," he says. His voice implies I've had more than I should, and that this matters.

"My mom called you, didn't she? Of course she did. Did she say to treat me like a child?"

He pouts; a youngest sibling, like me. "I don't know what to say. I don't know her, man, but she *is* worried about you."

"Did she urge you to go on this trip? Is that why you're even here?"

"What the fuck?" His pout becomes the stun of betrayal. "No, man. I wanted to come along for sure. I was just thinking how this is the best trip I've ever been on. Hasn't it been great? Relax, bro."

Don't call me bro, I don't say. *I have actual brothers. I also have actual friends.*

"I'm sorry," I say. "You're right."

I retreat with Hugo to our one-man tent. He plops down on top of my shins, all seventy pounds, and zonks out. No monsters under his bed tonight. Mine never seem to go away.

Outside, Brian says, "Conor, you're an amazing coworker, and the best adventure partner ever. If you need something, just say so, all right?"

"Thanks," I say. "I'm good for now."

He says, "King's Peak tomorrow, buddy!"

#

A fifty-foot fall can kill you dead. Or you may survive. I've seen both.

Avril agreed that my volunteering for Search and Rescue may have been the straw that broke the back, but now I think that camel was already cold. I thought it might spark something for her: her husband, a hero with costume and gear. A Gryffindor to the rescue. But relationship CPR failed.

The volunteer hours eliminated what little free time I had, all so I could help pluck stranded imbeciles out of the Wasatch, ill-equipped adrenaline junkies thinking they're invincible but winding up lost, injured, dehydrated, and often dead on the side of Mount Olympus.

One Sunday, in the middle of brunch at Cafe Niche, my phone buzzed. "Emergency call-out to Big Cottonwood," I read aloud. "Fallen climber." I wolfed down my last bites of hash browns, the arugula still untouched. I actually love arugula.

Avril picked at her French toast, looked at me. "I guess you need to go then, huh? We'll have to skip the aviary."

"Yep." I gulped the last of my coffee and hurried to my truck.

Dude fell fifty feet off the route known as The Façade. It was a common story: the climber believed he heard the belaying partner below shout, "You're on belay!" So he let go for a breather. Of course he was not, in fact, on belay. Climbing is so safe and so simple until you don't hear each other right.

In the ambulance, the patient was unconscious but technically alive. A vegetable. It occurred to me I should eat more vegetables. Then I chewed some Tums en route to Wendy's drive-thru.

#

It occurs to me that maybe Avril was being charitable, not asking for Hugo. Like I needed him so much more than her, looking after me full-time. Like she diagnosed me, prescribed this reasonable accommodation.

Or maybe she still wants a puppy and this is her chance. She had wanted a puppy before, and I urged patience until we had time to train it. But then a seventh grader told me her family was returning their three-year-old Hugo to the pound, and I pleaded a case for a trial run. Avril consented, and she came to adore him in no time, but my reversal became family lore and ammunition.

#

We wake up to rain. Typical Uinta summer is warm and clear, with thunderous microbursts many afternoons. We've had zero clouds until today, when we intend to reach the highest peak in Utah. Brian and I remark at the absence of lightning. We can hike in rain, but with any electricity, the summit becomes a hard no-go.

Brian smiles and says, "Good ole oo-intas," pronouncing Uintas the 'correct' way, with the u as in "umami," rather than the u as in "uniquely useless," like everyone else.

#

Our route up King's follows a moderate ridge along the shoulder, and the peak itself is quite dramatic, with a thousand-foot vertical precipice off the face. A spectacular view of it from the west where we've camped.

A thousand feet. Twenty times the fall that vegetable took at The Façade.

I *cannot* go back for next week's retreat.

#

She said she loved me, but not as much as she wanted to.

"You never talk," she said.

"I talk."

"Even when I get you to respond to something that matters, you only state the most basic message. You never share on a deeper level. We're supposed to be a team, but I never know what you're thinking."

"I'm sorry," I said. "You're right."

We called it a "Separation: Space to think about things and

decide what to do later." She Marie Kondo*ed* her suitcase, hugged Hugo, hugged me, and left. Rule Six.

#

Given the rain, Sullivan and I decide to leave our tents up with gear inside keeping dry while we hike. I pray for lightning to stop this idiocy. I've never been a peak-bagger. Hugo and I could lounge all day, rain pattering on the fly. Normally the Uintas sigh and rage, and I recognize myself in their tantrums. But this rain just keeps whimpering steady and light with no sign of quitting: very un-Uinta-like. I'm not sure I trust myself up those thousand feet. Breathe, Conor.

#

The peak is invisible all morning as we ascend. Just yesterday I saw it in clear skies, but now the mountain rises indefinitely into this mist, and my imagination draws a much higher pinnacle within.

Hugo hates rain, too. We should've stayed in our tents. But I never offered the suggestion. Sullivan's a moron but he's excessively agreeable. If I said I wasn't going, he'd stay back as well. And a "rest day" with him around, whittling and whistling—that might be more bothersome than a hike in the damn rain.

#

The wind is picking up, so it's even more miserable walking up this stupid scary ridge that from afar looks like an easy jaunt. The storm cloud looks stagnant, comatose. Will it ever get up and move on?

We come upon a trail runner hustling down off the mountain, each stride splattering mud up her legs. She looks thirtyish and like someone who subjects herself to long-distance foot travel. She slows down her jog as though to converse, but her chilly posture tells me it's not for inspiring reasons. She's not pointing out a herd of elk around the bend.

We discuss her situation, her friend's situation. He has a condition. And he's behind somewhere, not sure how far. He had to stop, with his condition.

I say, "He's struggling with a health condition ... and now he's alone up there?"

The running friend had insisted she keep moving to stay warm. He'd meet her at the parking lot.

"We do big runs like this all the time; it's the first time he's had any trouble," she says.

"I'm an EMT," I say. "And a member of the Search & Rescue team in Salt Lake." *A probationary member, I don't say, because I suck at knots and hitches—I'm too slow to tie them, and even then they come undone.*

I suggest she not run all the way down without him. She can go to my tent, warm up in my sleeping bag, and await her friend. We'll go check on him and make sure he gets there. I point out our campsite on the topo map, down below all these close contours, and then I point to it in the real world. She is thankful but non-committal.

"There's food in my bear barrel," I say. She runs away.

The friend emerges from the fog ten minutes behind her, slogging his way down the trail. He looks fifty or seventy. He's hypoglycemic, but not diabetic—a long story, he says. I start a SOAP note.

"How's your water intake? Time of last urination? Quantity and color?" He frowns, and I trim the interview. "Have you eaten? Take a Cliff Bar."

"No thanks. I have this whopper junior here in my fanny pack." He has hypoglycemia and a whopper junior in his fanny pack.

"Are you going to eat it?"

"What are you, my mom?" he says. *Checkmate.* "You sent my girlfriend where?"

He is irritated that I've asked her to wait, forced him an extra quarter-mile beyond his intended left turn to look for her. He does not recognize wisdom and magnanimity, and I hope a mountain lion devours him whole and leaves his whopper junior for the ravens. Or for me. He schlepps onward.

Sullivan asks if I'm obligated to investigate medical concerns in the wilderness. I don't know but it seems weird not to, I tell him. Even though it's a different county or whatever.

#

We arrive atop the King's left shoulder. Here, the trail becomes a vague course through a talus slope which, in the rainy fog, appears to continue forever. Cairns are piled about chaotically like dirty dishes, apparently by well-meaning amateurs. They seem to quarrel. This is the best way to the summit—No, no; this way.

Atop these jagged sandstone blocks, there is no good route for Hugo. The slick angles make him slip constantly, and he has to leap into one slippery awkward landing after another. He lands badly and yelps, shows me a lifted paw, asking: *What should I do now?*

My dog and I will not be summiting. We will not gaze reverently off the precipice. Sullivan and I will not offer a toast to the top of this weird state we live in. I suppose this also means I won't push him off the Uintas. He will not join the fifty-million-years process of their erosion, and nor will I. Not yet.

Sullivan has been scampering through the talus with ease in his Tevas, and he's nearly invisible in the thick mist. I holler, and he leprechaun-bounces back to us. We'll wait here for him to summit, I explain. He shouldn't miss out on account of it being too slippery for Hugo.

So Hugo and I hunker down and wait in the bone-chilling drizzle. His leg seems fine, but he's shivering, waterlogged fur clinging to his lean frame. How far is the peak from here, anyway? My vision is blurring.

#

Avril grasped my forearms to keep me facing her, how a parent delivers an ultimatum to a toddler.

"Remember when you took the students to Nicaragua last year? You never called until the night before your flight home, to tell me when to pick you up. A whole week, and I hadn't called you either. We didn't miss each other, Conor."

"I was too busy to think about missing you."

"I wasn't," she said. "But I didn't."

I could see she hated saying it. The devastation she knew it caused, her words treading right on through the horse shit we'd been tiptoeing around. That was our last big talk before The Separation. We sat in silence on the cracked cold leather of the couch, shoulders leaning into each other the way two friends grieve a third friend's death.

Then that grief provoked sex. The way two friends might determine to screw out of a glum curiosity, just to double-check. Artless foreplay. Bare minimum mouths. Bare minimum hands below the waist and overactive above, rubbing up and down the other's arms and flanks—the friction warmth you might share in line for a ski lift. Where shivering, you would suggest, knowing the other was reluctant to suggest it: *Should this be the last run?*

But it was so costly, reaching this mountain.

That's all right.

Are you sure?

So with minimal turns, no tricks or jumps, we slid to the finish. And afterward, though she didn't say so aloud, Avril seemed sure.

Laying spent beside her on the rug, there was nowhere in the keepsake-cluttered living room where my eyes could look that didn't hurt, so I squeezed them shut. Yet I pictured our younger faces grinning back from Zermatt, Tepoztlán, Mendocino, Provence. Smitten, and curious as blue jays, we flew to new environs, nabbing local tidbits to return to the nest and synthesize into the Conor+Avril shared bioculture, complete with fresh rituals and legends.

Hugo burst in through the dog door, his feather duster tail flapping wildly, and laid down between us. He rolled onto his back so we could pet his "itchy, itchy lightning bolt."

#

This headache is seventy-three times worse than any migraine I've known. Badgers are scraping new burrows behind my eyeballs. Sullivan is up the peak somewhere; how long has he been gone? Hugo is shivering wet. I no longer feel the cold or the wet. Badger burrowing, termite tunneling. Roaring mountain lions, thunder. Distant or from within?

You can estimate the distance of lightning by counting the seconds between the flash and the arrival of its thunder. You're in real danger within ten seconds: ten miles. But I can't see the lightning. I can't see at all in this stormcloud, this booming headache. The daylight, dim as it is, rips through me when I look upward. A flash.

Was that lightning? One one thousand, two one thousand—then the roaring in my head.

Hugo is barking toward the summit. *Good boy. Call to Sullivan.*

Useless to go get him, useless to wait for him. In lightning, separation is best. Keep apart to avoid a strike that spares no one. Gotta hurry off the mountain.

I shuffle down to the shoulder. I can hardly squint my eyes open enough to spot the trail ahead. The flashing, the lion's roar. I vomit.

I try jogging, then puke again. Hair is standing on my neck and arms, on the backs of my fingers that grasp the aluminum trekking poles. Aluminum? I hurl them into the grass. I'm a six-foot lightning rod on a treeless, 13,000-foot mountain.

"Go on boy! Get!" I urge, but he stays by me, incorruptible honey eyes agaze. His lush black fur oh my god is it standing straight up?

"HUGO!"

If only I could bury my face in that black mane one last time and—

#

This is a dream; I know dogs can't talk, not even Hugo. "Hello, Conor," Hugo says. He speaks in a low, doofy, Eeyore voice, minus the self-deprecation. "I don't have much time to tell you this. Gotta *carpe diem*, you know?" He's Eeyore fresh off a Costa Rican yoga retreat. "Look. You just gotta eat what's in your bowl," he says. "And when there's nothing in your bowl, you gotta pry open a cupboard. And if that doesn't work, you gotta jump a fence," he says. "Point is, self-fulfillment; fill yourself up. Got it? I have to go. Nice knowing you."

"But I have questions."

"I know you do, Conor. Belly rubs and fetch and all that. But you can't put in the work to get your tummy rubbed if your tummy's empty, so start there."

#

Tinnitus: a perceived ringing in the ears. I've always committed medical terms to memory with ease, don't know why. I remember nothing from the past few hours. Days? What hospital is this?

From my ECG I see that my heart is *lub-dubbing* along just fine. I suspect they've already got me on NSAIDs, but my whole body hurts like hell. I find a hospital call button on the bed rail.

What a waste of the last days of summer vacation. I should be with Avril and Hugo in the mountains. I remember the Uintas. Thimbleberry cobbler. I remember Sullivan. King's Peak. Why a summit? A *literal* summit? It held no magic for me; I forgot my why. Maybe Tafel locked it in his damn skeleton mug. I'm going to quit that job.

#

This goddamn ringing, I can't catch what this doctor is asking me.

"My dog, Hugo. Is he okay?" I'm not sure if I'm mumbling or screaming. She shakes her head and frowns a little. *No.*

She had better be saying, *I don't know.* She wouldn't know, right? She's not a veterinarian.

#

The Tribune once reported that a hiker and his Weimaraner were struck by lightning in Idaho, and the doctors told the guy that the dog "shared the electric charge" with him and she died, supposedly saving his life. They printed a photo of him giving thumbs up, his head all blood-crusted. Thumbs up? Despicable.

I'm so sorry, Hugo. I could see it in your eyes and you were right. I should've fixed things with Avril, talked it out. The stress, the exhaustion, the wrong career. The façade. I know you were hungry to help. You helped. I hardly lifted a finger.

#

My hearing is back to normal. All these annoying beeps and boops. Green zig-zags on a screen, each heartbeat just a blip on the ECG. Healthy blips, I think. Here comes that lady. She doesn't know I'm awake. "Doctor? Nurse?"

She smiles politely. "I'm Doctor Watkins. But also a nurse, actually. DNP. That's a—"

"Doctor of Nursing Practice," I interrupt. Then I'm sorry. "I'm sorry," I tell her. "But I couldn't hear you before. I need to know about my dog. Did he ... survive?"

"Survive?" she says.

"The lightning. Did it hit him?"

There was no lightning. A brain aneurysm leaked and ruptured, almost killed me. Sullivan did CPR. Some joggers were able to get quick help and I was evacuated by helicopter.

I'm getting woozy again. "Did I have brain surgery?"

A new voice responds. "Kind of. I think."

"Oh, hey Brian!" I say, almost cheering. I'm downright cheerful just to hear him, though I don't have the energy to turn and look. "Do you know what drugs I'm on?"

"Definitely something potent. You sound ridiculous."

Funny; for once I don't feel ridiculous. I just feel grateful. "Brian, I'm really grateful for you," I say. And having said that aloud, I feel a whole new kind of ridiculous.

"No worries, bro. I wasn't going to let anything happen to you. *Or* the Hugo pup."

Another swell of gratitude. I'm grateful for this gurney. It's so comfy. I roll my face into the pillow. Got to find out what detergent they use here, smells like bog candle blossoms luring me to sleep. But I can't fall asleep without telling Brian something:

"Sorry I've been such a *pendejo*."

I still don't look at him. Instead, I spot a good old analog clock on the wall, second hand and everything, and seeing these unfettered seconds dawdle away: it doesn't stress me out.

Brian says, "You're such a chill guy at work." He thinks I'm chill. "A little shy, but chill. But then on the trip, you were *scary* chill. And then you snapped." I roll over and look him in the eye, so sharp I think I can see my reflection in it, and I look terrible. I feel like shit. But I'm also okay. "I'm just glad you're okay," he says.

"Are *we* okay?"

"Yeah man, we're good. You should talk to Avril, though. She's asleep in the waiting room."

"How long has she been waiting?"

"I better let you two talk about that. And don't worry. I'll keep Hugo as long as you need."

"I'm really hungry," I say. Then I pass out. I sleep deeper this time, in the dark, velvety comfort of okay.

#

Next time I awake, Avril's watching over me, her freckled cheeks wrinkled with worry. She bends to hug me. I sit up and burst into a sob, the beeps of my ECG take off like a Great Blue Heron. Flap flap flap flap. Her warm hand rubs big circles on my chest. "Shhh, shhh, shhh."

But for once, I don't want to hush.

"I want to talk," I say. She nods, but it's not an agreement; it's a question. So I ask, "You got a minute?" She sneaks a glance out the door, the way one glances up from the trail to spot the next pass.

She grins and says, "I suppose I can stick around a little while."

"Okay, check this out," I say. "You know how mountain goats can basically climb anything?"

She cackles. I love her dopey cackle.

"Hugo chased one and got himself stuck on the side of a cliff!"

Then I tell her about the horses and she laughs even more. Eventually I tell her about the guy who almost died at The Façade, and she wonders why I never told her about it. I tell her I'm turning in my classroom keys, and my stupid superhero costume. Because sometimes I need rescuing, too; I suck at just saying so. She nods and nods, gnaws on her fingernails. And I tell her how Hugo and I are done with such long treks and she smiles and agrees. That I have new ideas for the bucket list. But first I'll ask about her list: what adventures does she want to go on?

Eventually—but not yet, when we're ready—I'll ask her who's coming along.

Billie Hinton is an award-winning writer and psychotherapist who lives in North Carolina. She keeps horses and bees, studies native plants, and wrangles cats and Corgis. Her work has appeared in Literary Mama, Not One Of Us, Manifest-Station, Riverfeet Press Anthology, Streetlight Mag and its anthology, Longridge Review, Minerva Rising, and failbetter, among others.

You can find her online at billiehinton.com.

We Are the Charm

We watch from the sweet gum tree the earthbound creature who tends the coneflowers we covet. She pulls the weedy things, making our descent to the seeded centers easier. We know she watches us from her windows, not as high as the sweet gum branches but higher than the coneflowers.

Sometimes we hear her exclaim with a chirp of delight, not unlike our own.

On summer days we perch in the sweet gum, wait for her to walk out to the box by the lane, and we fly alongside her, a cloud of yellow, from sweet gum to dogwood, then to oak and birch, where we wait while she collects things from the box, her own coneflower, we decide, whose seeds are much larger.

It's when she looks up to see us that she emits the chirp that means she's full of joy. *Ohmygod, ohmygod,* she chirps, and we fly to the next tree back in order to hear her make the sound again.

Sometimes when we want to hear it we fly and swoop, all in one, and she goes *ohmygod* and then *wooooowwwwww.*

Her song is different but has its own beauty.

Sometimes when it rains we stay in the tree by the coneflower bed and sing of sunny days, our own longing transmuted into notes that carry to her nest, and the earthbound one comes to the outside and looks up, trying to see us, listening. We sing louder then, just to feel her excitement.

We change color in the winter, our bright yellow dulling down to a sedate olive shade, similar to the coneflowers, also now brown, which she leaves in the garden so we can pluck the last seeds from them through the cold months.

She looks for us with her limited eyes, seems puzzled, so we swarm up in a cloud, not yellow but still to say, *it's us, we're still us, look,* and she lets out a muted *ohmygod* and we know she sees us.

When spring comes and the leaves on the sweet gum pop out, we get our shelter back, green and thick, and wait for the new coneflowers to emerge. It takes awhile but eventually they arrive, springing up from the earth, leaves and then stems, buds and then finally the flowers. We sing in celebration when they open and the new seeds begin to form.

The earthbound one watches with us, and she too exclaims when the first flower opens.

Soon our yellow feathers come and we gather and swoop across the grassy slope hoping she will see. Sometimes it takes a few tries but every year, in one singular moment on one day, she spies our yellow cloud dipping and diving, then arcing up high against the tops of the newly-green tulip poplars. Her spring song comes out especially strong. *Ohmygod, ohmygod, ohmygod!*

We've been waiting all winter for the flowers, for the chance to charm, for warm weather and nest building and the song of the earthbound one who sings but cannot fly.

JoeAnn Hart is the author of the crime memoir *Stamford '76: A True Story of Murder, Corruption, Race, and Feminism in the 1970s* (University of Iowa Press, 2019). Her novels are *Float* (Ashland Creek Press) a dark comedy about plastics in the ocean, and *Addled* (Little, Brown) a social satire. Her short fiction and essays have appeared in a wide range of literary publications, including Slate.com, Orion, The Hopper, Prairie Schooner, The Sonora Review, Black Lives Have Always Mattered, and others. Her work often explores the relationship between humans and their environments. "Flying Home" was adapted from Arroyo Circle, Hart's novel-in-progress about hoarding and wildfires in Boulder, Colorado, where she lived in the late 70s. She now lives in Gloucester, Massachusetts with some rescue livestock, her dogs, and a husband. www.JoeAnnHart.com

"Flying Home" first appeared in the Stonecoast Review, Issue No.15, Summer 2021. It was later anthologized in Among Animals 3, The Lives of Animals and Humans in Contemporary Short Fiction, April 2022.

Flying Home

Shelley woke to a high-pitched sound and braced herself for a nurse to come swooping in to see if she was dead. She wondered if that's how she was going to know it was over, with one long shrill beep. But the door did not open in a flurry of protective polyester, and at any rate, the sound had stopped. The machines that monitored her bodily functions seemed to be blinking and blurting with no special urgency. With great effort, and not a little pain, she turned her head to the window, smushing her oxygen mask against her temple. "Oh! Hello."

A red-tailed hawk was sitting on an iron rod that extended out from Boulder Community Hospital, right outside Shelley's room on the fourth floor. She'd noticed the rod before, when she first arrived another lifetime ago and had enough breath to stand up to look out the window and get her bearings in the world. A narrow side window was cracked open and it had felt good to feel honest-to-god Colorado air on her skin. But those few steps nearly did her in and the day nurse, Jeanette, looking like an astronaut in her baby-blue gear, had to help her back to bed. "Nice try, Shelley," she'd said. "But next time, you ring for me."

"I thought you'd say no," said Shelley.

"I will say no. That's why I say, ring for me. The last thing we need right now is a fall."

It was a moot point. After that, she never had the strength again. It took everything she had to breathe, but she was glad she got that one peek. If she hadn't, she might not know about the rod and then have to wonder what the hawk was sitting on, and it hurt her head to think. The rod was probably leftover from some sloppy repair, but this big raptor seemed to think it was custom built for his own private perch. It was a good-looking bird with its dark brown plumage and eponymous red tail, without which she'd be hard-pressed to say what kind of hawk it was. As it was, she didn't know her male from her female. The bird's intense, furrowed stare was aimed not at her – really, who would want to look at her now? – but at the utility courtyard below where there was a dumpster, and a dumpster meant rats. Probably plenty of them. Pickings were slim at restaurant dumpsters in town what with the lockdown, so rats across the city were starving, ravaging homes in search of food. Before she got sick, she'd seen them out on the streets in broad daylight, taking risks, exposing themselves to danger in hopes of finding food. The hospital dumpster was a good bet for untouched meals. The medical staff didn't seem to have time to eat, and most Covid patients couldn't ingest anything other than fluids by way of an IV. She first suspected she had the virus when she was making coffee and couldn't smell it. By the end of that day her temperature was over 100, and that night she was on her hands and knees trying to find a position where she could breathe. Eventually she crawled to her phone and called her son, who called 911.

Rats weren't the only ones interested in the dumpster. Crows, those vacuum cleaners with wings, were ripping their way, beak and claw, through plastic bags of cafeteria garbage, chattering away like shoppers. "Did you see this? Is there any more of that?" They soared across her view with the foul scrapings of hospital trays trailing from their beaks. It was a wonder they could get airborne they were so loaded. A baked potato shell, some strands of fettuccini, a gray strip of chicken skin. They certainly didn't want the red-tail staring down at them while they scavenged. It might get tired of waiting for a rat to dart out from the dumpster and choose one of them for lunch instead. It was a bird-eat-bird world. As she gazed at the hawk, a crow suddenly photo-bombed her view, trolling its nemesis with a swoop. But the hawk was unperturbed, and gave the crow a look that could have plucked him bald. "Stay strong, hawk," she muttered from under her mask. Just as her eyes began to flutter close, the hawk pushed itself off the rod and shot down into the courtyard. She stretched her neck, but she couldn't see if it scored a rat, and she never saw it rise.

Over the next few days, the red-tail and the crows became her entertainment as she struggled to breathe, giving her something to think about other than cement lungs. The hawk showed up on the rod at least once a day, but she never knew when to expect it. The crows were a constant, noisy presence but were rarely in flight where she could see them. Sparrows, who were thugs in their own right, often flew by in intimidating masses. Sometimes she felt the place was a little over-birded, but they were visitors after all, something not allowed otherwise. Her son and his family came once, at a prearranged time, and the nursing staff helped her to a wheelchair so she could wave at them from the window. It was exhausting for everyone. Dave held little Bennie in his arms and pointed at her window, which was certainly too far up for them to see anything other than a shadow. His wife Betsy was with them, which was alarming. She must really be sick if her daughter-in-law felt she should come along. They stood between the dumpster and a white refrigerated trailer and waved while the crows looked down on them from the budding cottonwood trees, impatient to return. The birds bobbed their heads and flew from limb to limb, making the branches bounce as if the weight of elephants had been lifted. She looked over the crows and beyond the hospital wing to the foothills and the snow-capped Rockies in the distance. When was the last time she even noticed the mountains?

When she looked back down at her family, they seemed so small. Her only child, her only grandchild. Small, vulnerable mammals. Sometimes she wondered if humans had any purpose at all. Keith, her ex-husband, had said we were here to protect the earth but that made no sense. From what she could tell, the earth needed to be protected from us. In fact, she didn't see where humans fit anywhere in what he called the great web of life. We devoured everything but seemed to be no one's primary food source anymore, unless you counted the virus. In which case, we were toast.

Jeanette came up behind her. "Shelley, we've got to get you back in bed. Wave good-bye." Shelley raised an arm tethered by a blood pressure cuff, and she saw her son mouth something. She leaned to put her ear to the open sliver of window, but Jeanette pulled her back before she lost her balance. She should have charged her phone so they could talk, but, in truth, she didn't have the breath, and her voice from under the mask would frighten Bennie. It certainly frightened her, but she was grateful it was just a mask and not a tube down her throat. That's what happened when they moved you from a regular Covid room, like hers, to the dreaded ICU. Endgame.

As Jeanette rolled her back to bed, she knew the moment her son and his family walked away because she heard the crows descend on the dumpster again in noisy celebration. She wished the window could open all the way so she could hear them better. The hospital walls were thick and her breathing filled her ears, not to mention electronic squawks and the noisy hallway. But no matter how loud it got inside, she could always tell when a custodian went outside with garbage because the crows made such a ruckus. A food delivery! And if she was at all awake, she knew when the hawk was on his way because a military detail of crows often mobbed him, trying to keep him away from his perch. Once, she saw them escort the hawk off the hospital property. Crows were persistent little buggers. Another time, she woke just as the hawk rose up from the courtyard with a mighty flapping of wings, a limp rat dangling from its claws. As much as she'd been rooting for the hawk against the crows, she felt for the rat. She hoped the end was quick. Suffering was a terrible thing.

She remembered once, when she was down with the flu, Keith trying to get her to sit outside in bone-chilling February weather to boost her immune system, insisting that natural settings were healing and would create a path to her soul if only she were open to the experience. It was such a Boulder thing to say. He was as annoying as a crow sometimes, constantly soul-questing, always trying to improve himself, forcing her to come along. After they got divorced, she never hiked again. What a brat she was. What she wouldn't do to be able to hike right now, to have that sort of breath. Funny she should think of him now. Those years began spooling out in front of her like colorful ribbons, the scenes vivid and magical like a movie, and she tried to grasp her younger, hopeful self to keep her from disappearing again. Somehow in the process, she pulled a tube from her arm, and Jeanette came in and loosely tied her hands to the bed with soft bandages, and that was surely for the best.

Later, she opened her eyes and there was a crow on the rod, looking in at her, first with one eye, then turning its beak to look at her with the other. Or was it a gargoyle? The creature was all beak and wing, hunched over and ugly, spouting words instead of rainwater. "Life is a near-death experience," it cackled before flying away.

Oh no. She was hallucinating now. That couldn't be good. What was that nursery rhyme about counting crows? One is for sorrow? There was some sort of commotion going on in the hallway. She side-eyed the hall window and there were gurneys everywhere, a traffic jam of the sick and dying. She was glad to have a bed. She heard a man call out that he was a lawyer. "This situation is actionable," he croaked. "When this is over, there'll be hell to pay."

If only she had the oxygen to laugh.

When there were no birds to focus on, she stared off at the familiar peaks and sloughs of the mountains. Spring was coming. The snow was melting, exposing the scarred landscape along the slopes, still black with soot from the wildfires that fall. That had been a scary time. You couldn't breathe from the smoke and ash. There were other scary times. She remembered going up a trail together as a family and coming across a fresh kill. The bloody contents of a deer had been hollowed out and devoured, the insides ribbed like the roof of a cathedral. Eviscerated was the word. She was uneasy knowing there was some animal, drooling red, waiting for them to leave so it could finish the job. Keith hardly gave the deer a glance, except to remark on the different types of flies on the carcass, then kept on his steady pace to the top of the ridge, but she and Dave stopped to gape. He was only five. "What happened?" he asked.

"Life happened," she said. "It's sad, but the bear or mountain lion who killed the deer animal needed to live too."

Dave's eyes grew large. "Is it dead?"

It took a moment for Shelley to respond. What constituted dead if not this? And yet. The blood was wet and the flies pulsed with vitality, making it seem as if life was just moving from one form to another. "The deer is definitely dead," she'd said at last. "Look at it. It's all eaten away." He squatted to peer into the carcass, and a cloud of flies rose up. "Let's go," she said and grabbed his hand. They continued up the mountain, meeting up with Keith and then, after she begged, they took a different path back down.

She told Keith it was for Dave's sake, but she knew it was for her own.

She'd do anything to hit that trail again, to be in the mountains where life could be reconsidered. To review all the options again. She'd felt like she'd been circling the drain for days, but at least someone had removed the bandages. Maybe the worst was over. Or maybe they had to untie her to flip her over onto her stomach to take the pressure off her lungs. That had seemed to help, but there was no more looking out the window, and the mask dug into her cheeks. A physical therapist came in to help her, as he called it, "visualize her breathing."

"Think of your shoulder blades as your wings," he'd said, putting his gloved hand on her bare back. "Now, pull your breath into your wings and feel them open. Expand your wings, Shelley. Good. Now let the breath go. Fold your wings and relax. Expand, and fold. Again. Good. Open your wings wide, Shelley. Excellent. You'll be flying in no time."

It was so Boulder. But it helped.

In between people coming and going to mess with her, she tried to sleep but the noise seemed to ramp up every time she closed her eyes. The beeps, the alarms, the announcements. Code this, code that. The crying out. The oxygen machine was so loud. Both she and the machine were working hard. She wished they'd turn it up. She heard people out in the hall say Covid this, Covid that. Wait. Or were they saying corvid? Corvid? She pressed her mind into action until it came up with the answer. A crow was a corvid! Counting corvids. Counting crows. Counting Covids. If a group of crows was called a murder, what was a group of Covids called? A slaughter. She laughed, but it used too much precious oxygen and she started gagging and Jeanette ran in with a syringe.

> One is for sorrow,
> Two is for mirth,
> Three for a wedding,
> And four for a death.

Later, after a team came to flip her right side up again, a nurse's aide brought her an iPad. "Someone wants to say hello." It was Dave and Bennie, and she sensed they weren't calling to say hello.

Dave said he loved her too many times. They were falsely cheerful, so she was falsely fine, then drifted off to sleep in the middle of a sentence. Wild visions, the sound of crows infiltrating everything. Humans in her dreams began to speak in caws and clacks. Telling corvid jokes. A corvid and a rabbi walk into a bar. Then Covid followed and they never walked out. No one laughed. This place has no fucking sense of humor.

At sunset, the crows were going wild and she opened her eyes. Something was up. She pressed the button to raise the bed upright. The nurse's aide had left the sides down after her sponge bath that afternoon, so she dragged one leg over the side, then the other. She sat on the edge to let the dizziness subside, then carefully plotted her path so she wouldn't yank out any wires or tubing, not wanting to set off any alarms. Jeanette would not be happy. She took her mask off and tested the air. There was no air and she put it back on. The clear tube was long enough to get to the chair by the window. Grabbing the metal tree that held bags of fluids, she slowly, excruciatingly, shuffled the three feet to the chair and flopped down on it, gasping. The crows were gathered in the cottonwoods, their attention on the double utility doors, and rats were leaping out of the dumpster. Garbage must be coming. Dinner. Someone in a black bomber jacket came out and set all the crows to cawing at once, but he wasn't carrying a bag. He didn't even go to the dumpster, but walked over to the white refrigerated trailer instead and unlocked it. When he turned to open the door, she could read the back of his jacket. Boulder Coroner. He waved to someone inside the hospital, and two women wheeled a gurney out. They wore the same bomber jacket, like a sports team. The Boulder Coroners. Their slogan, *Nature always bats last*. On the gurney was a white plastic bag, and the crows went berserk. The three coroners quickly maneuvered the body into the trailer, and when they stepped out, one of the women looked up at the hospital and seemed to sigh.

What had Shelley thought was in there? Had she never wondered? The women wheeled the empty gurney back into the hospital while the man stood guard at the trailer and they rolled out another body bag, and then another. The crows settled. Finally the man closed the trailer door and locked it, and the team went back in the hospital and the double doors closed behind them. One by one the birds raised their wings and floated down to the dumpster.

Alpenglow radiated pink behind the mountains and she yearned to be walking the foothills to be awash in that healing light, to be so high up she could turn around and view her life at a distance. She wondered if she could locate that trail again after all this time. She wanted to find the spot where the deer had been and collect the weathered bones in a pile, then top it with the skull. She wanted to sit and wait for the mountain lion who'd killed it, who surely watched her every move and knew exactly where she was. There was a lightness in her chest and she felt herself glowing with love for them both. She wanted to grab them together and hug them, like they were family.

She really needed to lie down. She had to get back to the bed, but she wasn't sure how. She'd used up all her strength and the call button was out of reach. She should just stay where she was and wait, but she had to lie down, now. She could do this, she thought. She'd done it before.

Shelley did not know how she ended up on the ground. She did not remember falling. Jeanette ran in and said "What the hell," and called for help on the intercom. Shelley's mask must have slipped off because she couldn't seem to breathe. More nurses in protective gear arrived and surrounded her. One nurse pushed the chair out of the way and glanced out the window. "I hear they have to bring in another trailer."

"Don't be looking out there," said Jeanette. "Get me the paddles."

Shelley didn't know what the rush was. She wasn't in any pain, although she sensed her body wasn't arranged quite right. Maybe her wings were in the way. She heard a long shrilling sound.

"Oh, the hawk," she thought. "The hawk is here."

William Burtch is a writer of fiction and essays. He was a finalist for the *American Fiction Short Story Award* (New Rivers Press) and is co-author of *W.G.* (2022 Sunbury Press), a historical biography of W.G. Raymond. He has been published in *Great Lakes Review, Ruminate, Northwestern Indiana Literary Journal, BULL, Schuylkill Valley Literary Journal* and others.

His work often gravitates toward the experiences and struggles of the rural characters he grew up around, as well as themes of survival in a culture of addiction. He is an avid fly fisherman, long haunting the waters from Pennsylvania to Montana. William lives in Columbus, Ohio.

Animal Crossings

High in the agave plant, the mouse starts its descent to the desert floor. Nearing the bottom, it spots a coiled rattler, its eyes colder than its blood.

Despite my tongue taunting that I had neglected to brush my teeth, Robin slips me her cell number. I'm to pick her up at her place, in Las Cruces. One of those complexes where the ladder climbers with decent jobs practically coagulate. Robin, whose given name is Bird of Spring, thinks I have a problem. She has seen it before. In her ancestry. Maybe I do drink too much. I'll need to hear more about her notion of surrendering, giving fully over to the universe. This idea of assimilating into something larger than myself. The animal kingdom knows and lives by all this shit, she explains. A glorious universal simplicity.

I design missiles for Uncle Sam, at the New Mexico Proving Grounds, in White Sands. Swaths of humanity in distant lands have come to know my work. While drafting schematics for these flying greeting cards, a haunting will suck me in. Like a dust devil. I will dwell upon a life's work measured by the degree of destruction I can pack into an ever shrinking container, hurled across ever increasing distances. As if these were actions mere mortals should undertake.

Pulling a swing of gin I quake, but manage to top off the tarnished flask for the drive to Robin's.

The mouse labors to keep its tiny eyes open. The agave flower ferments in its belly, like a double shot of mezcal. The rattler is placid in its self-assurance. The patience of Job.

Driving to her place, the white sand dunes reflect the moonbeams, and toy with me. I pull another deep gulp of gin. White fire.

Outside of town, not feeling well, I kill the engine. I stagger from the car, as if months at sea. By now I reek. As I double-over, the shrill screech of an owl in flight ices me. Some desert creature faces down its last breath.

The mouse surrenders to the weight of its eyelids. The snake breathes briskly now, intoxicated with anticipation. The reptile did not plan on the owl, a feathered missile, sinking its talons into the desert mouse. The owl and mouse ascend into an acrylic and unimpressed night sky.

I wake from sleeping on the hood of the car. I'm an egg in a frying pan. My skin screams the sun is starting to rise. I scan this apathetic desertscape. Fumbling with the keys I somehow fire the ignition, assaulting the harmony of the desert's morning sounds.

Back on the barren highway, I struggle to hold to the road, a sense of foreboding my loyal passenger. The desert dawn fools, as if the infinite grains of sand are a harmless, singular form. Masked is a treachery into which one can become trapped, taken. A monolith of bleakness, the pulse of life long evaporated.

I grope for my flask. A single swallow remains. As I begin to twist open the lid, the streaking mass of fur and hooves enters my line of sight to my left. The sickening crunch of flesh, fur and bone against unyielding metal overtakes me, before I know what hit me. The jolt propels my forehead into the steering wheel. I wrestle the car to a stop amid a shroud of dust and sand and blood.

The uncoiling of the rattler, resolved to seek new prey, is divine motion. Pure grace and pragmatic resignation. The ways of its world to be appreciated, never understood.

As the dust storm I created subsides, I spot the subject of this explosive collision. Attempting to stand, while pulling with its front legs, is a small deer. A doe. Grave wounds are evident in the entirety of her bony hindquarters. She spills to her side only to strain back up to her front legs, her rear legs dragging. I throw up.

Shoving the shifter into park, I jam the flask into my shirt pocket. Still intoxicated, I manage to get out of the car and seek some sense of balance, a stability of gait, to be able to advance toward the animal.

Placing one foot ahead of the next, I weave through the parched undergrowth to within a few feet of the doe. She is startled, in agony, crawling but a few inches only after great effort.

I reach for my flask. Her eyes stop me cold. Her large, dark imploring eyes. Eyes that do not question me, or scorn me, but that instead plead with me. Beg me to end it, to embrace the cold truth of this moment. I do not have to wonder what she asks of me. I have to wonder how. With what means?

And could I, even?

The largest rock I can find is not large enough. It would be savagery. I implore someone to happen by with a rifle, or strong drugs. Gleaning for miles in both directions of the highway, I see nothing but slithering heat waves. I know now that it will not be an implement of mankind's creation to finish the mess that yet another implement of man started.

I ponder the unimaginable. The absurd. Is it possible to strangle the life from another living being, all the while doing it with compassion?

By now, the doe ends her effort to flee me. She pants, her eyes pulling mine into hers. I survey the scene before me. I know it would be hours before she would surrender to death, of her own accord. After unspeakable agony. Maybe at last, and for all, I have discovered our true calling, the true meaning, of the lives of human beings—to bring an end the pain of those things without the means to do it themselves. When our paths may cross. Even, with a sick irony, as we are the witless source of most the suffering.

Gently, I place my hand on her side, which heaves from rapid breathing. She does not resist this overture. My body lowers behind hers. Almost into a spooning position. My trembling fingers caress her. She is in blinding pain.

Gradually, I work my hands to the side of her head. I speak to her in low even tones.

"Easy, easy girl. I am so, so sorry. Easy."

Before me, at long last in this cold life, is a pureness. The presence of innocence. And for me, a perfection of purpose.

I rub the side of her mouth. She trusts me, she surrenders. I feel it through my flesh and into my sorry heart. My fingers slide nearer her nostrils and gasping mouth.

Then I cover both.

***

I sleep with my arm around her body for a good while. The sun burns my face. Opening my singed eyelids, I am greeted by two buzzards, hopping grotesquely toward us, wings awkwardly flailing about.

I bolt to my feet, waving my arms and screaming hoarsely. The massive mangy birds are not at all impressed or deterred. Searching for something to hurl at the buzzards, I only find the flask in my shirt pocket, containing its one last swallow. I fling the flask, striking one of the birds squarely. They both launch skyward in a frantic fury of feathers. I know it is all futile. They will return, true to the way it all works. The unwavering way of our universe. The animal world accepts this from birth. Lives with this knowledge in their DNA.

Humans fight it to the end.

***

Back in the car I drone onward, tracking eastward toward home, winding through the jagged hills of scrub and sand, feeling more pulled than propelled. Ever smaller, with a numbness more akin to the peace of resignation than exhaustion.

The rattler settles beneath a scraggly mesquite. Intently focused on the present. Calm with the faith that it will feed again. Until its own time has come, as it does for all.

I call Robin. She tells me she is not at all surprised I never showed. Expected it even, given the predictable stage of my affliction. She tells me she will be at my place when I arrive. Says we can get breakfast. We will focus on now and forward.

"You must surrender," Robin says. "There are greater powers. Forces of which I will teach you."

"Have you ever witnessed perfect innocence?" I ask.

She tells me she is not sure it exists. In our world.

"Have you ever truly known love?" I ask her.

She tells me there are many kinds of love. All of them have their own truths.

"Even the kind where you would be willing to end another's life? If their pain is hopeless?"

Robin does not answer me. If she did, I did not hear. Or did not want to hear.

I drive yet deeper into the wastelands, the white sands. Through it all I drift, like the uprooted tumbleweed that dances on, well after death. Rolling and tumbling. No longer resisting.

Surrendering to the will of the wind.

Theresa Rice lives in Oregon where she spends her time hiking mountains, surviving modern dating, and keeping up with her dog and pony show. She was the 2018 Equestrian Voices Fiction Winner for The Plaid Horse Magazine, has written for Northwest Horse Source and Equus Magazine, and is currently querying her most recent women's fiction manuscript. You can find her adventures and writing at www.sassinboots.com

The Summer I Loved Three Fish

Summer came on like sunset in a cloudless sky. Slow and soft at first, subtle hints of the bright day slipping to orange, then amber mixed with peach. Finally, a receding crimson flame on the horizon as a darkening blue curtain rose in the opposite direction, glittering stars scattered across the expanse. My love for fish came on just as delicate. I never cared for fishing. Didn't even care to be alongside a man who was fishing. I thought a pole in the water and the slurping of beer next to a silent lake was irritating instead of serene. I didn't know about fly fishing yet.

A Tinder date cast a judging eye in my direction when I said I didn't like the movie *A River Runs Through It*. I dropped my head to take a sip of my drink, letting the gentle wave of my long auburn hair fall across my face to guard against his withering gaze.

"It's just a movie," I tried. "It's not like we believe in different religions just because I don't like it." I flipped my hair behind my shoulder and tried for a playful wink while biting my straw. Apparently it *was* akin to blasphemy that I didn't like the movie. He left me with cash to cover the drinks and an excuse about needing to let his dog out. My night annoyingly freed up, I decided to look up the plot of the movie, to remind myself what it was I hadn't liked about the story. What I found instead were the closing words written by Norman Maclean. Waters didn't haunt me, but the death of a brother did. A brother I desperately wished I could call for dating advice and how to fix my dishwasher. I knew there wouldn't be either of those answers in Norman Maclean's novella, but I thought there might be other answers in the story for me. The fish would come later.

Three fish.

The trout came first, on accident really. Once I decided I wanted to try fly fishing, I discovered all sorts of people I already knew who regularly went out casting lines into rivers.

"Heather, I could take you if you'd like." Dane, a friend of a friend, offered one night over a shared plate of fries and me sighing into a half-empty beer about my latest dating failure.

"You would?" I perked up, imagining all the great photos I could get. Now it wouldn't just be the men holding fish in their dating profiles. "I don't have any of my own stuff though, do you have a rod I could borrow?"

A smile unfurled across his face. "I'm pretty sure I've got a rod you could work with." At the same height as me, Dane wasn't tall but made up for it with the thickness of his arms and a smile that spread so wide and white you couldn't help but smile back, rosy cheeked.

I rolled my eyes at the flirty wordplay but a week later we waded into the McKenzie River, me trailing after him on the slippery river rock, my steps like a newborn foal. In water almost to my hips I casted for as long as I could, until I was shivering too bad to cast any good.

"Sorry," I laughed and wobbled back to the bank to warm in the summer sun.

He cast his line out, a graceful slash catching the light of the sun, back, forward, back again and then a tight loop arcing and landing a distance from his position in the water. "Is that apology for scaring the fish with all that stomping around?" He moved in the water with solid steps and gave me his grin full of trouble.

"For my bad fishing," I laughed back.

"No such thing. Come in and try some more."

I followed his beckoning and he passed me his rod. I bit my lip to hold in a repeat of our previous joke. He stepped back and gestured for me to get to it. With his eyes on me and the clumsy curve of my line, I struggled through my robotic ten-and-two casting positions. The rumored skittish trout rose to the surface all around me, leaping and gulping at hatches on the water, seeming to laugh and ignore my fumbling fly. I was warned about these suspicious fish, ducking away from shadows cast on the water, hiding in the shady hollows of rock or bank overhang. Retreating from any possible threat. They didn't care that my shadow was friendly and I just wanted a little of their time and magic. I was rebuffed. Repeatedly. I kept trying, thinking good thoughts for the friendship I wanted with these fish.

"We'll get you out again, and you'll catch fish for sure," Dane assured me as we packed up.

I shrugged in reply and picked up a Styrofoam cup left on the bank. "Bait fishermen of course." I waggled the container at him, "Bait!" spelled out in sun-faded blue italic letters.

He laughed. "You always pick up other people's trash? I think I saw a cigarette butt further downriver if you wanted to grab that too."

"Just doing what I can." I didn't bother sharing that it was something my brother had done when he was still around.

Two weeks later Dane kept his word and we waded into the McKenzie River again. "You just have to keep putting yourself in the waters of these leery fish," he encouraged.

I hoped he was right, I wanted to speak their language. Then, just as promised, I set my first hook. By luck, "on the swing" they call it. After I'd given up on my drifting fly and was about to reel it in, cast, and try again. But before I could, the curve of a little trout body broke the surface and grabbed the fly, both of us shocked to now be joined together, however momentarily.

"Keep your rod up," Dane called, miming lifting the rod straight up.

I laughed and fought to keep the fighting fish on my line, resisting me until the final moments when Dane scooped him into a net. Although my lack of intention made me feel as though I'd cheated, a caught fish is a caught fish. I beamed for a photo, my hand cupped under the wee little rainbow trout with the palest slash of iridescent crimson glittering down his slides. His slick body sprang against my palm, stronger than his size let on. I wanted more of that feeling, desperate for it. The sun heating my skin, the clear, cold water rushing by my legs, and the possibility of a small battle at the end of my line.

"When can we go fishing again?" I texted Dane late one Thursday night a few weeks later, hoping he'd offer up his Sunday afternoon, where we could fish for a couple hours and then share a beer on the riverbank where I'd convince him to grab dinner with me. A second delicate reeling-in I was attempting. I didn't get the answer I was hoping for. In fact, I didn't get any answer at all. As if I'd cast the completely wrong fly to him, he never answered. Never even broke the surface to let me know he was there and I just wasn't skilled enough to catch his interest.

I borrowed a different friend's rod and tried going on my own, tried putting into action all that I'd learned, fishing out of spite and wanting to prove to Dane and myself that I didn't need him or his fishing expertise. But the fish wouldn't rise, they wouldn't even leap and laugh at my fly, just ignored me altogether.

Confidence rattled, and confused at what I had done to be so disregarded, I slinked away from that fishing spot. I decided I didn't need a man to take me trout fishing. I booked the type of fishing trip most men only dream of: sockeye salmon fishing in Alaska.

"Heather, don't you think this vacation is an expensive over-reaction to getting rejected by a man?" my mom asked me one night over the phone while I picked at my cuticles and she ironed my father's dress shirts.

"No, not all."

The iron hiss-hissed over the phone. She clarified, "No to the expense of it or no to the overreaction?"

"I didn't just get rejected by Dane. The fish took his side."

Her throaty laugh reverberated over the phone, the iron hiss-hissing right along with her. "Oh my dear, always a penchant for the dramatic. Enjoy your Alaskan spite trip."

I landed in Iliamna, Alaska at the peak of the sockeye salmon run, ducking out of the 10-seat plane and into the welcoming wave of the lodge's head guide, Alden. Tall, thin, arms sculpted like a sailor's and the tan neck of someone who spends their days outdoors. I fell in step with him and looked up to his face as he told me with enthusiasm about the exciting week they had planned for me. The fact that yet another man was taking me fishing wasn't lost on me, but at least this relationship was more formal, with a payment due at the end of the week.

The guests were divided among the guides and on my first day out Alden drove me and an older couple from New Jersey to the New Halen River. We set up at a bend in the river, shallow water made of two currents: the icy teal water rushing downstream toward the lower falls and the dark shadowed mass of sockeye pressing upstream. While the other two guests repeatedly reeled in hefty salmon, I couldn't even feel the bump of a bite.

Alden approached me, slow steady steps on a different landscape of slick rocks. "Would you like some help?"

I smiled but wanted to cry in relief. And embarrassment. "I'd love some."

"Okay, please know that I'm teasing, but you know fishing is supposed to be fun, right?"

I laughed, shoulders dropping a little. "Don't I look like the picture of fun?"

A smile played at the corner of his mouth. "I'm sure you're lots of fun. But you look a little stiff. Your body's going to hurt at the end of the day if you keep holding yourself together like that."

I laughed again. If only he knew.

He laid his hand, light as the first leaf in fall, on the outside of my elbow. "Keep it close to your body, but not too close. Enough room for a bible." Heat from his hand permeated my sun shirt and further relaxed my casting-weary arm.

And then I started catching salmon. Once out of the water and their march upriver, their iridescent silver sides glittered, some of them darkening to dusky rose before they'd eventually turn brilliant red contrasted against a green head. The older boys developed noses hooked like beaks. I got good at feeling the bump of their mouth testing the fly on my line, I'd pull the rod back across my left shoulder, sometimes the force of their weight against the line a shock to my wrist. The guide stood close and kept me safe, watching for bears and reminding me not to go for the reel when the fish were in the middle of a run, lest I bloody my knuckles in a losing fight. I only had to be reminded a couple times before the pain was its own valuable lesson.

For the entire week Alden guided each one of my trips. I couldn't tell if it was on purpose until two days before I was set to leave. I walked out of the dining room, my thoughts on fish, wondering if Dane ever checked my Instagram and saw what great catches I was having and regretted his decision to cut me loose. I practically bumped into Alden, a glass of wine in each of his hands and his cheeks flushing pink.

"I was just coming to find you." He offered me one of the glasses. "Would you like to go for a walk?"

"I'd love to." I slipped the glass from his left hand and noticed the length of his fingers, their lean muscled look. We walked along the sandy pebbled beach of the lake and found a spot away from the lodge, under a crumbling ledge of earth and grass and sat down.

We gazed across the lake in silence for a few beats before he asked, "So, what brought you to Alaska?"

"To catch fish, silly." I laughed and took a sip of my wine.

"Mmmhmmm." He cocked an eyebrow. "Everyone has a reason beyond the fish."

I pulled my knees up to my chest and rested my chin on them. "I came to prove that I could fish without a man's help." I picked my head up and looked over at him. "Look how well that worked out." We both laughed. The warmth of the wine combatted the coolness of the sand soaking into my jeans.

"You fished just fine without a man. All I did was offer some tips and hold the net." He paused. "You try to do everything without a man?"

Now I really laughed, embarrassed. Shy, I tucked my chin behind my knees but answered honestly, "No. I definitely enjoy a man's company."

A lock of my hair, catching the light of Alaska's never-setting summer sun turned fire red, and fell forward, blocking my view of him. I tipped my head back and he tucked it behind my ear, his hand pausing at my neck, the heat of our skin passing electric signals back and forth, the moment still and filled with a rushing like the water of the McKenzie in my ears. I turned my face just a little, and nuzzled my cheek against his palm. He took the signal, rubbing the back of my neck with his thumb and then pulling me into him. Soon enough we had closed the space between us entirely, legs woven together, arms wrapped around each other. Later, in my room we laid in the messy bed, comforter on the floor, me staring at the ceiling and him staring at me while tracing the curve of my collar bones.

"What are you thinking about?" he asked, as his fingers took a detour down between my breasts, using my belly button as a roundabout and back up again. The sky made its best effort at twilight, filtering between a crack in the black-out curtains.

"Where fish come from."

"Ooh, I know this one." He grinned. "You see when a mommy fish loves a daddy fish—"

I turned my head to look at him and roll my eyes. "I know the mechanics egg laying. I mean in lakes. How did they ever get in lakes where there are no rivers or streams or fish highways for them to catch a ride into the water?"

I went back to staring at the ceiling. He traced the profile of my face, starting at the center of my forehead and, light as a whisper, followed the center of my face down to the tip of my nose, his finger coming to rest on the cupid's bow of my upper lip.

"Fish are magic," he answered, and tapped my lip, my nerves tingling at the tease.

I wanted to roll my eyes at him again but he was too sweet for my dating-hardened exterior. I continued staring at the ceiling. He stopped tracing my lines and propped himself up on one elbow.

"I'm serious. If there's a body of water, they'll make their way to it, somehow, someway. Maybe not the super fancy fish. But eggs hitch a ride on the legs of birds. Or a nearby river overflows and runs into the lake, leaving behind a family of fish. I mean, for sure wildlife departments stock lakes, but fish find their way to their waters."

He left me considering the pioneering habits of fish and slipped back to his room, not wanting our unsanctioned guiding activities to be discovered. The next night after dinner I opened the door to a soft tapping, he stood on the step rolling the bill of his baseball hat with those long fingers of his.

"Would you like to have another beach walk on your last night here?"

I smiled at him and grabbed my jacket, already feeling the warmth of his presence. Out of sight of the lodge he bumped my hand with his.

"Can I hold your hand?"

"You make me blush. I feel like I'm in high school."

"Is that a yes?"

He held my hand all the way back to my room and into my bed again. That night he held me until morning and I couldn't remember why I took a trip to Alaska or how I learned to fish and probably couldn't even have told you my name if you'd asked.

At the airport, waiting for the ten-seater plane for the ride back to Anchorage, he shook my hand. An awkward formal gesture between two people who'd seen each other naked only a few hours earlier. But I knew he didn't want people to talk. He leaned in and dropped his voice, though he didn't need to with the sound of plane engines drowning most everything out.

"I slipped my phone number in your fish box."

I laughed. "You slipped more than that in there." I knew he meant the wax-coated cardboard box announcing the bounty of my salmon harvest. After his initial instructions I out-fished the other guests and was heading home with 50 pounds of salmon. Forty-four fillets. Forty-four weeks of salmon meals in my future. I already had a list going of different ways to prepare it, Seven Ways to Salmon I'd titled the note in my phone. An effort to combat my worry I'd be sick of salmon after only a couple months.

Alden blushed at my smart mouth. "I hope that was alright?"

I knew he spent his winter seasons in Oregon, only about an hour from my town. I squeezed his hand. "It's more than alright." I boarded the plane in a fog of post-orgasm, salmon-abundant bliss. I had food for the winter and a man who actually wanted to talk to me after he'd slept with me.

I touched down in Oregon to record temps topping 100 degrees. Heat waves wobbled the dry-grass landscape out my plane window. After waiting at baggage claim for forty minutes, my fish box never arrived. I went home and waited for a call from the airline, my stomach tightening with each passing hour. Seventy-two hours later I finally got the call and retrieved my fish box. All the fish had defrosted, then heated, then rotted inside their plastic sleeves. Forty-four pink salmon bodies harvested for nothing. The folded piece of paper containing Alden's contact information had soaked up the condensation from the defrosting fish, melting the ink into an unreadable blob and tearing the paper.

A week after crying over the loss of my abundant fish, I called the lodge. "I'm trying to get ahold of Alden, one of the guides? I was hoping you could pass a message to him?"

The woman on the phone answered before I'd barely finished asking the question. "Sorry, Alden's gone home for the season."

I paused, trying a different approach. "Is there any way you could give me his email or a last name, perhaps and I could find him online?"

"Sorry, we don't give out staff information." She didn't try to hide her boredom with the conversation, which clearly was the equivalent of a middle schooler calling her crush's house and asking when he'd be home. I briefly realized this thought had to make me middle-aged, because kids now just text each other and avoid the voice-altering adrenaline rushes of having to talk to your crush's parents before having a halting conversation about Spanish homework.

"Hello? Is that all I can help you with?" The curt woman on the phone brought me back to the depressing reality of my current adrenaline-altered voice.

"Yes, sorry, I was just thinking there must be some way for me to reach him, he gave me his number but it—"

"Then why are you talking to me?"

"It got messed up on the flight home. I can't make it out. Could you maybe just email him and give him my number?"

She sighed her response, "I'll see what I can do."

There was a very good chance what she could do was exactly nothing. Three weeks going by without a text from him suggested the woman did nothing except hang up the phone. I had left the lodge feeling so sure of my abundance, in fish and romantic possibilities. And now my hands were empty of both. I called my mom.

She chuckled. "Easy come, easy go." Pausing, then a snicker. "No pun intended."

"Mother," I groaned, covering my eyes.

She lost no momentum. "You know what they say. There's more fish in the—"

"Don't. Don't be cute. All those caught fish for nothing. Dead. And he was so sweet and cute and treated me so well."

"No, you're right. The fish dying just to rot on some tarmac in Indiana or wherever the hell they had a layover is the real tragedy."

I sighed. "I called because I wanted a warm, fuzzy conversation where you told me everything was going to be alright."

"Everything *is* going to be alright. I promise. If the guide wants to find you, he will. Men find a way for a woman they want. And if he doesn't, well then, you had a great time in Alaska."

I disconnected and let the couch cushions swallow me up while I scrolled through fly fishing photos on Instagram. Gorgeous fisher-women beaming their just-caught-fish smiles, hair loosely braided, shirts tight under waders, holding fish that dripped water like diamonds back into sparkling rivers. All marked with hashtags like #5050onthewater and #womenwhoflyfish. How come everyone on Instagram looked like models but the guys on Tinder looked they'd just rolled out of bed? Complete with matted hair and saliva crusted at the corners of their smiles. You could practically smell the morning breath.

I sighed. My dating app photos were good, my own smiling fish photo cast out like a caddis fly trying to catch a bite. But I didn't feel like one of those accomplished fisher-women on Instagram. I couldn't fish on my own, I didn't even have my own gear. If the Alaskan trip was a spite trip, it was time for a real trip, to get better. And in my home waters.

I made a reservation on-line through the local fly shop, the blue glow of my phone screen the only light in my living room, which had gone dark with the setting sun. Two days later I received a confirmation email with, "Meet your guide!" in the subject line. A photo pasted at the top of the message showed a man with a mop of grey hair grinning and holding a fish in the bow of his boat. The name underneath read: Gordon Sullivan. His bio followed. I glanced at the photo again, his gold wedding band glinting in the sun.

At least there was zero chance I'd fall for this one.

The morning of the float I peed five times so I wouldn't have to go at any point during the trip. I didn't know what the bathroom breaks were like on a river trip. Probably they pulled over on some flat pebble sandbar with one bush and let the guys write their names on the river rocks. I would require far more privacy. I was outdoorsy-ish, but not low maintenance.

At the boat launch I found the drift boat with the fly shop's name plastered down its sides. But the guide standing in it with his back to me didn't look like the man in the emailed photo. Didn't look like a man in his sixties. Baseball hat, but no grey hair, navy-blue shirt pulled tight across broad shoulders, daily rowing-developed biceps curving out from under short sleeves. No pot belly pressing the seams of his shirt. This couldn't be the right guide, even though the boat had the markings of the fly shop. I stepped forward, about to introduce myself just as he turned to face me. This was definitely not the man in the email.

The morning light cast sparkling reflections from the water onto his face, lighting up the green of his eyes like the froth of an ocean. His beard dark against a summer-tanned face, and dimples that appeared as he smiled.

"Are you Heather?"

"Hi, yes. Um, you don't look like Gordon…"

"I know, Sorry to disappoint if you were hoping for that silver fox. I'm Cody Trout." He held out his hand. "Gordon came down sick so the shop asked if I could fill in since I didn't have any bookings today. They sent you an email about it this morning, not sure if you saw it?"

"No, I didn't. But that's okay. I didn't request him specifically."

"Oh good. Sometimes people can get frustrated with a last-minute change so I was hoping you wouldn't be too disappointed." He arranged a cooler next to his seat on the boat. No rings on his fingers. No pale mark on tan hands where a ring might normally be. "Cody Trout you said? Like the fish?"

He laughed, an easy smile broadening across his face, the dimples adding exclamation points of delight, like sunrise chasing off the dark. "That's right. Got lucky with the last name."

"Imagine if they'd named you Chase."

"Hey now, I don't want to chase trout, I want to catch them."

"Fair enough." I smiled, the crisp morning air prickling my skin, in anticipation and at the freshness of it all. Cody pushed us off from shore, hopping in with his pants soaked at the ankle, feet in flip flops that surely hid the lines of winter white skin. Then he launched into his rundown of safety requirements and started in on the anatomy of the rod and fly setup he wanted me try before pausing mid-sentence.

"Hold on." He grabbed a net and leaned over the side of the boat, snagging a Styrofoam fast food cup floating alongside us. He poured a little water out of it and then stashed it in a garbage bag. "Sorry. Personal pet peeve of mine. People don't come fishing to see garbage in our waterways."

I smiled. A familiar feeling unfurling in my belly, a heat and giddiness extending out in rings until they reached my face and I knew I was blushing. Not that he'd know why.

He waved his hand, a dismissal of the moment, and then handed me the rod he'd set up. "Let's get you fishing, lady." I shook the fly off into the water and stripped out some of the lime green line, letting the current take the end of it and pull it through the guides. Only three casts in and a little rainbow trout gulped my fly.

"Oh," I laughed in surprise.

He laughed too. "Sometimes they catch you off guard. The ones you don't expect are always fun. Now keep your line tight, strip it in if you need to."

I reeled in the line and Cody scooped the fish from the water and into our world. I posed for a photo holding the fish over the net, joy vibrating around my body. Done with the photo evidence, I leaned over the edge of the boat and faced the fish upstream, rubbing his belly and wishing him well. As soon as he could, he slid free of me and was gone.

"Wow, that was great. Cody Trout I think you're in the right business."

He smiled. "Thank you. Fish are magic, aren't they? They find their waters."

I knew he was joking a little, referencing his last name like a beacon for his career choice, but I cocked my head, startled and intrigued by the line I'd heard before from a different man. I nodded and repeated the phrase in agreement.

"Fish are magic."

NON-FICTION

SELECTED BEST IN NON-FICTION

Daniel P. Hoffman was born and bred as a young fisherman in Summit County, Colorado. His family moved to Alaska when he was twelve years-old. Working as a lodge staffer and fishing guide in the remote fly-out lodges of Bristol Bay's Katmai region, Daniel put himself through school while obtaining his Bachelor's degree in Wildlife Biology from the University of Alaska-Fairbanks. Ultimately transitioning to a career as a peace officer, Dan eventually retired as Chief of Police for the City of Fairbanks, remaining as a longtime resident of Alaska's interior while fishing extensively throughout the latitudes of the Far North.

He's been published in numerous periodicals, including: *Fish Alaska*, *Backpacker*, and *Alaska* magazine. In his first non-fiction work, *An Alaska Flyfisher's Odyssey: Seeking a Life of Drag-Free Drift in the Land of the Midnight Sun*, Daniel uses the book's introductory chapters of Winter, Spring, Summer, and Fall to relate the heartbreaking dichotomy of Alaska's seasons.

An Alaska Flyfisher's Odyssey is now in its second printing, and can be found in fly shops, bookstores, or ordered online. 50% of all profits from its sale are donated by Daniel to Trout Unlimited, in support of their Alaskan operations.

In Search of Flowing Waters: The Seasons of Alaska

(These four seasonal chapters comprise Section One of *"An Alaska Flyfisher's Odyssey: Seeking a Life of Drag-Free Drift in the Land of the Midnight Sun"* previously published by Sweetgrass Books, 2021.)

WINTER

It's been said that absence makes the heart grow fonder. As the frozen stillness of Alaska's Interior sinks into a pool of ever-increasing darkness, my thoughts of a flowing, fishable trout stream have become both intoxicating and torturous. Water is rarely wet here at this time of year; it covers most of the landscape in a layer of hoary and bone-dry insulation, the accumulation of which can vary widely from one winter to the next. In some places, a thin layer of frozen crust may cap the snow's surface – a lasting reminder of a brief, October warming trend that won't repeat itself 'til mid-April. In other spots, compaction due to wind or other activity will create a solid base of freeze-dried Styrofoam, where the pronounced squeak of one's walking will increase markedly in volume as temperatures head south of forty-below.

The rivers in our area have been locked-up tightly for many weeks now, with entire stretches of smaller streams freezing predictably solid. In a somewhat cruel twist of irony for dog-mushers and other wintertime travelers, the sudden appearance of lethally wet "overflow" can sometimes spring forth in sinister ambush. Here, the very deepest pockets of water – having thus far remained insulated and slowly flowing under winter's protective cover – finally fall victim to the weight of accumulating snow and ice overhead. As this crushing mass pushes downward with determined and inevitable force, the water has no choice but to escape via any available path. With the solid floor of the streambed supplying no viable alternative, it squeezes upwards through cracks in the ice. If prospective travelers are fortunate, the water will continue through the uppermost layers of snow, whereupon its flow will falter as it slowly glaciates, building layer upon layer of a highly slippery, yet thankfully visible, hazard on the trail.

Far worse, the most insidious of overflow will sometimes fail to breach the snow's top layer. Dependent upon temperatures and the timing of subsequent snowfalls, a thin, false icecap may form over the top of the newly liberated stream. Water now continues to flow over a base-layer of ice, while remaining hidden under an insulating – and dangerously concealing – new layer of snow. For those traversing the wilderness at thirty or forty-below, finding one's snowmachine or dogsled suddenly punching through the uppermost layer of snow and sinking into a liquid morass provides a sickening rush of fleeting insanity: free-flowing water simply *cannot exist* in these conditions! Or, at the very least, has *no business* doing so. (And yes, I said "snowmachine;" anyone this side of the 60th Parallel who uses the word "snowmobile" is clearly a southern tourist!)

Luckily, I have no such hazards to contend with on this early winter's day. It's morning, and I'm in desperate need of some coffee. As I set towards the kitchen in my routine and pre-caffeinated stupor, I can just start to make out the beginnings of a faint glow on the southern horizon. It's actually more of a tentative, atmospheric promise than that of any discernible daylight, with a slowly expanding blush that seems to defy gravity as it bleeds upwards at a deliciously languid, and maddeningly indifferent, pace. While a forgotten sliver of last month's November moon still remains inexplicably suspended in the southern sky, nearly all remaining stars have now retreated into the impossibly dark-blue expanse at the uppermost edge of my view.

It's nearly 10:30 a.m., and the sun still remains stubbornly hidden below its scheduled point of emergence. Far to the south at this time of year, its bashful, sloping trajectory has now sufficiently backlit the towering silhouette of an ever-present legion, dutifully rising to guard the Tanana Valley's southern flanks. Predominantly white when seen in full daylight, the currently featureless, black barrier dominates the landscape as an imposing, monolithic wall.

These colossal ramparts of granite, snow, and glacial ice comprise the mountains of the Alaska Range, with its paramount sentinels of Hayes, Hess, and Deborah standing resolute watch over the slumbering city of Fairbanks.

Denali, somewhat aloof in its placement at the far western end of the range, is still firmly ensconced in darkness. As North America's tallest peak, this massive general won't assume its vigil until early afternoon. There, it will stand in solemn observance as the fiery orange and yellows of a sustained, low-angle sunrise yield all too quickly to the soft, salmon pastels of an extended midwinter sunset. During these shortest days that bracket our northern solstice, the sun will trace a hopelessly shallow arc as it crawls just a few degrees above this mountainous horizon, with the entire panoramic progression lasting less than four hours. Laughingly mocked by the tilt of earth's axis in this "land of the midnight sun," December provides a scant amount of sun, while dishing out generous portions of midnight.

Another nightly stretch of extended darkness will inevitably follow. But, in a possible conciliatory gesture, the sun now offers its most surprising and wondrous contribution. Perhaps aware that the holidays are fast-approaching, and surely aware of the shipping deadlines imposed upon distances exceeding ninety-million miles, emissions of charged particles sent forth from solar flares have ensured the timely delivery of a billion small parcels, cheerfully dropped at the front porch of Alaska's upper atmosphere. As this multitude of tiny gifts accelerate through our planet's magnetic field, their collision with gas molecules will emit the shimmering and hypnotic palette of greens, purples, and glowing whites comprising the *Aurora Borealis*. Clear skies will ensure maximum visibility, providing a spectral show of northern light that's often bright enough to illuminate the vast, snowy expanse below. I live in a dreamworld.

Back to my coffee. It's exceptionally cold down in the valley this morning, and I don't bother to check our outdoor thermometer to confirm my observations. I've lived here long enough to accurately gauge the cold through a combination of visible and auditory cues, one of which was provided before I managed to drag myself out of bed. As I lay snugly next to my wife beneath two of her handmade comforters earlier this morning, I heard the first of the regularly-scheduled *Wright's Air* Navajos pass over the house, returning from the village of Fort Yukon or Tanana as it gradually began its descent towards Fairbanks. A twin-propeller airplane sounds distinctly different from their single-prop brethren, and both can be easily distinguished from turbine jet engines. However, whether a specific type of aircraft hums, buzzes, or roars, each has its own unique sound-profile, and they all resonate with a perceptively sharper crackle and pitch when passing through extremely frigid air.

"Shit," I whispered to Gwen, "...it sounds cold out this morning."

Throwing on some sweatpants and shuffling down the stairs, my view to the south immediately confirmed my suspicions. The plume of steam visible from the city's central power plant rose only a short distance skyward before bending sharply to the right, falling back slightly before flattening-out to form a suspended, wispy ceiling over the majority of town. Where the lights of civilization (I might argue that word later...) could be seen through the translucent haze, sharp and distinct columns of skyward illumination were captured within the fog's suspended ice crystals. These ghostly beams further confirmed the presence of extremely cold air, as this level of pronounced refraction doesn't occur when temperatures are warmer than minus-thirty or so.

While the power plant's horizontally-flattened plume confirmed that the city dwellers were trapped within a folded quesadilla of frigid air, foul moods, and car exhaust, the column's pronounced bend – occurring well below the level of my own vantage point – conveyed and confirmed a phenomenon that I'm often privileged to enjoy throughout these midwinter months. Our home is perched atop a crescent-shaped ridge a few miles north of town, and the nearly thousand-foot gain in elevation provides a benefit that rivals its expansive southern view. The predominant stillness most commonly seen in the lowlands combined with the settling of cold, denser air, results in consistent temperature inversions throughout the worst of the winter, often resulting in ridgetop temperatures twenty to thirty degrees warmer than those experienced on the valley floor.

"Time to trim the banana trees..." I smiled and muttered to myself, as I found a bit of creamer in the back of the fridge.

While I suppose it may simply reflect an amalgamation of adapted coping mechanisms, reveling in these small thermometric victories while getting lost in the sublime beauty of winter's frosted stillness and low-angle light, my current existence comes at no small cost. I'm a fisherman. Scratch that; I'm a *fly-fisherman*, and a predominantly stream one at that. And while Alaska has truly provided the stuff of my fly-casting dreams, particularly in the pursuit of trout, grayling, and salmon, the absence of flowing waters for several months each year has proved that nature can indeed be more than just harsh mistress; she can be a truly indifferent and cold-hearted bitch.

I've lived just outside of Fairbanks for nearly forty years now, and my wife was born here. As a fisherman, I've started to perceive this expanse – and my own measure of time – with a somewhat skewed perspective, much in the same manner as folks who earnestly discuss the relationships with their beloved pooches in terms of "dog years." While it's conventional wisdom to assign a one-to-seven ratio for such canine calculations, I figure that a roughly four-to-twelve ratio (reducing down to 1-to-3; thanks Mrs. Arno…) realistically reflects the limitations of the four-month, fishable season that currently occupies my annual trip around the sun. Now, I'd like to think that such a modest and reserved outlay of time and effort on the water would keep me roughly two-thirds younger than that of my angling contemporaries to the south. However, in a somewhat shocking turn of events, things don't seem to be turning out that way. Many of my friends in the Lower 48 seem to be getting in a lot more fishing than I do, while I continue to age in the same manner that I always have.

Thankfully, this hasn't been too big a problem over the past few years, as my life's accumulation of marketable skills and assets have finally allowed me to dance around the outermost fringes of the more economically well-endowed. Gwen and I have always prioritized the need for travel, particularly during the winter months. Through a combination of her warm and compassionate understanding (and my incredibly subtle application of psychology and campaigns of sustained whining) some of our tropical retreats have now been combined with a stop at a cold-water stream destination along the way. I've recently been able to extend my regular fall season through the entirety of October, visiting Colorado to chase rainbows and browns on the streams of my early childhood. We've also visited and fished some exceptional trout waters in both New Zealand and Patagonia during Alaska's midwinter, providing a level of seasonal escape that definitely bears repeating.

With everything finally coming up roses, I left my job in early 2020 to join my wife in full-time retirement, already plotting and scheming the course towards our next prospective fishing destinations. I suppose I should've predicted that it would only be a matter of time before a worldwide pandemic reared its ugly head, halting all non-essential travel and mandating that responsible folks "hunker down" for the coming winter. Luckily, when it comes to adopting marginally anti-social behavior, most of us Alaskans are already well ahead of the game. If staying inside one's own home, where niceties such as hosted cocktail parties (or just wearing pants, for that matter…) need not be observed, I can guarantee that I'm up to the challenge.

For now, I'll strive for contentment by donning enough layers to hike, skate, and ski in all but the very coldest of temperatures. When the mercury can no longer be coaxed from its baseline reservoirs, I'll work on inside projects, stopping to tie a few flies when I need a break from my more mundane chores. I'll help Gwen in the kitchen as we enjoy the bounty of moose and salmon that sustains us throughout the year, and we'll watch more than our fair share of movies in the evening as we gaze over the sparkling lights of Fairbanks below. I'll do all of these things as I continue to eye the southern horizon, waiting for the snow and ice to release their soul-crushing grip on my home waters. Hopefully, it won't be too much longer… at least not in "Dan years."

SPRING

It was the best of times; it was the worst of times…
— Charles Dickens

It's a great quote, but I'll come clean: I never read the entire book. However, the fundamental discord reflected in this simple, introductory phrase left a powerful impression upon me, as it fully encapsulates the torturous dichotomy that defines an Alaskan spring. The book itself did once manage to provide me with a somewhat more practical and useful platform; I'd photoshopped its cover to reflect *"A Tale of Two Dinners,"* providing an illustrative accompaniment for a rather pointed letter I'd penned to Alaska Airlines (Helpful hint: Should you ever be offered their "chef-inspired" turkey dinner, I'd suggest taking a hard pass...).

In my efforts to set a properly somber and dignified, literary tone, I began my missive with the appropriate preamble:

It was the best of meals, it was the worst of meals, it was the age of air travel, it was the scourge of coach, it was the epoch of hunger, it was the epoch of incredulity, it was the season of Alaskan winter, it was the season of Costa Rican summer, it was the Texas barbecue of hope, it was the Alaska Airlines meal of despair...

Luckily, the corporate staffer who received my correspondence seemed to genuinely appreciate my highly expressive efforts, as I waxed poetic while dissecting their culinary abomination in extreme detail. I suppose my letter may have provided a momentary distraction, and perhaps a welcome departure, from the angry and profanity-laden complaints that most airlines are likely to receive. As someone who apparently shared my sense of humor, and perhaps as a literary kindred-spirit of sorts, the agent graciously refunded the cost of our meals, along with providing a noteworthy credit for future travel. As airlines go in general, Alaska Air is among the very best. (Turkey dinners notwithstanding.)

But I digress... While not claiming to have full knowledge of the author's narrative with respect to that particular tale, the "best of times/worst of times" phrase has always stuck with me. Dickens apparently possessed a good understanding of the fundamental duality that could exist within circumstances, accompanied by the conflicting emotions that likely result. Accordingly, it leads me to believe that Charles ("Chuck" to his friends up here...) surely must've spent at least one springtime in the far northern latitudes of Interior Alaska.

As conceptual divisions of time go, defining spring as a true, full-blown "season" constitutes a bit of a stretch when one finds themselves north of the Alaska Range. Don't get me wrong; in terms of sheer import and overall transformational significance, there is no time of year that Alaskans greet with more frenzied excitement and anticipation. While these are indeed "the best of times," the issue – or perhaps more of a sticking point – is one of proportionality and delayed gratification. If placed within the analogous timeframe of a yearly holiday calendar, one can define the week of Christmas through New Year's Eve as a timespan roughly equivalent to that of a highly anticipated Alaskan summer. After enjoying a brisk New Year's Day, (which qualified as autumn in its entirety, in case you missed it…) you now spend the remainder of the year scraping frozen windshields, guarding against frozen pipes, and shoveling snow. Spring? Well, that would be represented by the stunningly short interval of Christmas Eve, when all of the giddy children eagerly await Santa and his sleigh-load of promised presents, too excited to fall asleep in anticipation for what they know to be coming.

Within some contexts, such a characterization may be a bit of an exaggeration. For those enjoying outdoor winter sports, the spring season can be considered to start a bit earlier, ushered in by the combination of gradually warming temperatures and (of significantly greater importance) the inevitable increase in daylight. As Fairbanks lies less than 200 miles south of the Arctic Circle, we gain only a couple of precious seconds of light per day immediately following December's winter solstice. Those small, incremental gains don't seem to add up to much, especially as one begins the long, slow slog through January and February. (And while the latter is technically the shortest in terms of calendar days, on a psychological basis it consistently proves to be the longest month of the year.)

Ahhhhh… but then there's March! The additional seconds have continued to accumulate, and as a function of the earth's orientation and position in its yearly orbital journey, the daily gain in daylight now begins to accelerate at a noticeable pace. Through the latter part of the month and on into April, we'll experience an addition of several *minutes* of sunlight per day, the difference of which is no longer subtle. This seismic shift in daily illumination now provides a significant mood-altering lift, as workers and students suddenly notice that both ends of their daily commute are no longer shrouded in perpetual darkness. This is the time of year when cross-country skis get their glide back, and when snowmachine trips become more a function of seasonal enjoyment, rather than one of perpetual cold-weather endurance and subarctic survival. We all know what's coming, and Santa's sleigh can't get here fast enough.

Unfortunately, I'm a fly-fisherman, and that brings us back to "the worst of times." While I'm as appreciative of the growing daylight and warming temperatures as anyone, it now only serves to heighten my impatience and frustration. Rivers and streams will remain frozen and covered with snow for several more weeks yet, and I take little comfort in knowing that the travelers who follow the creek's trails are enjoying the last of their springtime journeys. It'll still be quite some time before breakup. In years of particularly mild conditions, "ice-out" won't occur on the major drainages of the Yukon, Tanana, and Nenana Rivers until very late April; in most years we'll be waiting until May. The fishable, clearwater tributaries of the Chena, Salcha, and others will jealously guard their winter's covering parka even longer, as the larger downstream rivers must first open up and flow, eventually providing a pathway for the smaller streams to finally shed their loads of ice.

The month of May can best be described as "true spring" for the Interior Alaskan fisherman, in all of its frustrating glory. Streams will now begin to flow, though they'll likely rage and churn in high, murky runoff for a few additional, maddening weeks. Mid-term conditions will depend primarily on the depth of the winter's accumulated snow-load, as springtime precipitation is rarely a factor. May is often one of our driest months in terms of precipitation, thankfully hastening the thaw of remaining snow and returning area streams to their status as beckoning, fishable gems.

Water may be starting to flow in the country, but it seems to be backed-up to a standstill everywhere around town. Many of the subterranean storm-drains remain tightly frozen, in desperate need of a steam truck's attention. The largest lakes in Alaska – ones such as Illiamna, Becharof, and Tustumena – may temporarily lose their crowns to the new record-holders, as whitecapped reservoirs suddenly occupy the intersections of Airport Way, Cushman Street, and the Old Steese Highway. As the snow continues to recede from yards and alleyways across town, the discarded and long-forgotten detritus from the previous fall emerges in defiance, prompting a desperate need for cleanup. Such tidying chores may prove to be difficult; many areas are protectively surrounded by the emergence of several layers of frozen dogshit, accurately chronicling a record of the past winter's successive snowfalls in the same manner that tree-rings can be counted on a freshly cut stump. Now basking and thawing in the springtime sun, the preponderance of turds will add their own odiferous funk to the seasonal potpourri of the Far North.

Luckily, I won't be fishing anywhere too close to town. In true Alaskan fashion, the landscape in which I find myself is once again the product of stunning, visual transformation. The watershed valleys that define the boundaries of my local explorations are most commonly dominated by a combination of dwarf birch, alder, and Labrador tea in their higher reaches. As stream waters tumble to the lower valleys, they slow to eventually meander through broad stretches of poorly drained muskeg and black spruce bog, bordered by willows and interspersed with boreal stands of white spruce and a mix of birch, aspen, and poplar.

If you're used to carrying a compass in the woods, you needn't bother here. South-facing slopes receive the lion's share of sun, and are thus quicker to thaw and are inevitably better drained. The leaf-bearing deciduous trees dominate these expanses, showing a clear demarcation from the north-facing forests of spruce. These sharp divisions bisect all surrounding ridgelines, providing a clear signpost for geographic orientation.

An inspection of low-level flora upon the sunbaked microclimates of the uppermost, south-facing bluffs of the Yukon and Tanana river valleys reveals remnant populations of sage and dryland grasses, stubbornly clinging to their Pleistocene origins. Their presence serves as a surprising reminder of Northern Alaska's prehistoric past, where far warmer temperatures hosted the presence of mastodons and steppe bison as they grazed along semi-arid plains. One thing's for sure: The pre ice-age climate would've provided me with far more fishable months… saber toothed tigers be damned!

No longer on the lookout for woolly mammoths, I now bear witness to an impressive display of explosive synchronicity, as the budding leaves of area birch and poplar burst forth in coordinated and instantaneous fashion in the hills surrounding Fairbanks. This extraordinarily sudden transformation marks the area's highly anticipated "green-up" day, usually occurring by May 15th. While some of the less fortunate souls in the area can be seasonally derailed by the nearly crippling pollen counts that result from this over-the-top, seasonal explosion, I luckily have a high tolerance for such conditions.

Perhaps the most significant harbinger of the coming summer season is realized via the appearance of one of our most noteworthy residents: the ubiquitous Alaskan mosquito. The first wave of this annual onslaught can be easily handled, as the lumbering and drunken members of spring's first generation arrive to hover slowly and clumsily overhead, looking to score their first warm-blooded meal of the season. It's the second and subsequent generations that I'll need to mentally prepare for, as these smaller and considerably faster swarms of determined kamikazes will prod and pester without mercy 'til the first frosts of autumn.

Nearing the end of the month, I'll finally be prepared to transition into the three official months of summer: June, July, and August. May can still prove to be a real wildcard; it might well be snowing on us at mid-month, or it could already be soaring into the mid-80's, causing the first "red flag" fire warnings of the season. I'm uncontrollably antsy at this point, and I'll find any excuse to seek the season's earliest, fishable water. While I can always find nymphing water in the latter part of May, if I'm able to start catching grayling on any dries by month's end, I'll consider the spring to be "successfully average" within its yearly progression.

It's relatively easy at this time of year to quickly gather up my gear at a moment's notice, as I've had the entire winter to get things purchased, replaced, cleaned, patched, repaired, lubricated, categorized, stocked, organized, tied, wound, staged, sorted, hung, deflated, prepped, and ready. The side of my office dedicated to my tying bench and its adjacent closet would do any small fly-shop or sporting goods store proud, and the portion of my garage reserved for rods, boots, waders, and nets stands ready for immediate access. (Get back to me at the end of fall, and I'll let you know how things are looking then...)

Gearing up for my first exploratory foray of the season, I'll need to prepare myself for battle. Regardless of temperature, long sleeves and a neck cover will be the order of the day. I'm careful to confine the application of mosquito repellant to the backs of my hands only, in preparation for a quick smear around my face and neck. Any contaminating application carelessly applied to the fronts of my fingertips - or palms of my hands - would inevitably transfer to my fly-line and monofilament tippets, with disastrously corrosive results. If the bugs are particularly bad, I'll use the dope having a much higher percentage of DEET, though I absolutely hate the stuff. I have no doubts that the nauseatingly greasy, plastic-eating crap will inevitably prove to be cancerous, but I'm resigned to its use. We're on the cusp of summer, and I have fish to catch...

SUMMER

I've been banking my excitement and energy for nearly eight months now, and Mother Nature's balance is finally coming due. For those who've never experienced the feelings that accompany a Northern Alaskan summer, they're perhaps best compared with the exuberance of a teen's first unsupervised road trip, where a full tank of gas and a few cans of squirreled-away beer beckon towards a highway of limitless possibilities. Released from the shackles of darkened confinement, Alaskans will now seek to cram a year's worth of soul-wringing, exhaustive enjoyment into an intensive, hundred-day campaign of joyous and continuous outdoor activity.

I don't know what time it is... and frankly, I don't care. In marked contrast to the solar depravity of our winter's paltry efforts, the sun of our summer sky now boasts a roughly 340-degree procession, sliding beneath the northern horizon in the shallowest of dips for only a few dusky hours. Chirping robins and mournful thrushes can be heard at all hours, at least partially masking the ever-present hum of mosquitos. It's light outside pretty much all of the time, providing one less factor to consider when planning a day's – or night's – adventure.

As with many of our seasonal extremes, the specter of constant daylight is both a blessing and a bit of a curse. It can be tough to fall asleep (or to even realize that one's supposed to *get* sleepy) in the complete absence of any nocturnal cues. The continuous state of illumination can be a bit disorienting to outsiders, providing some predictable comedy as we observe the arrival of new summer tourists. The plaid pants, blue-haired crowd are now walking among us, having apparently followed the annual migration of America's waterfowl northward. (Sporting, in remarkably ironic fashion, their own goose-down vests as they emerge from air-conditioned buses, hopelessly overdressed for the Interior's 80-degree summer weather.) Arriving daily from Alaska's southern ports, these wandering adventurers are dutifully puked forth from their cruise-ship motorcoaches to bask in our constant daylight, remaining blissfully oblivious to the passage of time. We'll watch in bemused detachment as they scramble about tirelessly into the late-night hours, ultimately crashing in complete and inevitable fashion as their accumulated expenditure of energy finally outweighs their bodily reserves.

As a more knowledgeable local, I simply can't afford to waste any of summer's precious time as a wandering zombie. While I'll justify the minimization of sleep to the greatest extent possible during these weeks of high-octane activity, a certain amount will be necessary to fuel my campaign of extended streamside exploration. Planning accordingly, I'll transform our bedroom into an appropriate summertime sanctuary. While a cooling fan may be necessary to facilitate my rapid departure into dreamland during these surprisingly warm nights, blackout shades are the top priority. If for some reason they're not available, a layer of tinfoil applied to the window will do just fine. It seems crazy when I stop to think about it, but for at least a few hours each night I'll long for the return of winter's comforting blanket of darkness.

In another display of mind-numbing contradiction, I'll find myself occasionally cursing the very sun I'd been yearning for a few short months ago. Why? Because the damned, ever-present sunshine initiates an accelerated and sustained period of ridiculous, hyperactive growth for any and all manner of vegetation. While this thrills our local gardeners to no end, cultivating beautiful flowers and producing amazingly large vegetables to a degree that astonishes the tourists, for me it simply represents the starting gun for the encroaching jungle's race to surround and engulf my home.

I'll admit it, I'm not much of a yardwork, exterior-maintenance kind of guy. When it comes to a choice between going fishing – versus mowing, weeding, and brush-cutting for the day – you should be readily prepared to start packing our lunches while answering my questions regarding recommended tippets and prevailing hatches. Predictably, my avoidance of such chores results in our home adopting an appearance of increasing neglect and abandonment as the summer months progress, which chafes at my otherwise orderly nature. If only the grass were to grow during winter when all of our streams were frozen, I'd be *happy* to mow it!

In spite of my occasional bitching, I'm still firmly entrenched in the pro-sun camp. My little sister Diane lives in the small coastal town of Ketchikan, located at the southern tip of Alaska's Panhandle. Ketchikan receives up to 160 inches of rain per year, earning it the dubious distinction as our state's wettest city. Making her living as an accomplished musician and keyboard entertainer, I've often asked how she manages to work her piano's pedals while wearing swim fins. Perhaps she'll eventually answer in one of her letters, which I'll likely have to throw in the microwave to dry-out before reading.

Why do I fixate upon the sun and the rain? Because they provide the single most significant factor in determining the status of our Interior summer on a scale of livability and – more importantly – the fate of my fishing season. As a general characterization, our Interior summers are known to be hot and dry. The protective, curving arch of the Alaska Range blocks much of the moisture from the Pacific Ocean as it spirals and spins-off northward from the Gulf of Alaska, leaving the Interior to bask in relatively low humidity with a high degree of sunshine. Most of our summertime rains will follow the patterns common to inland regions elsewhere on the continent, where clear mornings often give way to the steady afternoon buildup of towering cumulous clouds on the horizon. Thunder, lightning, and sometimes intense showers may follow, with a return to clear skies by early evening. Given the millions of acres of forested lands that surround us, the lightening can pose a big problem.

With most sincere apologies to those in the western U.S. and elsewhere who've been adversely impacted by the recent spates of destructive wildfires, I'll readily admit that I'm actually quite fond of the faint, acrid tang of smoke blown in from distant, burning forests. A shift in June breezes will often find it seeping into my consciousness, providing an almost ever-present backdrop that (at least for me) defines the very essence of an Interior Alaskan summer. I suppose I developed this affinity in my teens, as I'd traveled north from Anchorage during the summers of my high school years to spend three transformative seasons at a Youth Conservation Corps residential work camp, located 30 miles outside of Fairbanks. Laboring to build hiking trails in the Chena River Recreation Area, the pronounced change in climate was a welcome relief from the damp, dreariness of Anchorage, where forest fires were rarely a concern.

Upon coming north, the noticeably deeper-blue skies and warmer temperatures of the Interior instantly brought feelings of both vitality and comforting familiarity, reminiscent of the Colorado mountains that I'd grown up in 'til the age of 12. While the common presence of wildfire smoke was a bit disconcerting at first, it soon embedded itself into the hard-wiring of my brain as an integral component of life in the Far North. After graduating high school, I decided to attend the University of Alaska-Fairbanks; I've remained in the Interior ever since.

Such nostalgia notwithstanding, over the course of the intervening decades we seem to have become firmly entrenched in an increasingly "either/or" model of devolving, summertime conditions. Either we receive *way* too much rain, swelling streams to unfishable levels, or we spend the summers cloaked in a suffocating mantle of excessive wildfire smoke, courtesy of the local lightning. The midsummer months of 2020 proved to be an extreme example of the former, as historically-high levels of rainfall in the Interior drove me (somewhat paradoxically) to the southcentral coast in search of fishable conditions. I can't remember *ever* having seen such rains around Fairbanks, as the home waters of my favorite streams ran high, murky, and un-wadable through the entirety of July and August.

Conversely, the preceding summer of 2019 found me struggling to spot rise-forms along the smooth stretches of my favorite Interior creeks, as my eyes were frequently stinging when looking through a dense layer of smoky haze. I had to frequently wet-down my protective facial buff; I'd originally purchased it to guard against excessive sun, but now commonly used it as a filter against the thick, choking smoke generated from nearby wildfires.

I try to roll with the punches when it comes to the weather and other related conditions, as I've gotten better over the years at shedding stress over factors that I can't control. If nearby conditions are good, I'll probably fish here. If chased off by excessive smoke or high water, I'll go in search of fish elsewhere. The most valuable commodities that I've found in retirement are those of freedom and available time, where the confinements of daily or weekly work schedules no longer preclude me from the possibility of an impromptu road trip.

With all that being said, it's finally summer! I'll frequently be on the move in search of optimal waters, and the possibilities are dizzying. However, as a denizen of the Interior, I'm immediately constrained by a fundamental and primary choice to consider, the determination of which will dictate my budgeted allotment of time, fuel, and hours (or days) spent behind the wheel of my pickup. Do I want to fish grayling, or do I want to fish trout? While there are certainly myriad, additional options that are frequently added to this list, (to include northern pike, sheefish, arctic char, lake trout, all five species of pacific salmon, and halibut) there are a few notable factors that consistently bring me back to this familiar and determinative fork in the road.

As you may have picked up on by now, the mountains of the Alaska Range play a pivotal role in my existence. While I've already addressed their importance as an impediment to both pacific moisture and wintertime sun, the formidable chain serves as a barrier of far greater pertinence to my life as a fisherman: It marks the northernmost boundary of Alaska's rainbow trout distribution. Save for the lower tributaries of the Kuskokwim and the mind-blowingly rich drainages of Bristol Bay far to the southwest, (travel to either of which would require a significant allotment of time and hefty expenditure in bush air-travel) a quest for trout in flowing streams will necessitate southbound travel down the George Parks Highway. ("Highway Number 3" in D.O.T. parlance, though most Alaskans would be hard-pressed to correctly identify any our major highways by number...)

Heading down the Parks to skirt the eastern flanks of Denali and continuing southward, I'll normally bypass the clearwater tributaries of the Chulitna for all but the briefest of windows in late August, when egg-seeking rainbows shadow the progression of spawning silvers and chums before immediately backing-down into their silty, unfishable home drainages. I may head to a few key spots that I like to fish in the middle-Susitna's clearwater tributaries during the height of the July king spawn, tracking the presence of some broad and exceptionally dark-colored 'bows that I consistently find in the upper reaches of a particularly favorite creek there.

However, If I'm indeed headed south in search of trout, another destination is far more probable. If I have rainbows on the brain, I'll likely be headed all the way down to the rivers and streams of the Kenai Peninsula. A drive of merely five to six-hundred miles, (dependent upon my most southerly target...) the journey is roughly equivalent to a quick trip from New York City to Raleigh, or a last-minute jaunt from Great Falls, Montana to Salt Lake City. In Alaska, our distances tend to be defined more in terms of hours travelled rather than in miles. Luckily, I have the time to spare.

While I do love to catch rainbows, most are a LONG way from my home. I'm therefore quite fortunate to have a solid alternative in much closer proximity, saving dozens of hours of prospective travel time every summer. The silvery-blue arctic grayling, perhaps best known for its oversized, sail-like dorsal fin, is my target of preference in the Interior. The answer to any fly-fisherman's most fervent prayers, the grayling perhaps best exemplifies all of the finest attributes sought in a gamefish. Requiring cold and pristine waters, grayling have remained plentiful here, while all but disappearing from most of their prior range in the northern and western portions of the Lower 48.

Voracious in their appetites and mercilessly predatory, the local grayling will serve me with a steady and sustained dose of fly-fishing over the course of the summer. Perhaps more importantly, they'll provide me with a strong dry-fly inoculation, with continuous follow-up boosters as necessary, to balance the preponderance of streamer and egg-pattern fishing I'll do to the south. While nymph fishing can be highly productive, especially in the caddis-rich environs of my favorite home water, I'll rarely have the discipline to stick with it for long. My addiction to surface takes is simply too strong, and in a rather gracious display of symbiosis, the local grayling's topside gluttony will happily satisfy my own insatiable cravings.

I have several favorite grayling spots located within close proximity to town, (i.e., within an hour's drive…) and many others within a reasonable, half-day distance. My closest friends know which creek I'll be found on during periods of extreme heat and ultra-low water, as they know what defines my ideal day. I've also recently discovered a couple of "new," highly productive upland creeks that I'd never bothered to fish before; these will thankfully provide me with some additional alternatives for escape when extended rains swell the streams of our lower valleys.

Now that I no longer have to worry about showing up for a regular job, I invariably don't bother to plan my calendar to the extent that I used to. However, I can't be too careless with this trait during the summer. There are several annual, required pilgrimages necessary for insertion amongst my normal streamside ventures, should I wish to keep peace in our family. Gwen & I will need to head down the Richardson Highway (Alaska Highway #2, changing to #4 after Delta Junction) in late June or July, taking advantage of the Copper River dipnet fishery to secure our winter's supply of fresh sockeye salmon. We'll head even further down the Rich to the stunningly beautiful town of Valdez on at least one occasion to fish the ocean waters of Prince William Sound, as I have yet to successfully catch a halibut in any of our Interior lakes, much less pull a pot of fresh shrimp. A camping trip to Homer at the southern tip of the Kenai Peninsula will nearly always be on the list, and my primary moose hunt has been shifted back to a ridiculously early date in August. (Thanks to the shooter that I commonly split the moose with, and his residential status within a federal subsistence management zone near Paxson.)

As summer moves toward its inevitable close, Gwen will push for at least one trip to the Tanana Valley State Fair, passionately professing the need to secure our annual photo button. I'll protest, but will likely be more willing if a decent band has been booked. (One advantage of our advancing years: Most of the bands of our youth are now considered has-beens, with many touring the summer fair circuits at rock-bottom, bookable prices.)

Overall, it'll be an exciting, hectic, and exhaustingly pleasing summer to be sure, where the more humdrum tasks of everyday life will predicably fill the remainder of any available spaces. Temptations for travel to the Lower 48 for specific events may occasionally arise, but will rarely be acted upon. To leave Alaska in the summertime for anywhere – or ANYTHING – is nearly unheard of, and may present cause for a clinical diagnosis. For now, the flowing waters of my beloved state will provide for yet another wondrous season of exploration, further filling the banks of my memory to a delightful level of overflow.

So many rivers, so little time...

FALL

Truth be told, it's somewhat difficult for me to even write this final, seasonal chapter. Autumn represents the most bittersweet of all transitions to be found in Alaska, echoing what I've come to recognize as a pattern of repeating, pronounced duality that defines my life in the Far North. The sudden appearance of shimmering yellows in the forests, combined with the astonishing transformation of upland hillsides into their fiery tapestries of crimson and gold, provides the most visceral and stunningly visual reminders that heaven is indeed a place upon this earth- and we are living in it. Fall is truly a wondrous time, yet its final, waning hours can be incredibly difficult to face.

As temperatures begin to drop, the nightly formation of crystalline ice along the edges of local waters immediately invokes a sudden, fight-or-flight response for those who live here. As the ice becomes more persistent, tentatively expanding its reach outward to the river's mid-channels, we come to grips with the inevitable realization that winter is but a few weeks away. Heavy frosts, hitting the low-lying basins first, will ambush those gardeners who tend toward procrastination, and those who don't have garages will scramble to find the windshield ice-scrapers that they'd casually tossed aside in the spring. The transition invokes both a profound love for the richness of the season, and a heartbreaking realization that our times of flowing waters are coming to their inevitable close.

Like so many other influences that have shaped my life, my intense love for fall as the most favorite of seasons was ingrained in the experiences of my youth. Growing up in the mountains of Colorado, fall was most closely associated with our family's annual deer-hunting and fishing trips. Traveling up to three hours to reach my father's favorite haunts in the southwestern part of the state, (the distance of which comprised an epic journey at that point in my young life) the excitement and wonder of those experiences were without equal when compared to the other activities of my childhood. Occurring within settings of cold, frosty mornings, brilliant blue skies, and the ever-changing palette of Colorado aspen, my distinct autumnal orientation towards the appreciation of life's vibrancy was born. For me, no other season comes close.

As is the case with spring in Alaska, fall can barely be quantified as a true season, particularly if one finds themselves north of the Alaska Range. Autumn's duration can be exceedingly brief – sometimes heartbreakingly so – dependent upon the weather in any given year. In general, for those of us living in the Interior, the month of September will usually qualify as autumn in its entirety. In the rarest of years, a protracted "Indian summer" will provide an extended period of sunny skies and warming daytime temperatures through the early part of October, bestowing an additional window of late season dry-fly activity that I'll shamelessly soak myself in. In other years, the snow that's received by mid-September will be here to stay for the duration of winter.

Autumn marks a time of extraordinary abundance, with residents invariably following the example of local Chickadees and squirrels as they scramble to locate and store their reserves for the winter. Close to home, potatoes will be ready for digging, and the crops of summer gardens will finally be ready for harvest. Cabbage, zucchini, broccoli, and spinach will all provide a tantalizing bounty- much to the delight of our local moose population, who'll blaze their paths of calamitous and pilfering destruction throughout the city and its outlying neighborhoods.

Most of the accomplished gardeners here are exceptionally generous, willing to share a portion of their bounty with those having less-than-green thumbs. This is frequently done in barter for salmon or game meat, as the skillsets required to encompass all methods of full-blown subsistence don't often overlap. While those providing fresh vegetables are greatly appreciated, the repeated, anonymous deposit of orphaned zucchini upon ambivalent doorsteps should perhaps prompt a clue towards restraint in one's planting. One final note: If you've grown a bumper crop of Brussels Sprouts and are feeling generous, you can do me a solid favor by leaving them for the moose.

Venturing afield, the lure of wild berries presents yet another opportunity for intense, preparatory hoarding. While raspberries, salmonberries, and currants are plentiful to the south, it's the pungent smell of fall's ripening cranberries (both highbush and lowbush) that provides the overriding, olfactory backdrop for Interior's autumn harvest. Slightly nauseating in its first fecal impressions, its peculiar odor somehow becomes increasingly satisfying as one wanders our birch-covered hills. One must set aside this particularly odiferous distraction, however, as another target of considerably higher prominence awaits in abundance.

In Interior Alaska, the blueberry is king. Its tiny, green, paddle-shaped leaves will have often gone unnoticed throughout the summer, gathering sunshine and rainwater in a bashful and unobtrusive manner. However, as the air of early September rapidly cools, the leaves will now sport a bold shade of vermillion, carpeting the landscapes of both low-lying bogs and brush-laden uplands in a blaze of autumnal fire. Tendrils and tangles of intertwined branches, having previously reached skyward with a cargo of green, un-ripened berries, will now droop sluggishly downward under the strain of their hanging, indigo burden.

Presenting yet another task in my list of mandatory, seasonal requirements, there'll be a spousal expectation for at least a couple of forays into our area hills, securing a sufficient quantity of blueberries for the coming year. Cleaned of excess leaves and twigs and spread in a single layer upon cookie sheets, the berries will be brushed with a very thin layer of sugar (to prevent sticking and clumping together) and frozen. This accumulated bounty of blue nuggets will then be stored in quart-sized freezer jars, ready for consumption throughout the winter.

I don't protest these berry-picking ventures for a couple of reasons: First, I recognize that the heavily laden bushes present a high level of attraction to our area's black and grizzly bears. While I have absolutely no desire to hunt these particular beasts in deference to their status as apex predators, I have no qualms in providing the requisite armed overwatch for Gwen, as her intense and directed focus will likely remain a few inches off the ground. Secondly, I've become increasingly fond of smoothies as a quick and convenient breakfast, with a concoction including blueberries, rolled oats, and peanut butter comprising my personal favorite. While I suppose store-bought blueberries could serve in a pinch, their deceptively large, water-swollen content doesn't hold a candle to the concentrated goodness of our local bounty.

While I've thus far emphasized vegetative concerns, don't get the wrong idea; I'm merely working my way up the food chain. One does not find a high number of vegetarians in Alaska, and the hunting seasons of fall underscores such a sampling. Moose and caribou are the most frequently sought-after game animals in the Interior, with a good-sized moose providing more than a freezer-full of meat for the winter. There are wild bison to be had in a few specific regions, though the Department of Fish and Game's raffle-style drawing permits required for such hunts have thus far eluded me. While a few friends of mine are diehard Dall sheep hunters, I'm convinced that the procurement of sheep flesh – in consideration of its overall caloric value – represents a net loss in total energy when tallying the significant expenditure required for a successful harvest. While I've packed-out more than my share of moose over the years, I haven't had to climb any 10,000-foot mountains to do so.

Of all the bounties that signify Alaska fall harvests, however, none is more centrally linked to our culture than that of our seasonal runs of salmon. Cohos (silver salmon) and chums (dog salmon) are generally the latest fall spawners, with chinooks, (kings) sockeyes (reds) and humpies (pinks) generally wrapping things up a bit earlier. All five of these species of Pacific salmon will die after returning to spawn in their native drainages, with their decaying flesh providing an ongoing source of protein and nutrients to enrich their respective home watersheds.

Following the courses of its largest of rivers, the Interior has historically hosted large runs of king and chum salmon, (with some other species to a lesser degree) returning to spawn in our region after making their highly circuitous journey from the Bering Sea. It can be somewhat surprising to see these fish show up so far inland, as their route must circumvent the formidable barrier of the Alaska Range as it follows an extended, clockwise arc around the mountain's western and northern boundaries. The placement of large fishwheels – traditionally constructed on a floating platform of logs and utilizing the river's current to rotate two opposing, trough-shaped baskets – can be seen continuously scooping fish along the banks of our region's silt-laden channels. The fishwheels have been utilized by subsistence users for decades, and can be found operating along the banks of the Kuskokwim, Yukon, and Tanana.

There are a few places where one can sport-fish for salmon in the Interior, as the fish depart from the confines of their large, silt-laden highways to spawn in the clearwater tributaries of their birth. Kings can be targeted in the lower Chena as it flows through downtown Fairbanks to meet with the Tanana, and late-season silvers can be found further south on the Delta Clearwater. While such opportunities exist to fish for salmon nearby, I've never had the heart to pursue them. Any salmon that can be glimpsed in the waters surrounding Fairbanks has already made an upriver journey of over 800 miles just to reach this point, transiting the Yukon, Tanana, and Chena Rivers respectively. Having eluded commercial fishermen on the open ocean, then dodging seals and beluga whales as they enter the rivers, they must finally avoid fishwheels, subsistence nets, bears, eagles, and anglers as they approach the terminus of their perilous journey. Banking all of this effort in the hopes of having sex just once before death, I figure I should cut them a break and leave them alone.

South of the Alaska Range, immense, black clouds of swirling humpies clog the mouths of oceanside streams as they stage for much shorter spawning runs. The largest of Alaska's king salmon push forward into the Kenai, with slightly smaller genetic variants of the same species heading up numerous other drainages. Impossibly large schools of sockeye flood the drainages of Prince William Sound, the Southcentral Peninsula, and Bristol Bay, providing a bounty of unbelievable proportion. Chums and silvers seem to fill in any available gaps, as the state's waters come unbelievably alive.

Having spent decades in Alaska, I've developed a somewhat strange orientation when it comes to salmon. Perhaps because they're destined to spawn and then die, I tend to view them primarily as a food-source to harvest when fresh, rather than as a sporting, catch-and-release resource. It's always a bit perplexing for me to see the late season, out-of-state angler proudly holding up a grisly, spawned-out sockeye as their "trophy" for a photo, perhaps ignorant of the fact that the garishly scarlet, humpbacked monstrosity cradled within their conquering grip is far past its prime, and serving out its final, desperate days before death.

Additionally, for any road-based, accessible stream found in Southcentral Alaska, the presence of salmon usually means people... LOTS and LOTS of people. I'll endeavor in subsequent chapters to try and best explain my orientation towards stream fishing and the peaceful, contemplative outlets that it provides. However, you'll be hard-pressed to find any section where I extoll the merits of having multiple pixie-spoons cast across one's line, or the wonder in witnessing the majesty and grandeur of a drunken midnight domestic as Joe-Bobb tries to extract a weighted Russian River fly from the brow of his girlfriend. (The predictable consequence of which, incidentally, I posit to be the *true* origin of the word "sockeye...") If people are crowding a stream in pursuit of salmon, it's highly unlikely that I'll be found amongst them.

Why, then, am I spending so much time addressing our state's Pacific spawners? The answer is inestimably simple and can be conveyed in a single word: TROUT. For me, the seasonal arrival of salmon in our Southcentral and Southwestern streams doesn't normally carry itself as a matter of primary concern. Rather, it serves as a cue for the development of a secondary condition; one of infinitely greater import, as reflected in the slight expansion of my earlier declaration: TROUT EAT SALMON EGGS.

Much of the referenced migratory activity associated with our various species of salmon takes place during mid-summer. However, the most intense and notable egg-drops don't occur until fall, when the salmon finally reach the uppermost portions of their drainages to culminate their spawning activity. Drawn like moths to a flame, the prospect of millions of fresh, protein-rich eggs being deposited over the course of a stream's gravel spawning redds presents a temptation that trout simply can't resist. Following the salmon upriver, sometimes for miles and often into drainages that are relatively barren and devoid of fish throughout the rest of the year, the trout will patiently bide their time, awaiting the autumnal buffet that's about to be set.

As a consequence, I'll let the combat fishermen duke it out on the lower portions of a stream as they target the latest wave of fresh, incoming salmon. I'm far happier when stealthily creeping to a stream's upper reaches, searching for the telltale presence of the comparatively dark and wavering, ghost-like shadows that hang just below the pods of scarlet and green spawners. Fishing small egg patterns or beads, ever adjusting the diameters and colors to best mimic the predominant eggs in the water, fall trout fishing in Alaska will fill me with the experiences and memories necessary to last through the coming winter. After happily catching and releasing fish to a point of satisfaction, I'll invariably head back downstream. While I'll still try to avoid the salmon crowd to the greatest extent possible, I'll occasionally meet one of their members on the trail, who'll likely want to commiserate after seeing my salmon-free, empty-handed status.

"Couldn't manage to catch any, huh? You know, they're pretty thick down below…"

"Yeah…" I'll reply in feigned frustration, keeping my long-practiced poker face, "I guess it was just one of those days…"

Returning to my home in Fairbanks after the last-fling trout trip of late autumn, (which, by definition, will have entailed a journey of several hundred miles) I'll casually toss my gear to the far-flung corners of my garage and office, now standing in abject, slovenly display as a tribute to an entire season's worth of rushed departures, sleep-deprived returns, and the inevitable, cumulative entropy that results. I'll have plenty of time to get things back in order over the coming months; I suppose I could dive in tomorrow and start straightening things up right away, but to do so would require admitting to myself that that the fall season has finally come to an end. I don't think I can handle doing that just yet.

Fostering a love of learning about global cultures, **Valerie Innella Maiers** teaches art history and museum studies at Casper College in central Wyoming. She has taught field studies courses such as Saints, Sovereigns, and Scholars: Scotland and Wales; Moorish Art and Design: Portugal and Morocco; Renaissance Dubrovnik; and Rome: Michelangelo and Galileo. Recent publications include the co-authored, "Creative Collaborations: Humanities Programming in a Natural History Museum" in the Journal of Natural Science Collections (2022) and "Humanistic Constructs: Creating Agency in a Natural History Museum" in Collections: A Journal for Museum and Archives Professionals (2021). Innella Maiers was awarded academic study of art in Jerusalem in 2023 and Scotland in 2022 through the University of Wyoming. She especially enjoys hiking new trails with her family in Wyoming and wherever adventure takes them.

Wyoming Four Ways

In the Rockies, the late spring morning sun bestows a virile white light that penetrates the curtains, permeates the bedroom, and the mind awakens acknowledging the bright promise of warmth under eggshell blue skies. Outside, violets raise their faces, emboldened on thin green necks. Then clouds roll over the mountain and unexpected heavy white slush encases the little flowers in glacier blue snow caves. Living where seasons confront with potency, our connection to nature is immediate. In the vast openness of the prairie, the air holds an invitation for exploration of forest royd and mountain gorge. The expanse also allows room for my dreams of dotted red lines inked on maps from Wyoming to diverse destinations. Perhaps this wanderlust stems from great grandparents who crossed the Atlantic to seeking a new home. Maybe even earlier ancestors were part of camel caravans stopping at Hans along the Silk Road or sailors who loaded spices such as cinnamon, cloves, and pepper on their caravels with the stars and sun as gliding lights. Seeking to experience unknown environments usually takes me sailing through the sky toward distant lands each early spring. Walking in new ways of seeing the world is the polka dot pattern on my monochrome. Each venture invigorates and months are spent saving, charting a course, prepacking, packing and finally, ascension. From sipping Turkish coffee while sketching Hagia Sophia to walking the cobblestone streets of Dubrovnik while hearing a local share Croatian political history, or holding palms in Budapest walking solemnly into a church with the faithful a week before Easter, the exotic is stitched onto my psyche. I fall in love with each site that envelopes my reverie and run my fingers over the smooth threads of memory. The slight nervous itch of not having control becomes a pop of pleasure when an itinerary works as planned. I was about to lift off to Amsterdam the day travel aboard was banned as the COVID-19 virus spread its shadow across the globe. Initially, in denial of the magnitude of the situation, I thought this would be a minor setback, a slight reschedule. Then, I became angry. No long walks along canals to windmills. No Rembrandt to feed the soul, the piercing light illuminating such emotional, personal content. No tulips, strolling the gardens, accepting the heady scents of new life. The pandemic stymied map plotting, as daily challenges of social distancing became paramount. Stress, stress, not sleeping, work, work, will we still work tomorrow? Worry about family, worry about others, worry about economy and depression. The handmade travel journals of study stock lovingly bound and adorned with notes to be used on adventures, became palimpsests for daily drawings of my tea cup, oatmeal bowl, or an apple on the table. Day after day, watercolor pencil and brush distracted from the ache for that launch into the sky, where from flying altitude, the Wyoming landscape appears as brown splotches with salt licks, beige and black cuts crawling with tumbleweed. Prickly pine needles on hiking trails and open endless terrain cracked dry; roads leading to foreign vistas. If I was up there, I would lean my head against the airplane window and view the quilt squares below, of the peacock feather emerald colored crops, rich chocolate brown mud circles awaiting planting, and blue streams of the agricultural landscape; a soft, warm earth blanket. Instead, I paint a crystal glass of opaque orange juice, which bitterly conceals notes on the orange as icon in 16th century painting and worry.

The last flight taken was on "repeat" in my mind. Like a worn cassette tape from my youth playing my favorite song over and over, I mused on the experience from air to land. Moving through time is a magic act but has casualties. Swollen legs, back ache, headache, and bloated body. The metabolism slows and less oxygen is taken; ascending into the clouds, I become a fog of myself. Sunlight glints on the wing of the jet and time is bent. Gaining precious minutes, lifting off from Wyoming usually showcases the barest traces of snow white on brown jagged peaks. I read my travel journals prepped and peppered with thoughts of meditation. From an antique book found on my shelf, *The Majesty of Calmness*, I repeat, "As waves lap onto golden sands, the breeze may ruffle the palm fronds but not uproot the tree. This is valuable life ebbing around each of us". I must not let the click, thump of tray tables unlatching and re-latching and squeak of drink carts rolling invade my serenity. Too hot, then too cold, then cramped and "hangry". Breathe, express profound gratitude. Look at the green veins in amber fields; horizontal clouds reflected in inky pools. I know when I land that seeing history illuminated in a unique visual vocabulary will be as exciting as any other adrenaline rush. From the slapping prairie wind to snatches of black cab traffic, the sidewalk chatter of uniformed children on the way to school, antique booksellers tucked in narrow alleys passed, while wandering a maze of medieval streets, landing in London was a contrast to the senses. On the silver thread of the Thames, humid, mudlarks trail treasure from the silt and bridges rise to span urban honeycombs. The sky was winter gray, clouds moody and a chill swept across the cobblestones at historic sites. Brown, black, and red threads were added to my soul, digesting the space around me from the wet leaves on the street to the pattern of the fencing around the urban garden square with row houses as sentries to this green oasis, their brick colored doors watching all who stroll past. Consumption of the wet air, city exhaust, and visceral treasures.

 Pondering the pandemic months later, I stood in a museum in front of the avian installations. Gazing at the majestically plumed quetzal, visions of wet tropical greens accented with neon yellow flowers, festooned with hanging bananas materialized, and the longing for further adventures intensified. Life had become hermetically sealed, no airborne pollutants could penetrate. I, too, perched on a ledge, others silent around me, frozen. Like the artificial museum environment, no sign of kinetic movement, not even one little ant on the prairie diorama broke the stillness. This inertia created an addict driven to check airline prices to destinations that could not be visited, spinning Google flights combinations like a Monaco roulette wheel. I internally promised that if I was allowed to fly, I would not complain about sore legs or jet lag. Attempting to quell the desire, which was more intense due to the simple ban on travel, time was spent sketching landscapes from postcards, images from a Venetian webcam of the Rialto Bridge, and exotic flowers such as the pink-petaled cranesbill of Madeira. The longing to wander plagued the spirit through the long months of spring snow dump as we sat still. As the sun's strength fostered iris and hops to leap from the mulch, and the daily drawings turned toward floral motifs in the garden, a flagging spirit resolved to find the "unseen" paths. To cultivate a perceptive eye for the bounty that still lay before me, charged with the energy of wild roses waving their hips in the wind, the rustle of aspen leaves as elk moved, the long legs of the brook hopscotching. My paradise would be found here; not "there". Yet, traces of the foreign were always evident; reminders of adventures past embellished the present. Patiently acknowledging and consciously absorbing the immediate world, this praxis would cease the freeze.

The Pleasures of France in Wyoming

Searing silent heat broken only by the weary hum of a small garden fountain motor elicited notions of Mediterranean landscapes. Staring at the shadow patterns cast under a patio chair from the glowing orb above, a plan was hatched to open the garden gate and explore beyond the lawn and perennial beds. In this "dreaming phase", as artist Kathleen Wille calls the logistical and thoughtful planning of an adventure, images of France crept into mind. Initially, these visions included the tall mountain peaks of the alpine region bordering Switzerland, then expanded to the vineyards of Provence leading to the sea. This first adventure would celebrate the bounty of Wyoming with an infusion of French artistry in a day trip to the southeastern part of the state.

Safety and gratitude were foremost thoughts, as picnic basket, watercolors and pencils, sketchbooks, and sunscreen were packed into the car. Lucky to be healthy, the goal was to approach any free moment with detailed consideration of the space around me. Whether stopping mid-walk to glean the various materials birds use build their nests to looking for patterns of light and shadow while sitting on the back step, this is an attempt to cultivate an appreciation for any space inhabited. Vincent van Gogh, the 19th century Dutch painter who famously painted the French landscape in Post-Impressionistic explosions of color contrasts and aesthetically pleasing lines, believed that the birds were artists, too, in the building of their nests. The first stop on our itinerary was Fort Laramie National Historic Site, where the historical buildings fostered a home for the bulbous swallows' nests in the gables of the rooflines. What a delight to see the little birds constantly swopping to and from their dwellings, standing in a landscape also viewed by multiple tribes, pioneers, soldiers, trappers, and those seeking their fortunate situation. Reflecting upon the convergence of all of these cultures, and their triumphs and losses, made the walk poignant. Continuing into the country, errant thistle and sage line roads filled with green rows. Salubrious warmth envelopes this southeastern corner of Wyoming where the white horizon washes to the blue, patterned with horizontal clouds stretched thin to cotton candy wisps crowning the open vista. At Table Top Mountain Winery, found by following two unassuming white signposts, the building was situated in an expanse of green with hay bales stacked on distant fields. Here, birds sang as they jumped from rows of vines with bundles of grapes still green. The light flooded the fields, reminiscent of van Gogh's paintings where purple shadows on the bare French earth provided stark contrast to the amber color compliment of the wheat sheaves. The glorious landscape, drenched in yellow glow, provided a picturesque backdrop evocative of visions of a French country garden where bees hover and land on lavender and giant sunflowers. Inspired by this musing, the picnic included homemade quiches, olive oil brownies, mint sun tea, grapes and cherries, and cheeses. The earth has given and I needed to stop running in my head and receive.

An Alpine Dream with Literary Notes

As the temperatures climbed, I realized that I live out an alpine cabin dream every summer. Over ten degrees cooler than the city, and painted with creamy clusters of yarrow, red paintbrush, pink wild roses, silvery sagebrush, and the accent of white bark on aspens, Green Mountain is a welcome retreat from the plains. The buzz of hummingbirds compliments a gentle splash of the brook trout stream over rocks. The scent of pine is a constant on hikes. The late sunglow over the adjacent ridge to the cabin provides the gift of late reading light. One can never have too many dreams or books. One of the pleasures of this locale is the proximity to Mad Dog and The Pilgrim Booksellers. Just past Jeffrey City (population 29) in Sweetwater Station (population of at least 2), a painted sign states "old books and fresh eggs". Any bibliophile can spend hours amidst the treasure stacks sprawling luxuriously over two floors. I have scored travel literature to take me around the world from Marrakech to the Balkans. There are even old Baedeker's guides in the mix. Classics, mystery, religion, history, fiction and nonfiction fill a magical space where seating in secluded nooks invites prolonged browsing. The shelves, the stacks on the floors, and even the back steps offer gems from rare or signed books and first editions to bestseller paperbacks. Children's classics were also in my stack of purchases this past summer, including *Heidi*, the beloved tale of a girl in the Alps.

Switzerland was on my mind; after hiking to high clearings filled with wild horses, deer, and antelope, I indulged in raclette. This traditional Alpine cheese was delightful over boiled potatoes and crusty bread. Before melting, I added salt, pepper, lemon thyme, garlic, and olive oil. This fondue experience was satisfyingly capped with dark chocolate and more reading, feet propped up and wrapped in a blanket to ward off chill in the evening air. In *Slow Train to Switzerland*, Diccon Bewes (2014) followed in the footsteps of the first travelers with Thomas Cook to "the continent" in the 1860's. The story of his journey also included facts about the package tour of this time such as "what to bring". Gentlemen, can you image packing to hike over glaciers and ride mules over Alpine mountain passes, for 14 days, with the following: "a small bag containing one clean shirt, pocket handkerchiefs, two clean collars, one pair of socks, toothbrush, writing materials, pocket comb, with umbrella and greatcoat"?! With food cooler, totes of clothes, toys, and snacks, we could have spent years on that vacation package.

At the picnic table, my young son built "stone people" from found rock tokens. Pinecone hats finished the bodies of his figures, which would also don bark clothing and hold meadow lupines at their stone arms. He paused and looked at this world, taking time to absorb the serenity. Wisps of wild grass gave way to a lone deer on a path. Both deer and boy observed each other silently. The summer stillness allowed a meditative reflection on the spring past. Mosquitos began to lurk from the cooler shadows and it was time for sleep; the deep travel in the land of nod that mountain air stimulates. Drifting to sleep, I meditate on gratitude and the opportunity provided by the generous landscape to be present in this moment.

Paradise on the Prairie

A notion of pleasure or heavenly realm may be called "paradise", a word that evolved from the walled gardens of ancient Persia. In religious theology, the concept of paradise also includes a garden with blooms infused with symbolic meaning. A garden in a Christian medieval monastery could have four quadrants representing the four Evangelists. The four rivers of an Islamic idyllic enclosure included milk, honey, water, and wine. This same concept was experienced in late summer, just west of Casper. Sheltered by the mountain to the south, the foothills are home to bees buzzing around wild carrot flowers, a stream running through a thicket oasis, and cows on a hill, a black accent to this vibrant tapestry of life. Vibrant red berries cling to green shrub branches, a William Morris print in situ. The musky scent of game is usually evident before the flash of antelope bolting from brush. While visiting Burlington House, an arts and crafts abode on the prairie, a 3 mile trail, worn into the land by cyclists, was discovered. Plank bridges provided safe passage over the water and led to an almost perfect triangle cone hill, which was used as a marker of hiking progress. The undulating landscape offered a variety of textures from soft minty grass patches to spiky thistle that poke at bare legs. Colors explode: the flashes of black, white, and blue as a parliament of magpies land in a tree with soft grey bark. When the sun sets, the lights of the town shimmer in the distance. Charm and silence fall over this land and the silvery soft lambs ear, blooming with purple blossoms, becomes a backdrop for the hummingbirds' flight path. The small green cactus disappeared into the shadows next to tall grasses where grasshoppers perch on thin blades. A picnic for this paradise included my own garden yield: carrots, red lettuce, onion, and tomatoes. This year, volunteer sunflowers gave shade to these edibles along with an array of herbs with both culinary and sensory benefits. Rosemary for bread, sage for tea to sooth in winter. The potatoes have flowered delicate pink blossoms that pop from the jungle of greens. Under the umbrella of giant radish leaves, tarragon and thyme flourished. While dining at Burlington, we moved to seating on different porches and nooks in the house. Small blooming wildflowers at the edge of the garden path, the vast expanse of land on the other side of Garden Creek's west ridge, each vantage point was a prompt for new observations and excitement as deer were spotted springing over the hill or Rufous zipped immediately over our heads. This was the embodiment of paradise, a moveable feast indeed.

Charming Britain in Big Horn

Even in late Wyoming summer, when the color palette of Wyoming shifts to corn husk hue, the tree-lined sides of this landscape bowl were flush with green. As we stomped divets at the Polo match between chukkahs, our picnic hamper laying on our floral picnic blanket, our eyes drank in the verdant landscape of Big Horn. Immaculately groomed grass lay welcome to skilled riders and amazingly beautiful horses with glistening manes. The sound of hooves galloping down the field broke the otherwise stillness under the intense sun. Salmon with capes, onions and greens, fruit, croissants with jam and infused butter enjoyed as the bright light sparkling on distant fields irrigated to their fullest potential. This was an adventure reminiscent of British countryside, where distant fields supported fuzzy white sheep. The pine forests of Story were also a part of this idyllic venture with their deep cool recesses supporting streams washing over moss-covered stones with bits of wild flowers at the banks. Our eyes expected Mr. Tod, the fox, to stroll from the undergrowth. At the Fish Hatchery, in the shade of tall trees, trout jump from their pond for pellet food prompting giggles from children. Resting on benches outside the bunkhouse of the TA Ranch, which features prominently in the Johnson County Cattle War, a further of appreciation of area history and the industrious and hardworking settlers that came to Wyoming washed over me.

These four ventures made visible what had disappeared in this landscape. A heightened sense of immediate surroundings created room for tangible surface qualities. I accepted this view. From this angle, the space was larger, continuous, open again to possibility. Highlights and shadows emerged on each petal of the burgundy chrysanthemum head; sage became gradations of silver and green. Grounded, the land is golden thread, a continuous arc where every step, near and afar, is in paradise.

Amie Adams earned an MFA in Creative Writing in Washington State, and her essays have been published in *Midwest Review, Relief, The Tiny Seed,* and *Pilgrimage,* among others. She was raised on the shore of an Iowa lake and is presently a walking tributary of the South Skunk River. Visit her website www.amieadams.space to read more of her work.

In Which Spring Makes An Appearance Once Again

A long time ago, it's unlikely that anyone knows precisely when, someone called a coot a mud hen for the first time. Looking back, this judgment was a sound one; for the American coot bobs its head like a hen. The coots were unfazed by this renaming, they had already chosen to be bog birds, waterfowl; rather they wore their name proudly, they became the first hens to paddle through the water, the first to migrate to Panama, the first to build fanciful floating nests in the marshlands. If a different birdwatcher from yesteryear had chosen to call them muskrats or swamp cats, the American coots would have become feathered muskrats or caterwauling swimming felines.

The coots' cool indifference to their nickname resulted in an unexpected outcome: the name's desirability. It became sought after. The coot, once ridiculed for its black-feathered breast became a symbol of strength and power. The coot responded with pride toward its new name. This chicken-of-the-swamp is joke of no casual observer, pauper in no mudhole. The marsh, where the mud hen resides, became its glory, because it is a place known for its vitality. A bird with less self-esteem would sink into self-pity when compared to a dirty chicken; a bird with the coot's self-esteem would chose to embrace its moniker.

Toledo, Ohio's minor league baseball team, the one that plays its games at Fifth Third Field, inspired by the coot, also chose to embrace its humble position. Many seasons of playing ball games in Bay View Park, amidst the ruckus of flapping wings and squawking alongside those mud hens inhabiting the nearby swamp, triggered an epiphany; the players saw the source of their botheration with new eyes, a mascot in the making. When the Toledo Mud Hens joined the American Association in 1902 their name reflected their humble standing, for they usually finished near the bottom of the league.

Like the baseball-playing Mud Hens, American coots have not acquired a large fan base; they paddle in their ponds like c-list actors. Most everyone recognizes their faces, but no one really remembers their names. After several springtimes, however, the American coot becomes memorable enough; and a young passerby on a walk with her father might stop by the lakeshore, look at the clucking mass of black-robed bodies, and ask her father, what are those birds called?

He will not be able to recall their true name, like we so often do with actors, so he will tell her the name he does recall. Even the most obvious creatures that signal the coming of spring cannot always be properly known. An American coot called a mud hen will go about its business as usual, like an intern who responds to anything, and do what a mud hen does; eating bright green algae, ending her long migration from the south and coming home to a reed-ringed lake, open marsh, or lazy river—any freshwater; swimming synchronously with other members of her raft and practicing her take-off dynamics in the open water, catching the red eye of a handsome male coot, responding to his initiation of the courtship ritual, touching her white bill to his with affection, forming a pair bond that will last for their lifetimes, forsaking all others to only perform this coot kiss with her partner, seeking a territory together to build a floating nest, constructing the nest-raft with nearby reeds neatly plucked with her bill, in order to keep it afloat as the heavy weight of eggs descends upon it in the darkness, when the moon is high and casts silvery shadows and glints off the coot's eye.

With their arrival from warmer climes, mud hens are messengers of springtide, numbering in the thousands and sending up a chorus hopeful enthusiasm. They descend from thermals of warm air, settling on slow-warming lakes, stirring up the chilly water with their busy feet, mixing and mingling with pelicans who may be passing through. How empty and quiet would the waters of northern lakes and ponds be without the mud hens to fill them!

Who would keep the fish company as the ice roof of winter is rolled back from their watery home but overbearing geese.

While mud hens summon the powers of grass greening and tree leafing, they alone are not enough to hold back an unwelcome May blizzard. The calendar might swing back toward winter so haphazardly that snow blankets a nesting mud hen, coating it in white, not unlike its snowy distant cousin by marriage—not blood—the common terrestrial hen. While white is an acceptable color for a chicken pecking about in an open field, for a coot and a charcoal brick and a magician's hat it is not. When a mud hen is surrounded by snow the white must frighten her, making her vulnerable, because her red-on-black face become visible to the calculating eyes of eagles. After an unexpected snowfall, the coot must take shelter in whatever hideaway is available to nestle into with her mate and sleep off the bad dream of winter and pray for the restoration of May. But a northern winter is a stubborn thing, and not even a thousand mud hens can conjure the return of tree-budding, flower-unfolding, sun-shining, bee-buzzing weather before its time.

***

One day, when mayfly nymphs molt, restless from their water-life, they sprout wings and fly, out into the air with its dandelion-brightness. They fledge like young birds. If you were on a walk by the lake watching pairs of mud hens swimming to-and-fro among the reeds and dining on their green algae, would you notice these newly flighted insects? Undoubtedly your pleasant stroll would be cut short, as you run away from the shore swatting the air until you escape the noxious cloud of quivering wings.

The nymphs pass from infancy to a stage called subimago, a teenage winged version of themselves. In some species, the subimago lasts only a few minutes, ending as quickly as it began. When the subimago turns imago and resplendent in its adulthood, it has until sunset to enjoy its brief life. Then the hourglass runs out; like the cruel timeline of a fairytale curse, the mayfly's life ends when the clock strikes midnight. Without a functioning mouth-part, the adult mayfly can only mate, dancing vigorously in the swarm, destined only to reproduce. Maybe this life feels like an exhausting rave that leaves everyone passed out and drunk on the dance floor. Maybe it feels like the selfless sacrifice of a parent who gives up everything for a child.

This primitive insect marches toward its life's end swiftly, dying as soon as it begins to live, careening toward the end of the day focused only on the whirling of the dance, on the dervish-like ecstasy of swirling in a cloud of its kin—the same cloud that sent you sputtering and choking on the writhing bodies of mayflies as you ran for cover, flailing, swatting, ducking for cover beneath your hands, feet pointed home.

The mayflies carries spring on their wings, like the mud hens; and they also find themselves bound to the celestial influence of the seasons—the push and pull of the light as days lengthen and temperatures rise, and by the marching orders of the calendar as it announces February, March, April, and finally May. You would think after all that time spent in dormancy that the day of flight would never come, that the mayfly would remain submerged in water for good.

Then something prompts the nymphs to interrupt their self-prescribed cycle of eating and waiting. They burst up the water and rocket past the bewildered mud hens, struggling to gain control of their awkward veiny wings, glomming onto one another as they all emerge at once, gathering in dense swarms large enough to be imaged by weather radar, filtering ultraviolet light through their upward and lateral eyes, searching for partners to mate with in the same air the streams uselessly through their empty digestive systems, catching a twirling partner mid-air, grasping one another tightly next to millions of couples dancing the same dance, dropping thousands of eggs per pair onto the surface of the water.

***

In another part of town, a boy plans a display of affection of his own; and once he finalizes the elaborate scheme, everyone one around him begins to sense within him a secret excitement building toward bursting, excitement that plants a seed of suspicion in his girl. The excitement grows like a pea shoot rooting its way up through the soil; it builds like a hot air balloon filling for flight; it lifts her like a nervous bottle rocket built by a ten-year-old boy on its maiden voyage, careening toward outer space.

    Even if spring does not stir the slightest pale pink flicker of delight in your winter-cold heart, does not pierce your melancholy gloom, if it does not fill your nose with anything but hay fever, there is an oceanic change taking place, that will seep into the air and soil around you like so many raindrops, soaking you with possibility, watering you with the secret thrill of a boy in love. And then you are utterly drenched in spring's return, and then you are a seed; and then you are an egg, incubating your own fledging possibility from a small bundle of cells, multiplying within the confines of its wall, fed by the mysterious nourishment of life growing from life, testing out your own beating heart for this first time, circulating oxygen through your ever-increasing cells and the first drafts of your limbs—a curved neck, two feathered wings, long legs, scaly toes—until you tumble out of your egg into a floating raft on a planet bobbing in space that defies all your assumptions that this world is like the one inside your snow globe.

Chris Waltz writes about outdoor adventure and semi-relaxing family vacations. Minor setbacks and humankind's complicated relationship with the planet are common themes. He grew up in a wooded subdivision in the suburbs of Cleveland and now lives with his family in Missoula, MT. His work has been published in Nowhere Magazine and Mountainfreak.

Read more at chrisjwaltz.com

A Geologist, a Bear and a Priest Walk into a Bar

So here we sit on weathered logs, our backs to an empty fire ring and an alder thicket where a chickadee flutters among twigs and leaves. In the uncluttered forest before us, sunlight pauses to reflect while lodgepole pines frame segments of a blue lake. Ray says he hopes no one comes by, which makes me laugh.

My friend spreads his hands, palms up, wondering what's so funny.

I sit up straight and shade my eyes, pretending to survey the landscape. We've crossed paths with four other hikers in the last three days. A breeze sways the treetops, a few scales of pine bark fall to the ground and go *tick*.

It's a Tuesday, the day before Independence Day in an empty backcountry campground in the Beartooth Mountains, Montana. A satellite image of the moment might show us just sitting here, but zoom out a few miles and there's a bear heading down the trail in our direction.

Ray says, "So this is *supposed* to feel like this?"

I exhale, shake my head, meaning, *Who knows?*

Ray looks toward the lake and nods his head, a sarcastic gesture since I'm not being helpful. He asks if we've made a big mistake.

"No, my friend. We just have to ride out this first part. But I do wish my heart would stop beating so fast."

"Your heart?" Ray says.

"And now everything I say echoes in my head."

"*What?*"

"There's a little delay between what I say and hearing myself say it," I say and then hear.

"Okay, good. So it's not just me. These are that strong. Wow."

"That appears to be the case."

"We're not getting much done today."

Over the last three days we've covered thirty miles scrambling through the alpine country between Huckleberry Lake and Granite Peak, navigating flowery meadows, boulder fields and remnants of snowpack while tracking lakes tucked below some of the highest peaks in the state. Given the amount of snow still on the ground, we considered ourselves lucky to get as far as we did without ice axes and crampons. Our good fortune was a regular topic of conversation, often pared down to mere syllables: *Wow. Dude. My god.* Blue skies over high granite, water and wildflowers everywhere. We stopped often to rest, gawk, listen. Afternoon thunderstorms let us be. Cumulonimbus clouds crept across thirty-mile views.

We'll be back at it tomorrow, shooting for Froze to Death Mountain on Froze to Death Plateau. In order to be closer to that trailhead, we broke camp at Huckleberry Lake this morning and hiked down here to set up a new camp. Before lunch we took a cold dip in Mystic Lake. We were standing on the wooden bridge over Huckleberry Creek when the pot in the medicinal Rice Crispy treat (RCt) we'd eaten after lunch started to kick in. The creek spilled over rocks and logs, slipped under the bridge and into Mystic.

When we were done watching the creek, we set out on what promised to be an easy hike to the head of the lake, but this is a spacious campground with a lot of trails veering off the main trail and leading to vacant campsites. We soon found ourselves back at our tent by mistake.

With tears of laughter in our eyes, we undertook a second attempt to leave. The sunlight was doing a wonderful job of shining through the treetops. Breezes aloft bobbed pine boughs and wafted beards of lichen. What felt like a separate breeze swirling within my rib cage was only my heart beating out of sync with the easy terrain. When Ray suddenly stopped because he thought he'd heard a voice, we looked at each other, thinking: *Dude*.

Ray asked, "Are you ... Is this ...?"

The friend who'd given me the ganja RCt had warned me, I'd warned Ray and now we knew. This paranoia was something we'd just have to walk off. A couple minutes later Ray asked if I'd remembered the bear spray and we headed back to camp, which consists of a tent pitched fifty yards from a cooking area, a stone fire ring surrounded by logs propped up on rocks, and two dudes who have failed to find their way out of an empty campground.

I grab the pepper spray and sit back down on my log. Ray looks at the forest and laughs. He rests his tanned arms on his knees and looks at me, shaking his head. He says "Jesus, dude."

In twenty-five years of hiking together, when faced with a choice between going too far and exercising prudence, Ray and I have often gone too far, and the older we get the greater the tendency to refuse to act our age. Even on a strange afternoon like this one, we could be covering a lot of ground, and I can't help wondering what we're missing.

I tell Ray that there must have been some extra marshmallow in the RCt because our asses seem to be stuck here.

"Or just a ton of weed," he says.

Ray and I have been through a lot together, leaning on each other in places like this and through the trials and tribulations of relationships and careers. We lend an ear and trust each other implicitly. Over beers or long-distance calls we'll rail against the Tweeting Ass of the White House and subhuman behavior in general. But when things go wrong out here, an unwritten rule keeps us from bitching at the same time. If a trail disappears into thin air or the switchbacks go on too long, one of us complains while the other laughs it off. One man's misery is another man's turn to prove he's the better man.

I can see the top of Ray's tent from here, and I notice that sunlight hits it just right. I suggest we go over and take a picture. Ray looks at me, and I know he knows that I'm just trying to take his mind off his mind. "Thanks, brother," he says. "I'm good here for now."

Three days ago, on the first evening of this vacation, Ray and I were making our way across a wide rockslide above the shore of Huckleberry Lake when we lost the trail. Each of the small rock cairns that hikers had stacked to mark their routes proved useless, as they delineated not the trail but merely the way someone else who wasn't on the trail had gone. With forty pound packs on our backs we side-hilled over boulder after boulder, high leg lifts and deep knee bends compounding into an exhausting paleo workout at the end of what had already been a long, hot hike up Rosebud and Huckleberry canyons. We were not as young as we used to be. Daylight would soon be seeping out of the sky and we'd need to find a place to camp.

In the narrow strip of trees between the rockslide and the lake, the forest had claimed all the ground between boulders, and near the head of the lake logjams scattered the creek across a wide course leaving little open space in which to pitch a tent. Around 7:30 we settled for a level patch too close to the creek and not far enough away from the trail. Ray, a stickler for a select handful of rules, was not happy with the set-up. He had put together the itinerary for this trip at the last minute when reports of a heavy snowpack in a different mountain range forced us to abandon Plan A. Here at Plan B there wasn't much of a view and the location of our camp made us look like amateurs. As for the bigger picture, we had no way of knowing exactly how much snow awaited us in the higher country, but from I-90 that morning the white patches above treeline had looked expansive. It was an ominous beginning for *Beartooths 2017*, and I could tell Ray was worried that his makeshift plan would be a bust.

We set up a kitchen away from the creek at the terminus of the rockslide. I ate sitting on a flat slab of granite and reclining against the angled face of another. The evening sun shone on the rocks, which radiated the heat of the day. Ray alternated between pacing and sitting. He reclined on a boulder and sighed. A few minutes later he stood and said his legs were toast. After looking up at the ridge and the sun slipping away, he turned toward me with his empty bowl in one hand and familiar camp spoon in the other, pointed the spoon at me and said, "So, dude. Why do we do this to ourselves?"

I laughed. "Habit?"

"Fair enough." Ray said. "This is no day at the beach, but we're here mainly for the fun of it, correct?" With the spoon he traced a circle above his head. "So what exactly is it about these mountains that gets *your* ass up here?"

Behind Ray there was a boulder the size of a shack. The side of the boulder facing the creek was undercut, forming a squat shelter over a patch of bare ground. On that ground were our backcountry stove and two flat rocks with metal pots on them constituting our kitchen. Growing out of the top of this boulder was a small island of forest, a layer of soil a couple of inches deep, a carpet of moss and lichen, white and yellow flowers, ferns, a few species of shrub and some fir saplings, all in a small fraction of an acre. The top of the boulder, the foundation of the micro-forest, was flat, but rough-cut shelves around the edges, also covered in living green, formed steps by which the cascading forest colony had made its way back to the ground.

"That boulder by our stove might be four billion years old," I said to Ray. "These mountains are made of some of the oldest rock on earth. The little bonsai forest on top of that boulder, I'm guessing, is a few hundred years of soil-building and several decades of colonization by plants. Our creek over there never shuts up, and the mountains keep repeating, *Time marches on.* Right now you and I are lucky enough to be taking part in the coincidence -- a convergence -- of all that's ever happened here and the practically accidental arrival of two big brains hauled around by upright bodies."

"I'm sorry. I forgot my question."

"Edward Abbey wrote that a person could write a book about one particular juniper tree in Arches National Park, meaning, I think, that the details add up to everything. The boulder with its forest tells the story. The creek tells the story. The shape of a mountain. The more you know, the more you have to wonder. Being out here stretches the imagination, exercises the old wonder muscle like nothing else can. The body's main job is to carry the mind into mountains."

"You will keep your old wonder muscle to yourself."

The evening thermals, updrafts of warm air, had made way for heavier, cooler currents streaming down the rocky slope. The breeze swept through camp and awakened the bonsai boulder, animating fern fronds, bending shrub and seedling stems, fluttering all the little leaves.

I said, "The little boulder grove appears to be vibrating."

Ray looked over his shoulder. "The breeze, is my guess."

"No doubt. But doesn't it almost seem like it wants us to notice?"

"It *wants*? You're speaking metaphorically I hope."

"Sure. These sentences are metaphors about my thoughts, which are metaphors about things in my field of vision."

"I suspected as much."

I was thinking that our bonsai forest was to the boulder what humans are to the planet, also that desire is a physical thing in the brain, a map-able response triggered by a person's relationship to what is and what isn't. The brain is a product of the raw materials of the universe wrought by natural selection. So, did desire just magically appear one day to occupy humans and make them act crazier than everything else alive, or had it been part of the mother ship's inventory all along?

I said to Ray, "The planet wanted to know itself, so it set about building a mind by seeding oceans with the most rudimentary life, the building blocks of evolution. Two billion years go by before cells develop internal organs. Another two billion before our species leaves the woods to become farmers, geologists, botanists, poets, strippers, priests. We've cultivated the wild, made up stories attempting to define ourselves, figured out how to date ancient rocks and trees."

"So is there an even higher mind behind this planet-with-a-purpose? Or are we just one of an infinite number of spin-offs of a lucky frickin' accident?" Ray asked.

Evening pastels softened the steep face of Froze to Death Plateau. On the cliffs above camp, solitary trees rooted in granite reached at uncommon angles into sunlight, suggesting an other-than-human will power, another terrestrial intelligence. I hoped the skies would remain clear and we'd get to see the canyon walls in moonlight.

About 4.5 billion years ago an asteroid the size of Mars slammed into Earth, and out of the dust the moon was formed. I wondered what sense other beings might have of our desolate companion, the lunar light and pull, the gravitational force that lifts an ocean like the center of a tablecloth and lets it go. Tides. We're not alone in being moved. Whales, for example; their world for countless generations has been hitched to the moon, as we are hitched to our most constant desires.

I said to Ray, "Anything's possible. To make sense of why we're all here we've defined a handful of possibilities and run with them. The word "faith" comes from Fides, the goddess who was supposed to oversee the integrity of the Romans. When I think about some of our stories, our religions and the trouble they've gotten us into or failed to keep us out of, the bloodbaths and bigotry, I see the devil smirking around the corner and I want to look somewhere else. It's comforting to think about this blue and green and brown miracle of a planet and the animal it crafted with a capacity for wonder out here on our own together, interbeing. No boundary between us, we breathe the same breath, consume the sun; the elements become our thoughts. You and I walking around out here, breathing heavy, gawking, thinking, we're just doing our part, earning our bodies, feeding our soul."

Ray looked at the plastic bowl in his hands. "Does your well-fed soul feel like doing the dishes?"

"Not even a little."

Ray picked up the plastic pint of bourbon and walked it over to me. "So," he said. "A geologist, a botanist and a priest walk into a bar in heaven…"

"God the Bartender says … 'What'll you have?'" I offered.

"Geologist says, 'Anything on the rocks.'"

"Botanist orders a … bloody Mary?"

"Priest says, 'I'm good.'"

We lingered on warm rocks until the sun slipped behind the ridge and it was time to hang the food out of the reach of bears and marmots. I tied our rope around a fist-sized rock and threw it over the diagonal trunk of a tree that had gotten hung up on a branch of another tree on its way to the ground. The rock went over the target, the rope caught on the trunk, the rock took a pendulous route toward my head. Ray was standing a few feet to my right, and I leaned in his direction as the rock swung past.

"Dude," Ray said. "That was close."

"Yes," I said.

"Okay, well, that would have fucked you up."

"True. Thank God I didn't hit myself in the head with a rock out here."

I untied the rock and tied the food sacks to the rope, hoisted the sacks up to the height of the tree and tied off the other end of the rope. Ray looked up and correctly observed that a big enough bear could easily reach the sacks and that the sacks were also too close to the tent. After lowering everything to the ground and untying my knots, Ray began coiling the rope, which had gotten tangled in some twigs. Ray cussed, called the rope a sonofabitch. I laughed. Ray said, "Goddam sonofabitch."

"Dude," I said. "We're on vacation. You might want to chill a little."

"I know. I just want to get this over with. That hike kicked my ass." Then he noticed another knot in the rope and yelled, "How is that even possible!"

I said, "Dude, let me rephrase that. *I'm* on vacation." I gestured toward the forest all around. "*This* is vacation. Blowing your top over nothing could inhibit my good time."

Ray looked at me. The creek babbled. Some of the tension washed out of his face. "I know. I know." he said. "Sorry. Thanks for saying something." He had finished coiling the rope, and now he picked up the sacks and said he was going to find a better place to hang the fuckers.

Later that night as the bourbon rations took full effect, Ray thanked me again for the intervention. I told him I was just doing my job as his lifelong friend, which led to us toasting a camaraderie that had brought us so many good times.

The next morning we'd discover that our imperfect camp was only a half-hour hike from timberline, ideally situated for what would be two arduous but hassle-free days of exploring some of the most glorious alpine scenery we'd ever set foot in. The first time we arrived at Princess Lake we took a left; the next day we went right. Both routes tended toward the highest mountain in Montana. Along the way, Ray's grit, generosity (I forgot my lunch the first day) and capacity for joy were on full display. My friend is a badass who needs these mountain escapes as much as I do, which helps to explain why when something goes wrong he takes it personally. Life back in the trenches of the day-to-day can be fragmenting, fraught as it is with compromise and false promise, so when we take some of our free time and come seeking what's whole and balanced and beautiful, a certain amount of tension attends the quest. Often things go well enough to bring a couple of middle-aged men just resting by a lake to tears.

Now on my way back from photographing the tent here at Mystic camp, I get cottonmouth. My water bottle is empty, and as soon as I pull the cap from Ray's gallon jug a fly darts inside, bringing to mind the cat hole I'd dug earlier behind the alder thicket and the squadron of flies that descended almost as soon as my shorts dropped. Now one of the flies is flitting around on the surface of our drinking water and I'm having an out-of-body experience watching myself try to coax a fly out of a jug. Ray, too, has been watching me, but he has no idea about the fly. There's just me talking to water in a jug, gingerly sloshing it around. Ray's enjoying a good laugh, but when I tip the jug, spilling sullied water and fly on the ground, his face registers the horror.

"Noooo!" he says. "Why?"

It looks like we'll need more water.

Fifteen minutes later the water filter and still-empty jug sit next to me on the log. As far as hiking goes, there's always Froze to Death Plateau tomorrow. Ray's been wanting to go there since he spotted it on a map six years ago. "Frickin' *Froze to Death*," he'd said. "How could you *not* want to go there?"

Being high, especially in nature, it's easy to comprehend inertia. If you're in motion, whatever's around the next bend keeps you in motion. Every yonder rise pulls you up and over it. On the other hand, if you're thoroughly at rest on a log, content just coddling your fear of moving, it could be a while before you make your way to the lake to fill your water bottles. Now, after an indeterminate number of minutes, it's finally go-time, probably. I begin gathering my water bottle. The jug. A cooking pot. The filter. I look toward the lake. I look at Ray. The corners of his mouth curl downward and his eyebrows arch. "Wow, my friend," he says. "Whatta … Where do you think *you're* going?"

We sit on the ground on the shore of a small peninsula. The lake water is clear and the sandy bottom slopes gently away from the eroded bank. Boulders in sun and shade, some driftwood, meadow grass, a breeze. The opposite shore is not far and the thick forest that covers it sparkles with sunlight reflecting off the lake. Above the forest, avalanches and the hammer of time have jumbled the steep, dry face of a high plateau. During our hikes the last two days we'd looked down on that plateau from ten miles away and watched afternoon storm clouds darken this valley, but now massive peaks to the west are awash in sunlight. Long sloping ridgelines usher our eyeballs toward the sky. The wind speaks the shape of things on its way from there to here.

    Meanwhile, all of the light and shadow from within the forest across the lake has come forward to that shoreline and I'm looking at a colossal hologram. My eyes are delighted, but my mind is worried. Sunlight and shadows flicker with the breeze, and the planet turns to the crinkly tune of a Jack-in-the-box playing on the other side of the moon. Next my mind threatens to leave my lazy ass for everything else out there, and the tension is riveting.

    Before long the jug is almost full. Ray is sitting a few feet away, facing me, lost in his own perceptual daydream. Normally he'd be looking for a way up every ridge and peak in sight, but for now his hands rest on his knees and his thumbs tap slowly along his fingertips.

    Suddenly his back and fingers straighten and he says, "Dude, black bear."

    I turn in time to see a bear emerge from a thin stand of lodgepole, walking along the trail. Ray and I get to our feet. A tall boulder to the right of the bear partially blocks my view of the trail. I'm holding my breath; if there are cubs there won't be room here for all of us.

The lake is at our backs. The bear, thirty feet away, steps off the trail, sniffing the air, coming toward us. Ray yells, "Hey, bear," and the bear stops, sniffs the air, lowers its nose to the ground, paws at the dirt. I don't know what this means. If it's a prelude to a charge, I better figure out what I'm going to do. Ray yells again and I think we're both thinking that the only problem so far is that this bear hasn't figured out what we are.

Ray says, "What are you doing, bear?"

I look over my shoulder and Ray looks over his. Would a black bear chase a man into a lake?

"Shit."

If this were a grizzly bear we might be into the carnage stage already. National park brochures, backcountry ranger briefings and visitor center videos have all instructed me to stand my ground against a black bear. Look big, sound threatening, stare it down (generally the opposite of what you'd do during a grizzly encounter) and the animal will know its place, move on. And yet, this one keeps coming.

I put my hands out in front of me. Ray says, "Bear, NO! Go on!"

This bear and *this* high; what are the odds? The unexpected is on a roll today, so I can't rule out an immediate future in which I've gone facedown fetal to protect myself and Ray is forced to fight the exceptional bear off my back. Hot breath of Ursus, the weight of it on my spine, slobber on my head. Claws, teeth. Ray's straining voice. Then I remember my wife and kids, and a mauling suddenly seems less likely; I wouldn't put them through that, would I?

The bear turns toward the trail, continues in the direction it had been going, stops, steps again toward Ray and me, gets yelled at and finally leaves. Profanity laced rhetorical questions fill the bear-gone vacuum. In a word, *What ... the ... fuck?*

I resume filtering water, my shaky hands in a hurry. Ray stands two strides away, facing the trail.

"Yeah," I say. "Just let me know if he comes back."

About a minute later Ray says, "Dude. He's back."

It all starts happening again. The bear steps toward us, sniff-sniff, worrisome head bobbing, the pawing at the ground. It's hard to say how big he is. Shoulders up to my belly maybe. We think it's a bad sign that it changed its mind about leaving us alone. The phrase *greater resolve* comes to mind, and I don't want it to apply to this bear. He's in prime condition; milk chocolate-colored coat with flashes of cinnamon and coffee here and there, especially when the breeze ruffles it. I have him pegged for a three-year-old male, based on the absence of cubs and the fact that his boldness or curiosity (or ignorance) suggests the equivalent of an adolescent boy. Maybe two-hundred pounds, including enough muscle to carry such heft over all terrain types every waking hour, to run it up steep talus slopes, pull it up a tree, turn over logs and boulders.

Ray picks up a small rock and lobs it at the bear. The rock thumps the ground near a front paw and the bear pivots away, tracking the rock, then turns again to face us.

I pick up a rock and throw it, but my aim is compromised by my lack of commitment to hitting a bear with a rock. I take a step forward and, like a cowhand, say, "Hep. Hep now, bear. Git now. Git." My strange words are plucky but my voice comes out high and fluttery. I have no doubt that the bear comprehends only my fear.

Ray turns around and picks up the cooking pot, starts banging it with the lid. The bear turns away, does a clumsy little shuffle, faces us again. I pick up two rocks and start clacking them together. This sounds like the hooves of a goat fleeing a predator across a rocky slope. *Never run from a bear!* I drop the rocks. I hear Ray say, "Okay. This is bullshit." I start to respond but my throat is suddenly so dry it could shatter. I spot the water jug on the ground on the other side of Ray, side-shuffle over and take a long drink. Ray looks at me, says, "Oh, no shit," and reaches for the jug. I laugh, aspirate water, cough, wipe my chin.

Ray repeats that this is bullshit. He bets the bear is just looking for scraps. "We need to get to our camp before he does."

The bear retreats to the trail and starts walking away. A very small part of me doesn't want it to leave. I'd love to feel safe again, but I don't want the part of my life in which I get to look at this bear to be over. Its legs rivet my attention. Long and sort of skinny, the hind legs look out of proportion to the rest of the body, and they swing stiffly, like the knees are bad, giving the impression that this bear is hampered by having to walk on all fours because of the damn horizontal spine. Now I think the legs look almost human, only cloaked in fur, and I'm a little spooked by the fact that the bottom half of a biped appears to be driving the bear, adding to the feeling that this animal is fucking with us.

The bear is going right, so we go left. The shape of the peninsula forces us to veer toward the bear, and then we're on parallel courses toward our camp. Ray and I start to run, the bear starts to run. Rounding a curve I jump over a steaming pile of green bear shit in the middle of the trail. Time does me the courtesy of slowing down so I can fully appreciate the novelty of this latest twist. My mind says, *So that's where he went.* I look over my shoulder at Ray dodging the bearshit. We don't even have to say it. *No f*****g way.*

It's taking longer than it should to get back to camp because the bear has engaged us in a game of chicken. Unless we're going toward him he's coming toward us. My instincts want to remind me that fear serves a purpose, but the bear keeps retreating upon our advances until Ray and I are back within our rectangle of logs.

There's a narrow trail between me and our tent, and the bear is on it, twenty feet away. Adjusting for the fact that the bear is a large omnivore, it feels even closer. He's doing the bob and weave and sniff thing again while taking tentative steps toward us. Ray says something about teaching him a lesson with the bear spray, and maybe he's looking for it somewhere behind me, but I'm not taking my eyes off the bear. I don't want it to know that I know he's the stronger animal or that I prefer the standoffs that come with actors and popcorn. This feels both too real and not real.

On cue, Ray says, "This is bullshit."

In the back of my mind is the fact that our campaign of aggression toward this bear was Ray's idea. Now I feel like I'm overcompensating for my failure to know exactly what to do back there at the lake. As I'm walking toward the bear once more I realize that I'm doing so partly out of an aversion to shame, like a soldier afraid to refuse to fight. The sargeant who thinks this is bullshit is somewhere behind my shoulder, and again the moment is upon us in which the bear will either be mauling me or not.

When the bear retreats to somewhere on the other side of the thicket behind camp, we pivot, tracking his trajectory.

Twigs snap and other things rustle. We brace for a nightmarish emergence from the thicket, yelling more *Go on's* and *Git's*. Next we see the bear near the far edge of the thicket, going away. More stern commands from the hominids, and the bear takes one last look at us before disappearing over a low rise.

We watch that rise for some time. Finally, we sit. We take turns standing and looking toward the rise. We talk about what just went down. We suddenly recall that we're super high then disagree about the length of the encounter. I think it lasted twenty minutes, Ray says forty-five. We piece it back together, scene by scene. Kudos to Ray for his decisive action, laughter over the sudden thirst, my cowhand alter-ego, the steaming pile on the trail, the fact that this bold bear happened along while we were so fretfully high.

We are by no means at ease, but recalling the scenes of the encounter nudges the bear into the past. Our laughter and, in time, our gratitude for the experience slowly erode the tension. To where in the body the adrenaline retreats we can't say, but eventually the experience goes from ongoing to a top-shelf memory; except at some point we'll have to return to the lake for water. We probably have enough to cook but not for doing the dishes and staying hydrated. Neither of us wants to go anywhere alone or to stay here and guard camp.

Sessions of sitting broken up by standing followed by a few aimless strides within a twenty foot perimeter of camp. After a long silence, Ray sweeps his head around from looking at the rise to looking at me. "So, dude." he says. "Are we really going to let *that bear* (with an index finger he stabs the air in the direction of the rise) keep us from cooking dinner tonight?"

"I think we are."

He nods and says, "Okay."

I think we're both relieved that we're not alone in being scared of being alone, too rattled to go to the lake. There's some bourbon, enough water to drink, some trail mix and a little cheddar cheese.

Eventually Ray announces that he might have found an alternative to his reading glasses. He's holding the discarded silica gel packet he'd found in the fire ring what seems like hours ago. He reads the warning printed on it and laughs.

"This print is *tiny*," he says. " And I could *not* read it before." He reads it again. "I think the weed has given my good eyesight back. Have you heard of this before?"

I have not, but Ray could be onto something.

"Maybe there's a way to infuse optical lenses with THC?" I offer.

"*Or*," he says. "One could just, like, *smoke it*."

"Good point."

It takes a while for night to fall, so when it does we're ready for it. Our day of rest at Mystic Lake has exacted a heavy mental toll. The RCt has almost worn off by the time we duck into the tent and settle into sleeping bags. Falling asleep feels like sinking into the womb. I dream-picture myself in a bear pelt hammock. Safe.

In the middle of the night I have to take a leak. I dare not go far from the tent because I'm in my socks in twenty-two million acres of bear country. The stars are shockingly numerous, like thousands of eyes suddenly at the window. The treetops are shadows on the constellations. The sound of urine hitting the ground breaks the silence and masks the footsteps of anything creeping up on me. I look over my shoulder. This anxiety, I reckon, connects me to primal man and to myself as a young boy in the woods running from Sasquatches of the mind. I finish, speed walk back to the tent and disappear inside my sleeping bag.

These Beartooth Mountains were originally coastal, on the western edge of a new continent. Much later an inland sea covered them. The mountains rose higher to shed the sea but remained buried in layers of sediment almost two miles thick. Uplift and magmatic intrusions, wind, rain and glaciers eventually eroded most of the sedimentary cap, washing it into the surrounding basins. Ray and I have wandered into the violent history of our planet, and now, awake in the middle of the night, a restless mind wants to wander a history of its own, like a dog unleashed. For every mile the body travels, the mind can do a marathon.

When I was in high school I went to Niagara Falls with a friend and his family. We looked at the falls from the American side, then the Canadian. The height and width of the falls, the rushing and concussive sounds, the incredible volume of water accelerating over the edge all made a strong impression. We took in every view we could without paying the price of a ticket to board the *Maid of the Mist*, which ferried passengers right up to the plunge zone. From high above we watched the boat churn through turbulent waters as passengers in raincoats lined the railings. Todd and I settled for running through the free mist billowing up and over the cliff face and onto the grass and sidewalk. In the visitors' center we'd read about the daredevils who'd gone over the falls in barrels, and I tried to imagine that feeling of freefall and the impact of landing. The noise inside the barrel must have been insane. Somewhere between a deadly stunt and just looking at the falls was where I wanted the experience to take me, but after an hour or so, it seemed there was nothing else to do with it. Across the street from the Canadian half of the falls the tourism industry was booming. Souvenirs, taffy, titillating museums -- Wax, Guinness Book of World Records, Ripley's Believe It or Not!

Inside the Guinness museum a short hallway led into a large room. Along the perimeter of the room, three or four dark alcoves made us wonder if we'd made a wrong turn. Todd turned and spotted a larger alcove just to the left of where we'd entered the room. "Dude," he said, pointing at a sign on a metal stand: *The World's Tallest Woman. Next Appearance: 1:30.*

In my memory the stage behind the modest marquee remains set: a small living room with wallpaper, a fake fireplace, a lamp on a table next to an upholstered armchair. A late-in-the-evening, 1920's sort of feel, hand-carved furniture legs, textured burgundy and gold fabric, tassels on the lampshade. Todd and I wandered off to see what else there was to see.

When we returned to the room just before 1:30, the world's tallest woman was sitting in the armchair reading a paperback, which was tiny in her hands. My friend and I stood in front of the display, glancing at each other sideways, most likely smirking. Was it okay to stare yet?

After a minute or two The World's Tallest Woman set the book in a drawer and stood up. I looked at Todd and he raised an eyebrow, nodding slowly. The woman's blue jogging shoes were large, polyester pant legs long and crisp, revealing no contour. Deep eye sockets, cheekbones and forehead prominent. I did not yet know she suffered from a life-shortening condition called gigantism or that one of the symptoms was widely spaced teeth. She wasn't smiling. Many years later I'd learn that her name was Sandy Allen, that she was from Indiana and worked at the museum for a total of eight years, that sometimes during her show she drank from a big soda fountain cup and joked with her audience about eating normal sized people for breakfast.

Maybe Todd and I weren't enough of an audience. Or maybe she'd overheard us making some smartass comment. Maybe we were supposed to ask her about her life as a very tall person. Whatever the case, she kept her eyes trained on the empty space a few feet to my right while her record-breaking body absorbed the intermittent stares of teenagers suffering an awkward silence. There would be no autographs or photos afterwards. The body's remarkable achievement was there for the viewing, but the museum headliner, at least on this slow day, was more like a sad pop-up book than an interactive exhibit. One of the natural wonders of North America was outside across the street, and maybe the rush of it seeped in once or twice when someone opened the front door. Otherwise, you could imagine a fake living room clock ticking. I wondered how long this showing would last, and whether she would exit through the door next to the fireplace or just sit back down. I would have liked to see her move again, but with an utter lack of showmanship she made her rightful claim to a humanity as guarded as the rocks behind the falls.

Outside in the daylight a few minutes later I was restless, wondering what else there was to see, or if there was anything more to the place than seeing. Was this how a guy ends up in a barrel bobbing toward the lip of the falls? We found Todd's parents in the taffy shop, walked across the street to their station wagon and headed down the road along the river to look at some apple orchards.

Now as I lay awake with this memory, I try to imagine our bonsai boulder at Huckleberry camp on display in a museum: The rock that grew a forest! It's more common than you think! Four billion years and counting!

Two days ago in the boulder fields below Avalanche Lake, Ray and I had stopped to rest in a flat patch out of the wind. Our hands and feet had been busy through acres of granite, ten thousand rocks struck with quartz zigs, zags and specks and colored by lichens and oxidation in shades of pink, jade and sage, black and flame. Single strands of spider's silk spun between jagged edges quivered in the breeze, glinting sunlight, and I'd tried not to break them. Thunder rolled in from far away. The prow of Froze to Death Plateau loomed a thousand feet above, and I wondered whether the rocks had fallen from there or had been dragged and dumped from the belly of a glacier. The face of the plateau was nearly vertical, and evidence of glaciation was everywhere around us in the form of hummocks, moraines and tarns.

"Glaciers or rockslides?" I asked Ray.

"Couldn't tell you," he said. "Which would you prefer?"

We enter these places tracking streams uphill until they are as thin as limbs in the territory of rocks, rocks like fragments of planetary memory I want to pry like a root, to course over like water and carry away. This is how everything that's happened here will dissolve in me, accrete into the wisdom mountains are patient to bestow. This is where I remember that our atoms are all the same. This is why I have to wonder what lies beyond knowing.

I try to imagine what Froze to Death will be like tomorrow. Whatever it has in store will be icing on the cake. The bear today was more than a sighting, the country above Huckleberry camp more than a jaw-dropping landscape. The Beartooths have been all that I'd wanted out of Niagara Falls half a lifetime ago.

In the morning it's last night's dinner for breakfast, gnocchi with instant pesto. By lunch time we've gained more than three thousand feet hiking six miles up and onto the sprawling alpine tundra of Froze to Death Plateau.

It's not as bad up here as it sounds. We're having lunch in a boulder garden next to a boggy stream. A marmot takes a roundabout way to a rock a few feet from where we sit. The plateau tilts upward toward the west, a few miles away coming to a point, the prow of a ship splitting a thunderstorm in two, one for each of the two forks of Rosebud Creek far below. Directly overhead, blue sky. A strong breeze ruffles the golden fur of the marmot, which, out of territoriality or familiarity with trail mix, keeps edging closer. It's about the size of a small beagle but looks to be fairly ripped under all that fur. He's close enough to spring onto my face, but there's no chance that he will. I'm sure I could take him if he did. I'd most likely experience some pain. What is it with these mammals of the Beartooths that seem to not know to be afraid?

Ray says, "Brave little pecker."

I pick up a stone and toss a warning shot. Marmot doesn't budge, except its nostrils, which pulse incessantly.

I flick my left hand toward the rodent and in a low, calm voice say, "Go on now. Git, marmot."

Ray says, "You tell 'im, partner."

After lunch we still have a lot of walking to do. I can't imagine a better place to watch a storm, or a worse place to get caught in one. We push on toward Froze To Death Mountain. To paraphrase Ray, how could we not?

John Jacobson lives in the Catskill Mountains of New York. His writing has appeared or is forthcoming in many publications including About Place Journal, Aji Magazine, The Dewdrop, Intima Journal of Narrative Medicine, Impermanent Earth and Talking Writing. His work has been nominated for a Pushcart Prize, Best of the Net and a John Burroughs Nature Essay Award. His essay "Between Grief and Hope" was a finalist for the 2021 Barry Lopez Creative Nonfiction Award.

Sprouting Leaves

New green shoots of grass have grown between old fallen hay stems and milkweed stalks across the field. Dandelions look like constellations of yellow stars in the path leading to the woods. Robins chirp. A chickadee whistles, "FeeeBeee!" "FeeeBeee!"

    I follow the path past a moss speckled fencepost with three knotted strands of rusty barbed wire. Wind sweeps across the mountain. I push my hands into the pockets of my coat. Tiny white flowers of harbinger-of-spring look like a dusting of snow under thornapples. A junco trills, Tetetetetetetete!" Another bird kicks leaves on the ground. They rustle loudly and swirl up into the wind. When he flies, he is the color of cinnamon, with a long tail. He perches on a low branch. I focus my binoculars and see that he is a brown thrasher. He opens his bill and sounds a low, guttural "Churrrrrrrr." "Churrrrrrrr." It's a strange sound for such a beautiful bird.

Sun slants through an opening in the clouds. It is warm in light, cold in shade. I imagine it was a day like this when Hades first saw Persephone gathering flowers in a lush meadow. He was smitten. He swept her up and carried her to the underworld in his chariot. Persephone's mother, Demeter, goddess of the harvest, wandered the earth in grief. There was a long drought. Plains lay bare and fallow. No crops grew.

Zeuss, the sky and thunder god, returned Persephone to Demeter, but before Hades let her come back to light, he gave her six pomegranate seeds to eat knowing they would bring her back for half of each year. Persephone came to this world again and spring bloomed. Crops grew. As fall came though, she was drawn back to the underworld by her memory of pomegranate seeds. Forever after, she spent part of the year in light among life, and part in the dark underworld. Persephone represents our changing seasons. I can't stop thinking though, about Demeter's grief returning over and over.

I enter the very different world of an old sugar bush through a gap in a stonewall. Giant dark maples in varying states of decay stand between spindly second growth saplings. The path winds down a gentle slope.

There is a soft scratching and tapping overhead. I sweep my binoculars up the dead trunk of a maple. Bark has fallen away near its top leaving bleached white and ochre wood cracked and pockmarked with old sapsucker wells. Bark beetle tracks look like hieroglyphics carved into it. The tail of a downy woodpecker protrudes from a partly excavated nest cavity. Its tail pulsates. Chips fall. The woodpecker emerges for an instant. It is a female, tiny, round and all black and white.

"Witchitywitchitywitchitywitch!" a common yellowthroat calls. He perches for a moment on a blackberry briar. His black mask and golden throat gleam. In my binoculars I see a glint in his eye that is focused on me.

It makes me self-conscious. Suddenly, I feel guilty for taking this walk. My wife Claudia is home in her hospital bed in our living room watching TV with her aide. Most of our trips together are to doctors. To get Claudia out of the house requires a Hoyer lift and wheelchair. To get into a car, two people push and pull her on a slide board. Everything she needs is carried to her bed and back again. Her care is exhausting for me.

I cannot know just how devastating her illness is to her. She was beautiful and strong once. She was independent. She was a Registered Nurse used to being in charge. All of that is gone. One day she wailed, "I want to be who I was! I want to walk with you in the woods again!"

Once I sat on a soft sofa in a social worker's office. I was struggling with something I couldn't name. The social worker was behind a big desk. She was professionally detached and spoke in flat tones. It felt like we were on islands separated by a dark sea.

"Have you ever taken care of anyone bedbound?" I asked.

She didn't answer. Instead, she said, "You need to take some breaks. What do you like to do?"

It took years, but I know now that I was struggling with grief. Today I would tell her about Demeter and Persephone. I would describe how grief returns over and over for a caregiver. I would say, "A caregiver's work is exhausting. Breaks are necessary. But grief overwhelms. It follows everywhere. It springs out of shadows, even at the most peaceful moments, even during breaks. It comes out as sadness and anger. It comes out as confusion. I never know just how it will be."

I would tell her, "I grieve for who Claudia was before she was ill. I grieve over our financial loss. I grieve for our better years. I grieve for time I no longer have. I grieve for our dreams that can no longer come true. Most of all, I grieve for the illusion that everything will turn out alright."

A break is not the first concern. Grief is.

When I return along the same path, I notice a black cherry limb lying on the ground. I had paid no attention to it on the way to the sugar bush. It came down in a storm last week. Even though it is broken, tiny olive-green leaves edged in rust have sprouted on its twigs. It seems pointless. They will soon shrivel, but they sprout anyway. I think about Persephone returning every spring. It's an extravagant gesture.

Isn't that how we live?

Kelli Short Borges is a writer of essays, short stories and flash fiction. A former reading specialist in the Arizona public school system, Kelli is a life-long reading enthusiast. She also enjoys hiking the Arizona foothills, photography, and traveling the world in search of adventure. Her work has been published or is forthcoming at *Across the Margin, Drunk Monkeys, The Sunlight Press, MoonPark Review, and The Dribble Drabble Review,* amongst other publications.

You can connect with her on Twitter @KelliBorges2

The Void

Previously Published by Her Story Dec. 7, 2021

I'm standing at the edge of a small, rocky precipice, deep in the heart of the Washington Cascades. Fear courses through me like a vise, squeezing so tight it takes my breath. Crusted with ice, the yawning gap stares up at me with cold contempt, challenging me to leap.

I know I must. After spending hours traversing the glacier below, I'm exhausted and shaking. The day is waning, the sun just beginning to make its descent, bright light slowly giving way to milky shadow. In the mountains, time is not on your side. I know this.

The summit, a stony, jagged gray peak, is just out of view, beyond this craggy spot. I'm here with my partner, Mariano, and our guide Margaret. Both have already bounded across the void before me, Tigger-esque, feet like springs. They made it look easy despite the crampons we wear, metal "teeth" strapped to our boots, meant to give traction on sloped snow and ice. On rock, they have the opposite effect, making me feel unsteady and unsure. Cold sweat begins to form, beading above my lip.

Trembling and on the verge of tears, I make my case to Margaret. "I can't do this with crampons." "It will actually be *more* dangerous if you take them off, Kelli. Come on, you can do it." I push back, glaring. "I don't like this. What if I fall and get really hurt, break my leg or something? We're so far from help." I picture myself helpless, seriously injured, waiting for a rescue that may not be possible this far up the glacier. Margaret's eyes meet mine, firm and direct. "Sometimes you just need to do it, even if you're scared, right? Push yourself, let's go!"

A flash of annoyance washes over me. *I've climbed to the top of this glacier and that's what she says? Haven't I already pushed myself, proven I can do hard things?*

Every cell in my body is screaming "NO," my most basic, primitive instincts kicking into gear. As I stare, frozen, unable to move, Margaret's voice rises an octave:

"GO!"

I glance at Mariano, searching his eyes with my own. An unspoken communication takes place withing a fraction of a second. I breath in, the sharp, icy air filling my lungs with oxygen, muscles tense and ready.

***

I met Mariano the year before, the summer of 2007. At the tail end of a heartbreaking divorce, I felt ready to meet someone new, but I was also colt-skittish, wary and slow to trust. The foundation of my failed marriage, built upon what initially appeared to be firm and level ground, had in actuality been poured over hidden, vast sinkholes. The entire structure inevitably collapsed, the void below swallowing us whole. Now, I scrambled to gain purchase, the dust settling around me, testing the earth beneath for the solidity I craved.

Set up by a mutual friend, Mariano and I met over iced coffee on a warm Arizona Friday in June. As I pulled up to the coffeehouse where we were to connect that day, I was nervous. I had never been on a blind date, and wasn't sure what to expect. My worries were quickly pushed aside as soon as I spotted Mariano, who offered a wide, welcoming smile. Soon realizing we had many of the same interests, minutes morphed into hours as we talked endlessly about our common passions. Mariano, a single dad with a grown daughter, had devoted the previous years to family and career. Despite this, he also found time to challenge himself, becoming a triathlete and eventually completing a full Ironman, an impressive feat by any measure. I was raising two daughters, then six and ten, and was a reading specialist in the Arizona public school system. Additionally, I had just earned my black belt in Tae-Kwon-Do alongside my eldest daughter, after years of hard work and commitment. We bonded over these commonalities, our first date leading to many more. It felt like Kismet.

A year later, we found ourselves planning a new adventure: a privately guided four-day long intensive mountaineering course in the North Cascades National Park. Mariano had summited Mount Shasta the year before, a towering, glaciated mass standing at 14,180 feet in northern California. Shasta is a challenging and technical climb, and Mariano had enjoyed this endeavor so much he was itching for another. This time he wanted me to join. I was nervous, but reflected that we had agreed early on to regularly challenge ourselves in new ways as a couple, and here was a chance to make good on that commitment. I took this pact seriously. Nerves aside, I was in.

We flew into Seattle-Tacoma International on a beautiful and sunny August day, the bright, cobalt sky welcoming us. Mount Rainer, royally majestic, hovered in the background reigning over its subjects, wispy cotton candy clouds kissing its tip. As we drove northeast toward Marblemount where we were to begin our adventure, we rolled down the windows, breathing in the fresh air, the spicy scent of sagebrush lingering. We would spend the night in Marblemount at a small inn before heading out early the next morning to meet our guide Margaret at the ranger station. From there, we would head to Boston Basin Trailhead, the launching point for our adventure. That night, sitting fire-side at the inn, accompanied by the crackle and dance of the flames, we toasted the challenge with earthy red wine, our excitement growing along with our nerves.

The following morning dawned crisp and clear, the first rays of buttery sunlight peeking through the window, beckoning with promise. The aroma of crisp, sizzling bacon welcomed us in the dining room as we grabbed our last hearty meal, knowing it would be freeze-dried food on the mountain for the next several days. Heading out, packs in tow, driving toward the ranger station, my stomach twisted in knots as I considered the challenge ahead. Mountaineering would be a completely new experience for me, and I wasn't sure what to expect. I glanced anxiously at Mariano.

"How far did you say the hike in was? These packs are really heavy."

"Just a few miles. We'll be fine."

"But our backpacks are fifty pounds! It's only a quarter of your weight. It's almost half of mine."

"You're strong. You'll be ok. I'll help you if you need me to."

Our packs were stuffed to the brim, but I accepted the reassurance. I was learning that what Mariano said, he meant. He wouldn't leave me hanging. It was a new comfort for me.

Margaret was patiently waiting at the ranger station. Six feet tall, with closely cropped.

blonde hair, broad shoulders and an athletic build, she smiled and shook our hands with firm confidence. She certainly *looked* capable, and, reminding myself of her outstanding credentials, I felt reassured. We double checked our gear, and with a thumbs up from Margaret walked to the trailhead. Hoisting our packs with a grunt, we headed out, Margaret taking the lead, the whooshing sound of distant streams providing a musical backdrop.

Boston Basin Trail is an unmaintained climber's route, the first mile or so gently following the overgrown and eroded remnants of an old mining road. *No big deal*, I thought, as we trudged our way up the trail. Breathing in, I closed my eyes, the woodsy scent of local pine and cedar carried by the wind. Heaven.

My moment of bliss was quickly interrupted when we turned a corner and caught a glimpse of the path before us, which ascended precipitously up a rocky, brushy gully. An avalanche chute in the winter, it was the only way up. Boulders and fallen trees littered the path, and I turned to Margaret, confused.

"Is this the trail?"

"Yep."

I stared ahead, eyes widening.

"How do we get up it?"

"We climb, pull ourselves up."

I watched as Margaret tackled the challenge, at times on hands and knees as she ascended. I was next. Hoisting myself up a boulder, pulling with all my strength, I suddenly lost purchase and fell with force, my pack pulling me backward like fifty pounds of wet cement. Heart pounding, I yelped in fear, the possibility of broken bones, a concussion, flashing through me like lightning. I knew this was going to be bad. It was a long way down. Suddenly, I felt a firm weight pressing against me, stopping my fall. It was

Mariano. Sure and steady, he pushed me forward until I was able to grab hold. Leveling myself, I pulled back up using the thick, gnarled root of a tree for leverage. Shaking, adrenaline sprinting through my veins, I turned to Mariano. "You ok?" he asked, brow knit in concern. Still trembling, palms slick with sweat, I managed a smile. "Yes, fine."

Crisis averted, we continued up the path, which finally wound through a sloped, gentle forest, the lush, leafy canopy above providing a welcome break from the heat of the day. As we trekked, my thoughts drifted back to Mariano. Reflecting, I recognized a shift, however small, had taken place.

Our foundation was being strengthened, laid brick by brick, each placed squarely upon the other and cemented by the strongest of bonds. I was beginning to gain confidence as the months passed, that those bricks were real, that they were solid, unbreakable. That they would last.

Still, there was an uncertainty I couldn't shake. I had been hurt badly in my marriage, and like a small child hunched over, protecting a wound that had bled bright red and not yet healed, I held my deepest fears close to my chest. Unfurling myself completely was a step I was not yet ready to take. Sensing this, Mariano was patient, but we both knew we could not truly move forward, build a life together, until I fully opened up, trusting enough to expose my vulnerabilities.

The rhythmic gurgling of rushing water pulled me from my thoughts as we came around a final bend and caught our first glimpse of Boston Basin. Relieved to have arrived and easing our packs down with weary gratitude, we stopped and reverently took it in the ethereal beauty of what would be base camp.

Rimmed by spectacular, snow-capped peaks on all sides, Boston Basin is wide and expansive, with dozens of streams and sparkling waterfalls cascading gloriously toward the main creek, which lies a short distance from camp. Lush greenery and wildflowers abound, sweetly floral lupine and Indian paintbrush washing the valley in riotous color- blush, magenta, deep crimson red. Huge slabs of speckled granite litter the valley below Quien Sabe Glacier, which lies north of camp and just below Sahale Peak, where we would make our summit attempt in just a couple of days. Taking it in, mouth agape, I reflected on the Zane Grey phrase "Climbin' up through hell into heaven." It seemed an apt description for our grueling trek to the paradise before us.

Setting up camp that afternoon alongside Mariano and Margaret, I hummed to myself in relaxed content while we worked. Local marmots, abundant in the area, chirped along with me as the day waned, welcoming us to their home in the wild. That evening, work complete, we sat around the campfire talking with Margaret, trading stories and laughs as we shared our first dinner in the basin. At last, blanketed by the glimmer of what seemed a million celestial fairy lights, woodsy smoke from the fire lingering, we crawled into our tents and collapsed, exhausted.

The Boston Basin has been called a compressed version of the Swiss Alps due to its moderate altitude at 6,000 feet, and easy access to the surrounding peaks and glacier. It's the perfect outdoor classroom, and the next morning found Margaret headmaster, teaching us our first new skill: how to build a snow anchor, used to provide stability and safety when descending a snow couloir, a steep gully in alpine terrain. Snow anchors are created using an ice axe, climber's rope, locking carabiners (oblong metal rings used as connectors), and a metal picket.

Margaret began the lesson, showing us how to use the ice axe to dig a capital T into the hard-packed snow. Next, she embedded the metal picket horizontally and securely along the top of the T and attached a carabiner. Threading rope through this metal ring, she connected the other end to her harness using a figure eight knot. This creates a pully system that provides leverage for climbers on steep descents.

Mariano and I were next, each digging our own snow anchor, practicing the necessary skills again and again, then checking each other for accuracy and safety. As we worked alongside one another, I realized we were truly a team out here on the mountain. Mutual faith was not only necessary, but vital. As Mariano steadfastly lowered me down the slope, I felt safe, secure. I realized at that moment that day after day he was showing he was dependable, truthful, a solid and stable anchor not only on icy and treacherous terrain but in my life, *our* life. Out here, feet planted firmly on the mountain, Mariano slowly and safely guiding me, I felt incredibly lucky to have him as my partner. I wondered if I could be the same in return. He deserved to have someone just as sure, someone ready to fully trust. A partner who was "all in."

I pondered this as we wrapped up the day, heading back to camp as the sun set, framing Johannesburg mountain to the west in its honeyed, celestial glow. I was quiet that night as we ate, the hazy, pungent smoke of the fire an obstruction to clarity, paralleling my internal struggle. Leaving Mariano and Margaret to chat, I retired early, physically and emotionally drained, and fell into a fitful sleep.

"Good morning, guys!" chirped Margaret as we crawled out of our tent the next day, wearily rubbing sleep from our eyes.

She explained that today we would be learning a technique called "glissading," when a climber sits, then slides down a steep slope of snow or ice with the support of an ice axe.

"Margaret, that sounds dangerous. I thought we were supposed to build snow anchors on steep slopes?" I interjected.

"Yes, but this technique is used when the slope is a bit gentler. It's another choice for descending, and much faster than building an anchor."

Curious now, we grabbed our day packs and headed up the mountain, crampons crunching as we made tracks in the snow alongside those of local critters, a chilly breeze biting our exposed faces. Pulling my woolen beanie a little lower, I shivered in anticipation, wondering if I had the nerve to slide down the icy glacier, relying only upon myself.

Arriving at the glacier's base, then climbing up a bit, we finally set down our packs and grabbed our ice axes, the only glissading tool required. Margaret demonstrated, sitting first, then holding her ice axe firmly, right hand just under the base of the blade, left hand crossed over her body, securely holding the wooden handle. She began sliding, slowly at first, then faster, suddenly flipping her body over, chest to the slope, swinging the pick of her axe squarely into the dense snow on top of the glacier, arresting her fall. Mariano was next, making it look effortless as he started to slide, then quickly turned and struck his axe firmly into the snow, completing the exercise.

It was my turn. I picked up my axe, white knuckled and palms sweaty despite the chill. Shaking visibly, I sat, griping the axe tighter. The slope looked steeper from this angle. Biting my lip sharply, gathering courage, I pushed off, quickly gaining momentum as I slid faster and faster, heart pounding wildly.

"Now!" yelled Margaret, my cue to self-arrest.

I flipped over onto my belly, heaving the axe in an adrenaline-fueled burst, planting the pick deep into the snow and quickly coming to a halt.

"Perfect!" encouraged Margaret, as I whooped with joy.

I felt a burst of pride as we practiced again and again, trusting myself a bit more with each attempt. Day by day, on the mountain, I found my confidence growing, the wounds of my past healing with each reminder that I was capable, strong. I felt a rush of joy as I acknowledged this unexpected shift. Glancing at Mariano, elated, I laughed with glee, feeling like a kid on a playground as we slid. Finally, forced to pack up by the setting sun, we headed down the slope toward camp, ready to tackle what would be our big day, tomorrow's summit attempt.

We awoke to the sun's first fingers just reaching above the eastern peaks, sky bright and clear, a good omen. Huddling around the campfire, we wolfed down peanut butter sandwiches and slugged steaming mugs of coffee as we discussed the day ahead. It would be a long trek, Margaret explained, nine to ten hours total, and we would need an early start to make good time. Donning our packs, we set out for our final push.

Nearing the glacier, we pulled on crampons and securely tied rope to our harnesses, each connected to the other for security. "Roping up" is an important part of glacial traversing, each climber acting as an anchor for others. If a team member slips, others immediately self-arrest using their ice axe, which is always kept in hand. I reminded myself of the arrests we practiced successfully the day before while glissading. The stakes were high, but I knew I could do this. Determined, I stepped onto the slope, thirty feet behind Margaret, Mariano trailing at the same distance, a measure of safety.

Hours passed like minutes as we crossed the glacier in tandem, our steady breath and rhythmic footfall a moving meditation, the sun's warmth welcoming us in its gentle embrace. As we came around a final bend the lull was broken as we approached Sahale Col, a narrow ridge we would need to successfully navigate before reaching the peak just beyond.

Stepping onto the rocky ridge, uncomfortably exposed, the mood shifted as a frigid, howling wind suddenly pushed against us with force. Shivering, we turned and viewed our last obstacle, a gaping precipice rimmed with ice. Deep and too wide to step across, we would need to jump, crampons on.

***

Frozen, legs unsteady and trembling, I stare at the chasm before us. The summit lies just beyond, taunting in its proximity.

"Almost there!" encourages Margaret, leaping gracefully across, followed quickly by Mariano. They turn, beckoning.

My breath quickens. Can I do this, take this final leap? Squeezing my eyes shut, reflecting on the previous days and all I have learned, I deliberately, consciously, push fear aside. Blocking vision, light, and sound I slow my breath, place a hand over my heart, feeling it beat, slower now.

I open my eyes, glance at Mariano. He nods, eyes warm and reassuring. Suddenly, I know. In that split second, that fleeting moment of time, an undeniable truth, one that has been building day after day, crests, washes over me, engulfing me in its certainty. Despite the icy void before me, my quivering legs, the unwieldy crampons, despite everything, the ground below has never felt so solid and sure. I see Mariano on the other side, patiently waiting.

Breathing in, I leap.

Monica Devine is a writer, poet, and ceramic artist. Her most recent book *Water Mask* (a Finalist for the esteemed Willa Literary Award), is a collection of stories reflecting on motherhood, place, memory, art, and perception in the natural world. She is a Pushcart Prize nominee, a First-Place winner in the Alaska State Poetry Contest, and her piece "On The Edge of Ice" won First Place in Creative Nonfiction with New Letters journal. Her stories and photographs have appeared in a number of anthologies, and she has authored five children's books. Her children's book *Iditarod: The Greatest Win Ever* was a nominee for the celebrated Golden Kite Award. Monica splits her time between the awe-inspiring landscapes of Alaska and New Mexico, where she hikes, bikes, skis, and alongside writing, creates figurative ceramic art.

View her books, photographs, essays and sculptures at: monicadevine.com

Many Things Were Visible When the Earth Was Thin

Just now a rock took fright
When it saw me
It escaped
By playing dead. —Norman Mayer

On a retreat in New Mexico, I woke up one morning and looked out at red clay mesas and sandstone chimneys propped up like cut-outs against a coal-smudged sky. Only 50 feet from my door, the ground pushed up in mounds of red clay that begged my hands to sculpt pots. Rain spilled hard during the night (praise the sound of moody tin roofs), and I was surprised to see snow powdering the hills. Not unheard of in early October at 5,200 feet.

Only it wasn't snow. It was gypsum rock, an abundant mineral in the area that is usually covered with a thin layer of red dust that gets washed off by rain, then covered over again by wind. Up close the stones looked like Chiclets scattered over wide swaths of red clay. I had climbed these hills many times, stepping on the tiny white stones knowing exactly what they were. But that's not how I saw them that morning. I raced into the ranch's kitchen to tell friends of my snowy discovery. As soon as the words left my mouth, I was reeling them back in with apology.

I thought of Anaïs Nin's famous quote: "We don't see things as they are; we see things as *we* are." One only sees what one knows. This is the time of year the mountain slopes of my Alaska home collect termination dust, signaling the transition from fall to winter. A change in light and a good washing after a night of hard rain made those tiny stones tumble into the foreground of my vision. Fresh from sleep I interpreted them as the first official snow of winter.

The experience of "different" seeing happens to me all too infrequently. I wish I could recreate a sudden jolt of perception through will or effort, but I can't. What I *can* do is stay alert and open to possibility so its occurrence won't pass me by unnoticed.

And then it happened again, though this time it was a sudden perception I couldn't make sense of. A summer day, late August. Driving home from a painting class, I was stunned by cottonwood trees shaking with a vividness of color I'd never noticed before. A strong wind blew as the leaves twirled and vibrated in rhythmic waves. Varying shades of green pulsed through the leaves like light from a stroboscopic lamp.

I was not surprised to learn the word *strobos* means "an act of whirling," because that is precisely what happened. The leaves whirled against a backdrop of high-octane light. Had my right brain, the nondominant language side, taken over my perception temporarily? Was this a vision or an act of clear seeing? Or was it an altering of consciousness that bypassed thinking and went straight for the jugular: pure, ineffable awe? To be fair, the vision, or whatever it was, lasted only a few seconds. But it felt like much more than simply witnessing pretty trees on the side of the road. What had caused such a jarring shift in perception, a sporadic moment of magic? Whatever it was I wanted more. I was having dinner with seasoned painters later that night. I could quiz them about the act of perception.

I wondered how artists are trained to see. Do they paint a mirror image of a scene or go for their own best interpretation? Perception is as unique as memory. A dozen people viewing the same scene paint it with wildly different perspectives.

One painter friend said he looks at the landscape and sorts elements related to shape. What is striking in the foreground? Where do strong lines meander, and do they move diagonally: left to right, up and down? What shapes stand out? Another friend said she keys into color and mood first and notices where light and shadows meet. Whether you are painting a landscape, an object, or a portrait, the interplay of light is central to how you will create the form.

Weeks later, walking a horse trail south of my casita, I saw a large misshapen stick on the side of the trail. I'm always careful to notice what is directly beneath my feet in the high desert, whether it be friend or foe. I toed the stick with the tip of my boot to view its other sides. The bottom was pocked and whitewashed. Clearly it was a bone, a single bone, probably from cattle. I walked on, prodding with my hiking pole, aware that I could run into a rattler. I spotted another stick, long and curvy, that looked like a snake, or was it just a twisted juniper branch that resembled a snake? I stepped back just in case. My eyes were playing tricks on me again.

Storm clouds idled above my head, a common late afternoon occurrence in these parts, and I walked faster to make it to shelter before the daily deluge. My stride kicked up dust, and I caught a glimpse of something dark, the size of a small backpack. It zipped past me in a blur and ducked under a spray of creosote bush. A jackrabbit perhaps. Quick movements and layers of shadow were tricking my sight as the darkening sky bled away color and definition.

You have to lose your mind before coming to your senses, a famous psychoanalyst once said. You have to lose the stickiness of thoughts, discard the roaming bandits of conceptualization, and let feeling and awareness have a say. You have to know where you are in every moment, as horses do. Always alert, they prick their ears to unfamiliar sounds. They throw their heads back, inhale, and open their nostrils wide to new smells. Their sensate bodies are acutely aware as they draw information about everything around them. Surely artists and photographers are privy to technical knowledge when they create, but intuition and feeling are equally as valuable. Led by their senses, artists become completely immersed in their subject matter. The late painter Georgia O'Keeffe sketched and painted thousands of landscapes of the acreage around her home in New Mexico. She walked the land daily, gathering the smell of the air, the mood of the sky, the color of the mesas when diffused by the light. She collected the weathered skulls and pelvises of deer and antelope for her studies, keying into the perception of starkness in the desert, and used a minimalist color palette to depict animal bones in her paintings.

In her pelvis series, using only blue and white paint, the bleached white bones look as though they are floating in space. A cerulean sky shows through the holes in the bones and gives the anatomy an abstract look. The forms appear ambiguous in shape and the contrasting effect of bleached white on the deepest of blue is stunning to the eye.

Sometimes I wonder if we humans aren't missing out on something. We know that because of the structure of their eyes, deer see color differently than we do. They see a bluer blue than we are able to perceive. Just as we humans can't hear some sounds, our eyes can't take in some elements of light, like the invisible wavelengths of ultraviolet and infrared. Deer sense colors toward the violet end of the spectrum so they can see a wider range of blues. Would a deer see the blue of my jeans in a bluer blue than I see? Is there an enhanced world out there we're simply unable to process? Surely an artist's paintings would be more vivid and alive if her perception of the world was amplified. If we could perceive an enhanced range of color and light, everything around us would throb in an ultra-shimmering way, like my experience of the stroboscopic leaves. If our feelers were super sensitive though, it would be hard to manage such wild stimulation. We'd become unhinged.

"Many things were visible when the earth was thin," said Alma Keyes, a Yup'ik elder from Kotlik, Alaska. Keyes was speaking about the thin veil as she understood it through her ancient tribal people's worldview. "Things were distinct when the land was thin," she said. "Not the way it is today."

Celtic mythology points to the notion of "thin places" too, where the visible and invisible worlds join, and we experience these thin places when we unexpectedly encounter shifts in perception or heightened states of mystery and joy, perhaps even in suffering. My interpretation of the thin places, as experienced by ancient peoples, goes something like this: Imagine for a moment a hunter going after his prey as if his whole life depended upon it. There are no thoughts in his head other than the moment. He is not thinking about building a fire or what a clan member said earlier in the day. His attention does not stray from his immediate experience.

The hunter learns of the animal's thinking by examining its tracks: how the animal hesitates and turns, how it stops or stutters in its movements. Following his senses, he is ultra-aware of everything arising around him because his very existence depends upon it. To call the animal out, the hunter may mimic its sounds. To experience the animal up close, he may make the same movements.

Like a bird in suspended flight the hunter waits for the right moment to spring. He is focused and aware of his own actions and at the same time alert to the actions of the animal, the feel of the air, sounds of footfalls, sticks breaking under his feet, motion in the leaves. He imbibes a diffuse attention that includes everything around him, all at once. He is so attached to the animal's movements and rhythms that he and the animal become one. By worshipping the animal he is pursuing, the hunter adopts the material world as his spiritual world. He can turn into the animal he is seeking, and the animal becomes his guide in the spiritual realm.

Lest you think I'm a person, as you go, glance back at me! says the hunter to the animal. The hunter does not look up to the heavens and plead for a favorable outcome. This is unnecessary. The divine has its presence in every moment of his existence. In his world, everything is awake and aware: rocks, lakes, animals, wind—all things are brimming with consciousness. This may be why some people feel, wherever they go, they are among the spirits of their ancestors. Everything they encounter in life is considered with a bare reverence, a reverence that makes "the center hold." The direct immediacy of nature is what guides them through life events, their experiences requiring no filtering through a priest, rabbi, or guru for interpretation.

The psychological state of all of us is ruled by our patterns of attention. The veil between the object world and the self is clearly thin in young children, who are fully alive and engrossed in each experience and immersed in the pleasure of their senses without having any reflective thoughts about them. They simply enjoy a solid communion with each new and interesting moment. They don't stop and reflect. They don't make judgments. There is a clean slate between their perceptions and the object itself. In piercing the veil, could I, too, become attuned to that which is invisible? I often find myself standing outside this circle of reciprocity with the moment, yearning to get in. I want to become part of the whole. If I could, at every turn, open to an expanded sense of seeing and feeling, then perhaps everyday moments in my ordinary life could be perceived with more depth and joy, even surprise. Everything that exists can teach me something, I reason, if only I slow down and take notice. I can temporarily experience a thin veil like children do if I pay attention to something without desperation, longing, and judgment. Without having any kind of mental construct about the object or experience. If I drop my thoughts of past and future, my awareness will become razor sharp. If I converse with all the elements in my world, perhaps I would see that everything in my midst does indeed shimmer.

Marcel Proust said the secret of life is to be found in the art of attention, what he called "exaggerated attention." His writings describe pointed sensations of an activity where the mind is focused on minute details rather than thoughts of other things. Shifting our perception can lead us to other facets of reality. When an old woman asked Buddha, how does one meditate, he replied: "Watch your hand when you draw water from the well." That is all. He succinctly described meditation in motion, a way to become immersed in the task at hand, a way to relax the mind of unnecessary thinking, like the ancient hunter does.

Proust wrote that shining awareness on the task at hand may lift the ennui people often feel, the sense of dread as if their lives are passing them by. If we mindfully observe the small things as Proust did in his famous description of becoming completely immersed in savoring a madeleine steeped in tea, our absorption in the moment will set us free. With vivid awareness of the tastes and smells of the experience, there would be no dread in the moment. And if we could keep it up, there would be no dread in the next moment, or the one after that, and the one after that. Now I finally understood the meaning of the words from the poet William Blake: "If the doors to perception were cleansed, everything would appear to man as it is ... infinite."

Another way we can pierce the veil and feel totally alive is when we are in the presence of great beauty. We can be delivered naturally to a heightened state of awareness when we take part in great art, music, and poetry. In these moments, our mind is idle, and time and space cannot touch us. On a recent trip to Italy, I was rapt by the beauty of the exquisitely carved, replicated statue of *David*. I slowly circled the work of art, gripped with awe by its beauty. The statue was so engrossing, for long moments I simply couldn't look away. In those moments, *the I that is me disappeared*. A seamless place rarely noticed in my everyday life took over and my thinking mind stopped.

I once read of a rare psychological disorder in which foreign tourists standing in the presence of miraculous beauty were rushed to the psychiatric ward of Florence's Santa Maria Nuova Hospital. One woman collapsed while viewing a Raphael painting. Another panicked at the foot of Bernini's *Ecstasy of Saint Teresa*. I don't know if this is true. Immersed in the serenity and power of *David*, I was glad to have left there sans an episode of fainting. Though breathless, I think I may have come close.

Shifts of perception can be remarkable in the natural world too, even in modern times. Wild animals often cross our paths by way of scent and movement and sometimes just by plain curiosity of the human-hiker-woman wandering the tundra, passing through their mountain homes. Never before had I experienced so deep a connection with a wild animal as the face-to-face meeting with a hoary marmot I surprised on a rocky outcropping while hiking up to a chain of alpine lakes. To be honest, he wasn't the least bit surprised; I was the one who stopped, stunned in her tracks.

After climbing a steep slope flanked by hemlock, I paused to rest where the tree line turned to alpine tundra. Blue, glacier-scarred ponds decorated the terrain. Rounding a bend, farther up the trail, I was startled to see a huge marmot sunning on a flat rock about 10 feet above me. He sat calmly on the bedrock bench, observing his world like a king surveying his kingdom. He was resting, perhaps, after his daily occupation of digging burrows and searching for food. Taking in the afternoon sun, he lounged unperturbed by my presence. Silently I stepped off the trail and when I stopped, he noticed my movement. He looked sidelong into my eyes. Now we were taking a great interest in each other. Alert for predators, marmots sometimes make loud whistles when alarmed, but he remained quiet and still. Our gaze held. I could feel my physicality, the material sense of my body in relation to his. I was watching him, and he was watching me. I wondered how long our encounter would last. His gray coat rippled in the wind. Neither of us flinched. In a momentary trance, our sentience melded.

David Abrams, in *Becoming Animal*, writes, "Many undomesticated animals move in a fairly constant dialogue, not with themselves but with their surroundings. It is not an isolate mind but rather the sensate, muscled body itself that is doing the thinking. It is a kind of distributed sentience, this intelligence in the limbs and body."

The marmot sat motionless, sniffing the air, the smooth arc of his body still. He continued watching me until I finally broke gaze. I was not drawn to this charming moment by the tundra grasses stirring around me or by the magnificent blue alpine ponds; those were beautiful sights to consider, all alive in my peripheral vision. I was drawn to the moment by an act of absorption as this motionless animal split my perception like a boat's bow through water. In a sudden shift in awareness, I became fused in an event of spontaneous interaction where my gaze lingered in the eyes of a wild animal. I imagined him thinking: What is this long-legged creature carrying a heavy backpack and sporting a bouncy ponytail? I stepped back onto the trail feeling refreshed and alive.

Tin skies. A cold fall day. I am walking a beach on the shores of the Bering Sea in Nome, Alaska. Waves break the shoreline as a cold wind bruises my cheekbones. I zip my hood and cinch its ruff around my face. Sifting through stones, I notice a white one with a pale blue vein running through its middle. I bend over and pluck it from the gripping sand and stroke it between my fingers. Its presence in my hand seems to light up as the graying sea and sky shrink into the periphery. An ordinary stone to be sure but as I hold it in my hand, I give it vitality.

I claim the stone as mine. I rub it between my fingers, feeling its cool contours and admiring its subtle beauty. I remember reading about a shamanic practice called "rock seeing," in which you choose a rock that gathers your attention, hold it in your hand, and simply observe. Besides noting its physical features, I ask myself what type of wildness resides within this stone? Where has it been? Where is it going?

Cold to the touch, I think, there are stories in this stone. Awash and carried by stormy seas, it has been pushed, tumbled, and coughed up on this shore. It has seen many things over the ages. Perhaps stacked in a heap on the beach, where someone built a small cairn, marking a trail for others to find their way. Or maybe part of an ancient or contemporary ritual, where each member of a tribe or family whispers a prayer to the stone and then stacks them on the grave of their beloved.

I believe we have the perceptual ability to *extend* our awareness out into the world, and not solely with living things. Baudelaire observed, "Man walks through forests of physical things that are also spiritual things, that watch him with affectionate looks." The rock will respond once I make the decision to become an active member in the reciprocity of its nature. All I have to do is feed the rock with my thoughts and consider it an object of reflection. In turn, it prizes me with an image or feeling that heightens my curiosity. I put the stone in my pocket and carry it home with me, aligning it on a shelf in my studio. We would talk again later.

On a cold early morning at my casita in New Mexico, I hear a slight wind gearing up outside. The sound is eerie at first, a low nasal humming. Picking up momentum, it makes an instrument of my vibrating clothesline; my jeans and towels rise up, slap-flapping. Updrafts gather under the outdoor chairs, shaking all sorts of metal parts. Even the windowpanes are shaking in their casings.

I open the screen door and step out. I'm a large woman, and I can hardly stand up in the turmoil. I look across the yard to where the wind, blowing in all directions, bangs against a lonely horse trough, causing a ruckus wherever it touches. And then, just when I think its momentum is nearing a peak, it stalls. Quells in an instant. Where did it go? Just as suddenly it drums up again, the wail strengthening in layers. A dust devil coils, then lets loose. I watch and wait for the fury to die out, licking my lips of grit.

Apparently, I can't trust my seeing *or* my hearing. I'm not always 100 percent sure of my perceptions and what the wild elements are trying to tell me. Intuitively I know the afternoon heat that bears down as I climb mesas in the high desert is remembered in my body in the same way as when I'm walking a cold sand beach on the Bering Sea. Both places possess their own particular mysteries, remembered when my senses and my heart remain open.

I praise the mountain energy night and day, said the female mystic poet Mirabai. *I walk the path that ecstatic human beings have taken for centuries.*

Scott McMillion has been writing about wildlife, conservation, hunting and other issues in the American West since 1988. He edits and publishes *Montana Quarterly*, an award-winning literary journal. He is the editor and a principal contributor to *Montana, Warts and All*, a collection of the best entries from the magazine's first ten years, and is the author of *Mark of the Grizzly: True Stories of Recent Bear Attacks and the Hard Lessons Learned*. He has been a featured essayist for *The News Hour with Jim Lehrer* and his work has appeared in *Audubon, Nature Conservancy* and many other magazines. He lives in his home town of Livingston, Montana.

This piece was originally published in the online journal Narratively, *April, 2016.*

Hunting Among Wolves

Winter landed hard in Montana last November, about the time we learned that a new wolf pack in the neighborhood had pushed the elk out of our honey hole. But we kept trying, my grandson and I. One more day of frozen eyeglasses and icicles in my beard, we decided, and we'd hunt someplace else.

The next day at dawn, we spotted two sets of elk tracks, hot ones, the first we'd seen since the snow had blanketed everything a few days earlier. We crept up the ridge, where I really thought we'd find elk grazing in the meadow. But all we got was track soup. And a story. Smooth and fresh as a clean sheet, the snow told a tale. The elk had come through before dawn, walking north in no particular hurry, facing the wind. Then they bolted south, fast. The snow told us why.

The elk had stumbled into five wolves, sleeping in the sparse sage. We saw the wolves' icy beds, places where they had dug at the frozen ground, tussled and played, peed on the shrubbery, trampled the snow with their feet. The wolves hadn't chased the elk but turned east instead. Maybe they'd been caught napping and saw the futility of pursuit or maybe they just weren't hungry. But the elk weren't sticking around to find out. As a hunt, it was a frustrating scene, but it was a pretty damned interesting morning, figuring out the story, drawn on a whiteboard bigger than a football field.

At the age of thirteen, my grandson Dylan is already a good hunter. He's got the lungs and legs for it, and, more importantly, the tenacity and steady patience it takes. He's already taken one elk and a couple deer and I expect he'll get a lot more as the years unfold. He'll make memories that will or won't fade, but I think that morning's story will stick. I know it will for me.

His story and mine have different roots.

I grew up hunting in Montana, but it wasn't wolf country then and I'm still trying to wrap my head around the changes. The federal government brought wolves to Yellowstone National Park, about an hour's drive from my home, in 1995. It was very controversial at the time. The federal government and environmental groups wanted to restore wolves to their natural role in the ecosystem, to bring back an animal that had been hunted and trapped and poisoned to extinction in that area decades earlier, and they had the law on their side. The wolf was protected by the Endangered Species Act and the courts ruled that reintroduction should proceed, despite the fears of some that cattle ranches and game herds would be wiped out. As the years passed, the wolves multiplied, traveled far from the park and established territories in places that hadn't heard a wolf howl in generations, including our honey hole on a friend's ranch, a place that has filled my freezer many times. One small pack had roamed the ranch for several years, but I never saw more than a track, and elk had remained plentiful there.

Today, Montana has hundreds of wolves. The government recently counted 536, though biologists stressed that is only a minimum estimate, that the number is at least 30 percent higher than that. And the population is holding pretty steady, even though we've had a hunting season on wolves for several years, ever since Congress stepped in and forced the removal of federal protections in 2011. The state of Montana immediately set up a hunting season for them.

I'm not interested in hunting anything I don't care to eat, and I don't care to eat a wolf so I don't hunt them. Still, people value the beautiful pelts and plenty of folks relish the chance to shoot a wolf. For some, I think, it's a chance to stick a thumb in the eye of the federal government they maintain has forced wolves upon the West.

I suspect that's what happened to my honey hole; human resentment took over and stirred the pot. The ranch owner told me his neighbors had killed several of the wolves living in the area and a new pack had moved in to claim the old pack's territory. In their attempts to figure out this new ground, these animals had chased the elk somewhere. The ranch owner – no big fan of wolves – wasn't happy about this development. He figures he was better off with the wolves that knew his ranch and didn't cause trouble than he was with new ones that had some exploring to do. I think he was right about that. The old pack knew how to take down a meal without chasing away the whole herd and closing down the store. The new pack flubbed it and likely will have some hungry days as a result.

As an apex predator, wolves change how ecosystems operate; how the elk and other prey species behave and where they spend time, which changes plant life, which effects streams and erosion patterns, and therefore fish and bugs and all sorts of things. Biologists call this a "trophic cascade" of consequences and people are still learning new things about how it all works. As a reporter, learning and writing about wolves was part of my job for many years and I enjoyed it a great deal. Now I'm learning how to hunt among them. It's a new thing for me.

Dylan, on the other hand, has never lived in a world without wild wolves. He spends plenty of time on his cell phone and iPad, but he's an active kid, a good athlete eager to go outside most of the time. Like most of his friends, all Montana kids, he's an avid hunter and wolves are part of the only landscape he's known, a place where I'm teaching him to harvest clean and natural food, from mushrooms to meat. These are things we could get much more easily at the supermarket, but we like doing it this way, because it's not just about food.

For his generation, having wolves in the woods is just something that exists; like the rule that makes you take your shoes off at the airport, it's always been that way for them. But he's learning that wolves add complications to the hunting equation, and, as the biologists say, complexity is good, but not necessarily easy. It adds resilience and strength to a place. This is the world in which Dylan is learning to read tracks, to open his eyes and nose and ears all at the same time, to control his breathing and heartbeat. I'm glad he has the opportunity. He's learning more and learning it faster than I did at his age.

The day after we found the wolf beds, we tried a different spot, not so far as the bird flies but with a lot of human boundaries in between, roads and fences and such. Those fences create yet another complication, one that Dylan is also learning. They generally indicate property boundaries. Some people will allow us to use their land and others won't, as is their right, and we respect that. We found a couple hundred elk, but they were on the wrong side of the barbed wire so we started hiking away from them, to public land that is everyone's property, hoping to find more elk. We found fresh tracks and beds, which was exciting, then a scrape tree, where a buck or bull had displayed his lust during the rut, mangling a scruffy lodgepole pine with his antlers, leaving his scent in the bark and probably getting some pine sap between his ears. And there, just above the scrape, we saw bear scratches, claw marks ripping the wood. Predator and prey marking the same spot.

And that made for a second interesting morning, even if we didn't bag an elk.

Just over a small hill, we could see Livingston, the town where I grew up and where I live now. We could hear trains and traffic on the highway. Somewhere between us and town was a herd of elk, inaccessible because of the fences and the human decisions they indicated. In this case, wolves had nothing to do with putting our prey out of reach.

When I was my grandson's age, still too young to drive, my friends and I would walk to this area from town, pitch a tent, cook some beans and fantasize about the animals we would kill, come the season. The man whose land we crossed didn't care about our wanderings, as long as we didn't set the place on fire or harass his cattle, but I don't remember ever seeing an elk there in those days. Nowadays, if I set up a spotting scope on the deck of my house, I can sometimes see hundreds of them from town. But I generally can't hunt them, because new people own the land and they've made it clear that I'm not welcome. For Dylan, walking from town and going where his nose leads him really isn't an option, unless he wants to risk being arrested for trespassing. That freedom doesn't exist for him.

Twenty-first century Montana is a wildlife-dense environment, including predators. Black bears and grizzlies, wolves and coyotes, mountain lions and bobcats, all make a living on the land, often by killing something. They all owe something to hunters, who financed countless conservation projects over the past century, improving habitat with their license fees and the taxes they pay on equipment and ammunition. We have more predators now partly because we have more prey animals.

Still, human hunters outnumber other predator species, all of which want wild meat, but for the humans, the meat is not a physical need. It's important to us, but we won't starve without it. And the nonhuman predators have at least one advantage: they don't have to pay attention to fences.

The state abounds in prey, despite all the teeth and bullets out there. When the wolves were reintroduced, the silliest of the critics predicted *canis lupus* would create an ecological desert, basically wiping out everything from moose to moles. Quite the opposite happened. Montana has more elk in more places than it's had in a century thanks in part to hunters, the habitat they protected and the biologists and game wardens they hired with their license money. But that doesn't mean it's any easier to hunt elk, mostly because of all those fences and the "no trespassing" signs they carry.

That's why I worry about the current movement to privatize the public lands across the West, places like the National Forest land where we found that scrape tree. People such as the Bundy family famously puff up their chests for the cameras and stage armed standoffs in Oregon and Nevada, but their fellow travelers in state capitols and Washington distress me more. They're trying to force the federal government to get rid of public land, to turn it over to corporations and individuals, so people can make money from it and shut us all out. If private landowners lock their gates, I'll accept it without much surprise simply because I've seen it happen too often. But I'll do everything I can to keep that from happening to public land, property that belongs to you and me. And to my grandson and yours, whether you hunt or you just want to go look at a scrape tree.

For hunters, wolves have changed things, but not as much as people have, especially the ones who lock the public's wildlife away from the public. As in most of the West, Montana is seeing big social changes and people are cordoning off more and more land. Sometimes it's because they don't like hunting. Sometimes it's because they want to make money through selling guided hunts. Sometimes they just want their privacy. It can be frustrating when wolves chase the elk to the wrong side of the fence, but I believe the wolves have as much right to elk meat as I do and the elk will return to our honey hole sooner or later. I just have to work a little harder now and that probably won't hurt me a bit. Dylan understands the work. For him, it's always been that way. And the "no trespassing" signs have always been there as well. They're a lot more common than wolves are, and they scare me more. That's why we need to keep our public lands in public hands.

Plus, the wolves wrote out that story in the snow. They gave that story to my grandson. And they gave it to me. It will last a lot longer than an elk steak and if we hadn't all been hunting the same ground that day, how could we have learned to read it?

Continue reading the entire collection. You can order volumes one and two of this best selling anthology direct from our website: www.riverfeetpress.com

Other titles from Riverfeet Press

THIS SIDE OF A WILDERNESS: A Novel —Daniel J. Rice

ECOLOGICAL IDENTITY: Finding Your Place in a Biological World —Timothy Goodwin

ROAD TO PONEMAH: The Teachings of Larry Stillday —Michael Meuers

A FIELD GUIDE TO LOSING YOUR FRIENDS —Tyler Dunning

AWAKE IN THE WORLD V.1: A Riverfeet Press Anthology

ONE-SENTENCE JOURNAL (winner of the 2018 Montana Book Award and the 2019 High Plains Book Award) —Chris La Tray

WILDLAND WILDFIRES: and where the wildlife go —Randie Adams

I SEE MANY THINGS: Ninisidawenemaag, Book 1 —Erika Bailey-Johnson

LOOK AT ME —Stephany Jenkins

AWAKE IN THE WORLD V.2: A Riverfeet Press Anthology

FAMILIAR WATERS —David Stuver

BURNT TREE FORK: A Novel —J.C. Bonnell

REGARDING WILLINGNESS —Tom Harpole

LIFE LIST: POEMS —Marc Beaudin

I HEAR MANY THINGS: Ninisidawenemaag, Book 2 —Erika Bailey-Johnson

KAYAK CATE —Cate Belleveau

PAWS AND HIS BEAUTIFUL DAY —Stephany Jenkins

THE UNPEOPLED SEASON: A Journal of Solitude and Wilderness —Daniel J. Rice

WITHIN THESE WOODS —Timothy Goodwin

TEACHERS IN THE FOREST —Barry Babcock

BEYOND THE RIO GILA — Scott G. Hibbard

WILTED WINGS — Mike McTee

NO GOOD DAY TO DIE —James Wolf

BETWEEN ROCK AND A HARD PLACE —Maggie Anderson

CPSIA information can be obtained
at www.ICGtesting.com
Printed in the USA
JSHW051255060323
38542JS00006B/43